Kerwall Town

Kerwall

Town

S.D. Reed

*This book is dedicated to Vourn, Tony, Liz, and Lin.
My cheerleaders. A simple thank you is not enough.*

This edition first published in 2020.

First Published in Great Britain in 2020 by KDP.

Copyright © S.D. Reed, 2020.

Managed and edited by Footnotes Management, Rachel Hewitt.

The moral right of the author has been asserted.

Cover design by Iain Henderson.

Content Warning: This work contains depictions of sexual assault and suicide, should you be affected please use the contact details available at the end of this novel.

Every effort has been made to trace copyright holders and obtain their permissions for the use of copyright material. The author apologises for any errors or omissions and would be grateful if notified of any corrections that should be incorporated in future reprints or editions of this book.

ISBN: 9798692396648

"The strength of the vampire is that people will not
believe in him."
Garrett Fort

"If a fear cannot be articulated, it can't be conquered."
Stephen King, Salem's Lot

Dear Friends,

Once again, I thank you for joining me on an adventure. It has been my ambition since I was 11 years old to become a novelist. I remember vividly at around that age when I read *The Fantastic Mr. Fox* by *Roald Dahl*, that becoming a story teller was what I wanted to do. It wasn't until later on that I discovered I not only wanted to write stories, but to also have each of them connected in some way. Much of that inspiration came from *Stephen King*. I'm fascinated with classic monsters, always have been, and I had longed to pay homage in some way to that section of literature.

There are also more mature themes in this story and it's certainly a lot darker. So, if you are of a nervous disposition, hold my hand and I will guide you. I must warn you though, if something grabs you while we're in the darkness, it wasn't me. There are legends of demons, witches and even vampires in this part of the country. So, if you feel the hair on the nape of your neck stand on end from an icy cold touch, run.

Run and don't look back.

Your Fiend... Excuse me, I mean, Friend,
S. D. Reed

27th December 2019

S.D. Reed

Part One

Kerwall Town

1

The New Town Mayor

Like most buildings in Kerwall, Terry's hardware store was a dilapidated shell. The owner, Terry Jr., who was no junior at all at 83, refused to leave. The whole town was a failed government experiment, built on top of the remains of a previous failed government experiment. You wouldn't find it on any map of England, because, *technically* it doesn't exist. After the First Great War, a select number of people were paid to move there and it was branded as the 'town that would rebuild Britain'. To the credit of the government, it had a modicum of success for a couple of years, however, when the mines got shut down things started to go south. Investors stopped investing, the younger generations moved away a decade ago, the only tourists that were 'visiting' were ones who had stumbled across this ramshackle of a town, trying to get to somewhere else. Some stayed permanently, somehow drawn in by the charm of the town, or lack thereof. Others gawped at the buildings, whose signs hung off their failing hinges, with plans to fill their photo albums with Polaroids, before heading back out into the real world.

The population of Kerwall was 915, with very few residents under the age of 25. Official censuses at the time of the 'Boom Period' listed the population as almost 30,000. A fact no resident would, or could, forget.

"Have you seen the remote?" Calls Dotty from the sitting room.

"Checked down the side of the sofa?" Terry is busy on the shop floor.

"Of course!"

"Well, I don't know then."

"Oh, just come and help me look for it will you, Tez!"

"I'm working, Dot! You know that." Irritation is rising in his voice now. They've been married for so long, it's almost like they have become the same person. Their souls have completely entwined, that doesn't stop them bickering over small things every now and then though.

"Come off it, will you! There hasn't been a bleedin' customer in this town, let alone this store, in almost three months now. What makes you think today will be any different?" She's now joined him on the shop floor.

"Hope."

She brushes his snow-white hair with her life worn fingers, strokes his cheek and leaves her hand there for a moment. Gazing into eyes she's stared into a thousand times before, she kisses him on the cheek before leaving to continue her search.

They had met playing Lawn Tennis many moons ago and, by all accounts, it was love at first sight. If anyone was absolutely made for each other it would be these two. Their birthdays, for example, are exactly a month apart, their eyes, both a deep blue, could be a mirror image, and they both had their first white hair within days of one another. They had not been apart from each other for more than a month since they first laid eyes on each other, not counting the dreadful months when Terry was away in the Second World War.

Terry had inherited his hardware store from his father when he had passed away. The mortgage had long been paid off when business was at its peak - back in the good old days. It was a long and rambling store with every DIY item your heart could ever wish for. There was an upstairs too, but it was scarcely ever used by either Dotty or Terry now, climbing stairs belonged in their past after numerous hip and knee replacement surgeries. Before that became their reality, Terry had the foresight to build a ground floor suite, comprising of a small kitchen and living room, bathroom, and bedroom. This made it much easier for Dot and himself, knowing that their waning mobility would restrict their vertical movements. What had been their room was seldom used, save for when their grandchildren, Jack and Donna, were able to visit. By now, the upstairs was home to a plethora of spiders, webs and quite possibly a few bats too. They often hear fluttering at night but choose to pay it no mind.

"Found it!" Dotty shouts from the kitchen.

"Where was it?"

"Under the bleedin' table. I haven't been on my knees that long since we were courting." She's now by Terry's side and he sees the wry smile on her face.

"What's got into you today, Dot?" He strokes her hair gently. "Not that I'm complaining." He adds with a cheeky wink.

"Can't a wife just love her husband?"

Terry kisses her lips for what must be the millionth time but, as ever, it feels like the first. The moment they shared their very first kiss was on their third date. He had taken her on a picnic and as they sat, digesting their homemade sandwiches under the oak tree, he leaned in and kissed her. It was a somewhat perfect memory.

They would have continued to lock their lips had it not been for the sound of the bell above the door. A tall, thin man, with an even thinner pencil moustache, stepped inside. He was wearing a dark charcoal suit, accented by an oil green tie and matching shoes.

"I am very sorry to interrupt." His voice, devoid of any distinguishable accent, had steady, melodic pacing to it. Terry thought that if you listened to him long enough you might become hypnotised. He disliked and distrusted him instantly. A feeling which was shared by Dotty.

"Not at all. How can I help?"

The strange man laughs, a peculiar sound which almost seemed to make the atmosphere of the room thicker.

"I think the question should be, how I can help *you*." He pulls out a business card from his inside suit pocket, handing it to Dotty. She was careful not to touch his hand, even though they were inside leather gloves, it was an impulse that she couldn't explain.

Frances Lloyd-Chatman
Kerwall Town Owner and Mayor

The lettering seemed to jump off the small white card. They were a striking green, perfectly coordinated with his outfit.

"What's this supposed to mean?" Terry reads the card over his wife's shoulder.

"Exactly what it says, Mr Smith." He placates the statement with a smile like his mouth had been tugged at the ends by a thread.

"How do you know our name?" Dotty raised an eyebrow.

"As Owner and Mayor of the town, I think it's my business to know, or at least try to know, all the people that reside here. Especially the proprietors of such an age-old establishment."

"We didn't vote on a new Mayor. What happened to Richard?" Unease was building in Terry now, evident through the rising urgency in his words.

"Don't worry about Mr Percy. He is enjoying a holiday in Devon as we speak. His lovely wife, Lorraine, is with him too. They were such gracious hosts. My business associate and I were there until the small hours of the morning smoothing over every detail."

The Smiths, without knowing the other was doing so, twisted their hands into knots. Something wasn't right with this *stranger*. His uneasy smile, his strained laughter and that moustache that belonged in the Art Deco period of time, or some Hammer Horror movie.

"Do you know when they're coming back?" She tugged at her sleeves.

There it was again, that strange, empty laugh like something nefarious was inside of him and was trying desperately to claw its way out.

"Their stay in Devon will, I feel, remain... permanent." He stretched out that word for all it was worth. He was now surveying the store, walking up and down the aisle close to the counter. He picked up a hammer and lightly tapped it on his gloved hand.

"As you are aware, they have a holiday home there, and as I'm *sure* you know, they've had their house on

Kerwall Town

the market for some time now. Nice house, big, spacious… private." He puts the hammer down slowly and walks over to the counter once more, where they are both stood, almost frozen.

"The Percy's, my associate, and I struck another deal last night too. I can tell you are both wise citizens, you wouldn't be at your grand age if you weren't wise after all. Yes, I'm sure you know by now that the other deal we struck was to buy their house. I must admit we paid a substantial amount over the asking price but it was certainly worth it." Once again came that chilling laugh. "Now, I must be off, there are other pressing matters to attend to today. Do be sure to be at the town hall this evening at 7 p.m. … Sharp." He smiles and stretches out his gloved hand. Terry and Dotty watch it for almost a second too long and then Terry shakes it. He could feel the muscles in the stranger's hand and knew, that if Mr Lloyd-Chatman wanted to, he could crumple his hand into dust without any effort. The stranger lets go of Terry's hand and stops at the door, pulling a black umbrella from where he had left it by the front of the shop. "Don't forget, 7 p.m., sharp." With that, he was gone.

Dotty put her husband's hand in hers and rubbed it gently.

"He didn't hurt you, did he?"

"Pah! Not a chance… Although, he scared the bleedin' life out of me."

"You and me both. I'll put the kettle on, come and sit down for a minute."

Terry does as his wife says and takes a seat by the counter.

Moments later, a crash comes from the kitchen and Terry's heart rises in his throat. He runs in, as quickly as his frail body allows him, to find his wife slouched on the floor. His panic turns to confusion when he sees her laughing. Kneeling beside her, he strokes the hair out of her eyes. There is a small cut just above her left eye and it's bleeding freely, making a stark contrast with her aged, greying skin.

"The cloths are in the middle draw, Tez. Get one out and wet it for me slightly, will you?" He's amazed at the calmness in her voice, even so, he was still confused by the laughter surrounding her words, he thought that perhaps it was a defence mechanism against shock. He seemed to think that he had read that before, but couldn't recall. He'd come to realise in his 80's that there were a lot of things he couldn't remember. The things he did want to forget kept him up at night, taunting him through dreams. Terry was sure that he wasn't the only soldier who was plagued by such dreams. He had told Dot about a few of them, mostly the ones which held him in an icy grip of fear. They were always the same; being caught by an unknown enemy whilst deep in the trenches, the rain beating down on his face turning to blood, or the gun he was holding turning into the bony arm of his fallen comrade. He hadn't thought about those dreams for a long time and it wasn't until this strange encounter that they came flooding back.

"How we looking on that wet cloth, Tez?" She breaks him from the stillness. She was still laughing as if this was the funniest thing to ever happen to her. He kneels beside her, this time his knees go off like the crack of a whip, sending a hot bolt of pain up his body. He ignores it as best as he can and tends to his wife's wound. She winces against the pressure momentarily

Kerwall Town

and then presses her hands over his, pushing down on the cloth.

"Say, what's so funny, Dotty? Are you ok?"

"Of course, dear. I just feel like a fool, that's all, and the best way to treat a fool is to laugh at them. That's what you told me, many moons ago." She kisses him on the lips. "Now, come on, help me up off this bleedin' floor."

As he lifts her his free hand finds the small of her back and pulls her in. They dance around the kitchen. There is no music, only the beat of their hearts to follow. There is no dance floor just the old linoleum beneath their feet, not that it matters as their minds transport them out of 1977 Britain. They are in the Jazz club where Terry had asked Dotty to be his wife. They had always believed that the happiest place in the world is in the arms of a loved one.

The Smiths weren't the only store owners to get a visit from the stranger that day, and those that didn't get a visit found out the details anyway; news travels fast in a place as small as Kerwall. By mid-afternoon, everyone had heard about Frances Lloyd-Chatman. Most thought he was impossibly handsome, while the rest were a little dubious about his ambitions. Talk of his silent business partner was all speculative, with no one having met her, except for Peter Wright.

He was the town's local drunkard and, by all accounts, a habitual liar. So naturally, when he told the others that he had not only *seen* the silent business partner but *spoken* to her, no one believed a single word, after all, why would they. Fifteen years prior, when the town still had a flicker of promise, Peter was a well-respected member of the community. He had a

18

prominent job at the manufacturing plant and doted on his wife and son. Talk around town, though, was that she wasn't so loving to him, rumours circulated that she had been sleeping with half of the men, not only in Kerwall but in the next town over too. When Peter had discovered this, he infamously succumbed to a fit of blinding rage, although instead of lashing out at her, he stormed through the pub doors where he remained for the night. The following day the town was awoken by a huge blaze at the Wright residence. Peter came staggering home to the commotion of it all, sobering him instantly. He had run past the gathering crowd and the firefighters, who tried to restrain him, and straight upstairs to his little one's room.

Shock turned to outright horror when the crowd saw him burst through the front door moments later with the charred remains of his son held tightly in his arms. There was a confusion of screams. A team of firefighters had to pry the lifeless body out of his death grip, while others were patting out the small fire that was melting his clothes to his back. The air had filled with a sickly smell. Peter was screaming, not because of the pain of his skin, but the pain of his world shattering.

Many people had pinned the blame on him, even though he was acquitted of all crimes by the court. It was on that day that people started calling him a liar, the irony being was that he was one of the most honest people in the town. No-one truly knows who started that blaze and really, it doesn't matter. The town had already found their culprit, and the sentence they bestowed upon him was the label of town drunk and liar. He simply was not to be trusted and was treated with the utmost contempt. His work dismissed him and he fell behind on payments for his house. Despite things working a little differently in the self-governing town of Kerwall, the then Mayor, Richard Percy, took the house away from him 'as a precaution for his health'. The house now stood derelict, not a soul had entered since that fateful day, but that was nothing compared to the nightmares and PTSD that tormented his, almost, every thought. He had tried to nurse the nightmares away with a strong bottle, when that inevitably failed, he turned to drugs to numb the pain.

When he came across the two new town members that night, something stirred in him. There was a pressing thought in the back of his mind telling him that he needed to stop begging for spare change in the next town and to stop drinking altogether. Yes, that was more important than anything. He had always listened to that little voice deep in his head. It was the same one that had told him to come home from the pub that fatal evening. He had tried for fifteen years to drown that voice out and he had been quite successful for a number of them. But that *touch*. Even now, recounting it, sent a shiver through his spine. It was the touch from the tall woman with the infinitely black hair, save for the green highlight. When he had seen them both walking down the path, and observed how well dressed they were, he had stood up and tried on his most winning smile. She had taken his hand in both of hers, distinctly coated with long gloves that wouldn't have gone amiss in the 1930's. He could feel her bones writhing under the gloves and he tried to let go, but she only held his hand tighter. Her voice was soft, and her eyes were a deep jade, when his gaze found hers, he couldn't stop staring into them. He felt like he could drown in those eyes and be lost forever. He had no recollection of what she was saying, only the melody of her voice and that she was smiling, showing just a glint of perfect white teeth. He recalled that there was a man with her too, he had flipped two coins into Peter's tattered hat, lying on the floor. Peter seems to remember that they both wished him a good evening, although he couldn't be sure. When they had left, he began to laugh uncontrollably, he didn't think he would, or could, ever stop, until he started choking. What seemed strange was that he hadn't laughed for as long as he could remember. Stranger still, he hadn't a clue what he had been laughing about.

2

Town Meeting

It was at 6:45 p.m. when the town hall held all of its residents inside. Most, however, had already arrived outside by 6:30 p.m., all of them eager to uncover what was going on. They weren't averse to town meetings, quite the opposite, nonetheless, it was a rarity for everyone to attend. They were a good place for the week's gossip and, most importantly, who would be hosting this month's Tupperware Party. The town may be small and it may be almost dilapidated; but there was a sense that the residents of Kerwall town resonated with the outlandishly resilient plastic. Some went as far as to say that the residents and the plastics were one and the same. However, some would argue that Kerwall town was, instead, the persistent tomato stain on life. At one point, the parties generated almost as much money for some housewives as a full week's work would for their husband. Others claimed to have earned even more. One family had, apparently, earned so much from the parties in just one year that they up and left the town over-night, now living in a holiday home on the coast somewhere. Despite not generating nearly half as much as that these days, the draw of the possible is what keeps them popular.

Peter was the last to walk in and take his seat at the meeting. He chose one right at the back, hoping to avoid the eye-line of the new strangers. Terry and Dotty, on the other hand, were sat on the end of a row towards the centre of the crowd. The town hall was extremely, and unusually, large and at one point in its life, it could hold over 1,000 people at a time with nothing left but standing room only. The walls were adorned with fading portraits of past Mayors, in dirty gold frames. Ordinarily, the previous Mayor's portrait would be hung on the navy-blue wall at the back of the stage, flanked by two red velvet curtains, which were ever so ostentatious. This evening, however, there was no familiar portrait of the smiling Richard Percy. This evening it was replaced by a striking image of a man with a pencil-thin moustache, with a slight smirk etched upon his pointed face. His hair, although long, wasn't of this time. It was slicked back so tightly that his deep green eyes commanded attention, particularly when set against his porcelain white skin.

At 7:00 p.m. sharp the two strangers walked onto the stage; gasps escaped the few mouths that had formed distinct 'O' shapes. No one had ever caused so much commotion in the town. Not even that fateful fire 15 years prior. In just a few short hours, these two people had not only elected themselves Mayor but bought the town outright. The seemingly strangest thing about all of this was that no one kicked up a modicum of fuss, there were small, yet readable, traces of delirium and hope. There's an old saying about hope which circulates around Kerwall; some say it's the best of things, whilst those who have been scorned know

Kerwall Town

just how dangerous it is - with the power to steal everything away from you.

The tall woman, in strap heels and a long black evening dress, which fell to just below her knee, took a seat at the back of the stage. Her complexion was the whitest of whites, and her eyes were such a dark green they could almost be mistaken for black. The long, highlighted strand of hair, that Peter observed the night he had met them, formed a stark contrast. Looking at it now, it perfectly matched the colour of the man's tie. The woman was also clad in long black gloves, covering up to her elbow, and clutching a small dark green purse.

The slim man, Frances Lloyd-Chatman, walked to the lectern and tapped the microphone with his long finger. The sound reverberated through the two speakers on either side of the stage.

"Good evening."

The last little bits of murmurings from the crowd fell away instantly, the whole room unanimously captivated by his smooth voice and flawless skin.

"We are both so delighted that you have all made the... effort to be here this evening. For those of you who don't know by now, my name is Frances Lloyd-Chatman. This stunning lady sat down to my left." He gestures with his hand as a magician would to his assistant. "This is Ms Victoria Viridi. We have been business partners for as long as either of us can remember. Our working relationship has stretched continents and when we saw the opportunity to reinvest in a town with as much history as Kerwall, well, we were on the very next flight over." There it was again, that signature laugh, sounding like a part of him is dying as the sounds pass his lips. He glances over to Ms Viridi, who nods for him to carry on.

"You may have also heard that I am the new Mayor of this fair town, do not worry, I have all the correct documents to prove this." As he said this a strange thing happened; most of the people in attendance nodded in agreement, some of them cheering too. Mr Lloyd-Chatman waved his hand away dismissively but was smirking despite it all.

"Friends. May I call you all that? I feel that 'citizens' is far too formal you see, if we are to all live and work together, then I would rather have you all as my friends than my citizens." More cheers followed in response to this, with one or two townsfolk even standing up to cheer. "Now, I know that times have been tough for you all in this town, for several years now, but I can guarantee you that we *will* make Kerwall town the place to be! We *will* make Kerwall town prosperous and we *will* keep Kerwall town Alive!"

Rapturous cheers arose from the crowd upon hearing this, and almost all of the residents were now on their feet. The old Mayor, Richard Percy, could never elicit such a response.

"Friends! Friends!" He continues. "I am now going to pass you over to Ms Viridi." A wolf whistle escapes from one of the crowd members lips as she stands and strides up to the microphone. She waits until they are all seated and silent once more, before addressing them.

"Ladies and Gentleman." Her accent is nondescript, much like Frances', with a strained ancient langue, and her words hold weight. Her high-class bloodline is evident through each syllable's crystal-clear enunciation.

"Thank you all for welcoming us with such open arms. I will not keep you all too long."

The hall is silent, you could hear a pin drop. Every single person was hanging onto her every word. Even

Kerwall Town

Peter has been encapsulated by her, but something inside him tries to resist the hypnotic gaze of this beautiful stranger.

"As of tomorrow, the mines *will* be operational once more and the manufacturing plant *will* be in extended operations. There *will* be new vacancies for every single one of you in this town. You *will* all, no matter your ailment, play your part to make Kerwall town great and you *will* be victorious in your efforts."

Terry and Dotty had noticed that the strangers were overemphasising the word 'will'. They were also two of the only people who hadn't stood or cheered; it certainly wasn't because of their age. They simply outright refused to buy what these two strangers were selling. They had been on God's green earth long enough to know when they were being had.

"There is nothing more to say on the matter this evening, other than to wish you all a very good night. Get yourselves some rest, because the next few days and weeks will be the hardest you've known. But don't worry, it won't be long before you see the fruits of your labour. Trust me."

With that, she exits the stage. Peter noticed how her pointed heels didn't clack on the wooden floor. Instead, they were completely silent. The uneasy feeling that they both gave him had returned. He had made a mental note of all the people who didn't stand or cheer with the rest of the crowd and thought that it was highly imperative he spoke to them before the strangers did. If he noticed it then they absolutely would have too. This all sounded crazy, but with a mind now free of the desire, 'no', he thought, 'the need to be inebriated and to numb the pain'. He was thinking clearly again. He had heard about withdrawal symptoms, and the dangers of going cold turkey, but whatever had happened to him with the strangers that night seemed to have been some miracle cure, still, he didn't trust them.

Mr Lloyd-Chatman left the stage not long after Ms Viridi. The townsfolk didn't move for a few moments, it was almost as though they were in a sort of trance. Later into the evening a good many of them would suffer from a bout of hysterical laughter, some would even pass out.

When the strange veil, or whatever it was, had lifted from them, they left the building, chatting silently to one another. Peter was the last to leave, save for Chris Kempo, the town's custodian and chief key keeper. He was a middle-aged man, with brown eyes, and short, greasy, brown hair. He was never found out of his dirty grey overalls, with goodness knows how many years of oil, dirt, and quite possibly blood stained into them. Peter had observed that throughout the whole meeting Chris was slouched up against a wall, with a mop in one hand. He had been paying attention to the strangers but didn't partake in any of the fanfare.

"Chris! Got a minute?"

"Not for a drunk like you, get out! I'm locking up for the night."

"Look, I'm not drunk alright. I need to talk to you!"

"Just fuck off will you. I haven't got any spare change, and I'm not giving you any more booze." Chris was struggling to find the right key. He had a key for every establishment, even the ones in disuse. They were all hanging on a large, silver, circular chain attached to his waistband. He was now muttering to himself, completely oblivious that Peter was still there.

"I'm not drunk and I don't need any change! For fuck's sake, Chris, just listen to me, alright? For one minute, it's important."

Chris is now furious, with not only the arduous task of finding the right key but with the local drunk harassing him. He swings a punch at Peter and it connects directly with his nose, breaking the bone on impact. A river of blood cascades out of it instantly.

"I won't tell you again. Fuck off! There's a new horizon in fair old Kerwall. Didn't you hear? And everyone is to play their part. I don't suppose a drunk... and murderer, will know what that feels like, but the rest of us do, so why don't you do the whole town a favour, and piss off for good. And do you want to know something? The whole town wishes it was you in that fire, not your wife and child. Sure, she was a bit of a slut, but she weren't no murderer." He punctuates the tirade by spitting in Peter's face. He then pushes Peter out of the way; already off balance and trying to deal with his broken nose, Peter falls to the ground in a heap. Chris finally finds the key he had been looking for and locks up. Not even bothering to look at, let alone help Peter, he walks away.

Peter was used to this hostility, but not from Chris. Although they had never really spoken, he had assumed that he was one of the good guys. On this new evidence, he couldn't be more wrong. The pain emanating from his nose was immense. He was trying to stop the blood flow with his T-shirt, but within minutes it was soaked a deep red. It was dark now, and he was alone on the street. The doctors would be shut, not that they would help him anyway.

Most of the town chose to ignore him, and the rest treated him like vermin.

An hour had passed since the first town meeting under the new ownership, a meeting being hotly debated in most households, generally full of praise. The men were secretly in awe of Victoria, and all her beauty. The women, for the majority, were having secret fantasies of their own about Frances. There was a small contingent, however, who thought it was all a load of bullshit. They all, at least, had one thing in common though. They were all in their warm homes, with loved ones, and their bellies were seldom empty - if they were, they could just whip up some beans on toast, even sit in front of the television while doing so. Peter had no such luxury. His idea of four-square meals recently consisted of half-eaten food from the bins and drinking from the town fountain. When times had gotten really bad, and there were too many to count, he had resorted to braining rats with nearby bricks and cooking them using a campfire in the local woods. It was a neat trick he'd picked up from the scouts when he was younger, he had never thought he'd be using it, least of all to cook rats for his tea. On the rare occasions when he did have money, it would be shot up his arm, or down the local pub. Not now though, if he even thought of either, a wave of sickness engulfed him.

This evening he was sat in the alleyway between the hairdressers and the supermarket. He was wrapped in a thin patchwork blanket, which didn't keep the cold out one bit, and the blood had dried on his T-shirt. The headache he was suffering from, as a result of his broken nose, was threatening to tear open his skull. It was a welcomed distraction, however, from the usual ache in his stomach. He thought about fixing his nose

Kerwall Town

himself but chickened out the second his fingers touched his misshapen snout, sending a fresh wave of pain up and down his body, forcing his stomach to flip. His eyes were starting to shut now too, he thought it must be from the swelling.

Just then, he heard the unmistakable sound of footsteps. Clack, clack, clack. He prayed that it wasn't the strangers, he would do anything on this earth to not see them, especially right now. He drew his legs up to his chest and held his breath. The footsteps grew closer. Clack, clack, clack. 'Just walk on by, and leave me alone, please!' He pleaded desperately to himself, shutting his eyes, wishing to make himself invisible.

"Peter..."

'Shit', Peter thought.

"What on the earth's happened to you?"

"H ... Hello?" He says with a voice so small he didn't recognise it to be his own. He opened his eyes, slowly wincing from the pain.

He hears the sound of the footsteps getting closer still, and then a vice grip on his shoulder. Peter turns around so fast that he would have fallen over if it wasn't for the steady hands that came with the voice.

His vision grows clearer and he is flooded with relief seeing the friendly face of Terry.

"What happened to you, Peter? You're bleedin' everywhere," adding, with some hesitation, "let me smell your breath."

Peter complies, breathing lightly into the cold night air. Terry can't detect an ounce of alcohol on him. He scratches his white hair. "So how did you come to end up like this if you're not drunk?" It was a genuine question, and Peter could tell there was no malice in the tone. Terry and Dotty were some of the few people who didn't buy into the lies of the town. Peter knew that they tried, for the most part, to keep their business and everyone else's absolutely separate.

"Never mind what happened for now. Can you fix it for me?"

Terry surveys the damage to Peter's nose, touching it lightly. A fresh wave of pain engulfed Peter, who pulled away instantly.

"Well, I'm no doctor, but it looks like it's broken. You should book an appointment with Doctor Sharpe in the morning."

"Oh, come off it, Terry, you know he won't see the likes of me. Remember when I broke my arm a few years back? He told me to 'piss off', so I had to get it fixed in the next town over. That was, of course, before I knew that your wife could mend bones. Do you think she would fix my nose?"

"I don't see why not. She's in the house warming up our dinner." A pang of guilt struck Terry. Here he was, talking about his family, his house, and warm food on his table - to a man who has none of those things. The only thing that Peter has, that Terry doesn't, is a broken nose, and he was glad of that. "Why don't you stay with us for the night, and fill your stomach with some food. Dot's a better cook than she is a healer you know."

Peter was touched by this generosity. It was the polar opposite of his encounter with Chris. He was now wishing he had spoken to them first, avoiding the pain of his broken nose.

3

Small Town Talk

"Look who I found on my walk." Terry walks through the kitchen door. Dotty, who is plating up their dinner, turns and notices Peter. She doesn't completely see him until she double-takes. Rushing over to him, she takes him by the arm and sits him carefully down. The swelling around his eyes was beginning to make him look like he's just had twelve rounds with Muhammad Ali.

"Oh my, what happened to you, dear?" She tuts. "You're not drunk, are you?"

"No, ma'am."

"He hasn't said what's happened yet." Terry chimes in. He looks at the two plates on the side, then into the saucepan on the hob. There's still plenty of stew unserved. Had there not been, he would have subtly scraped some off of his own plate.

"It doesn't matter for now. I can already see it's broken. Terry dear, get me something he can bite down on."

"Wait, what? Bite down on? What are you going to do?"

"Well, what do you suppose I do with your nose, leave it crooked? And there's no other way to fix a broken nose."

"Aren't you going to give me some medicine first?"

Dot laughs. "We're not a hospital, dear."

Terry hands her a small hammer from under the sink. Dot looks at it for a moment, then concurs, it's probably the only thing to hand that will do the job. She thanks him and then asks him to pour a cup of tea with two lumps of sugar for the shock.

"Ok, Peter, I'm going to place the handle in your mouth. All you have to do is bite down on it. Bite down as hard as you can... and think of something happy."

Peter gives her a look as if to say *are you mad,* but he obliges anyway. There really was no other option. In the other half of the kitchen, the kettle, white with a black handle and adorned with flowers, began to whistle as if it were merrily mocking its audience. Terry attends to it, making sure to put two lumps of sugar in, just as Dot had ordered.

Dot's age weathered hands found the misshapen nose on Peter's face. She had done this countless times before, during her time as a nurse. She rubs it slightly, causing him to wince away from her. Dot grabs the sides of his head to pull him back, and places her fingers either side of the swollen feature. She suddenly snaps it into place. Peter lets out a flurry of curses under his breath as he feels the cartilage in his nose pop back into its rightful position. The dried blood coats his nostrils, the pools on his philtrum and lower lip have hardened to a deep red. Dot dampens a cloth and gently wipes his face clean, Peter was flinching with every touch.

"There, all done." She says, standing up.

Peter is clutching his nose, which is now in the normal position. White-hot pain is still emanating, but it is improving with every passing moment. His stomach, however, was doing somersaults. His eyes were still puffy, Dot assumed they would be for a couple of days, at least.

"Tea up, Peter."

Peter takes it eagerly from Terry. He's hunched over, his face deep in the mug of tea, with his hands clasped either side while Dot drapes a knitted blanket over his shoulders and rubs his back.

"How are you feeling now, dear?"

Peter takes his face from the mug to answer. "Much better, thank you. Thank you both."

"Kindness is free, remember that." Terry smiles. "Now, are you staying for stew? I hope you are."

"If you would have someone with my reputation, then I would be eternally honoured." Peter gives a slight bow.

"Reputation stands for nothing if the people who bestow it on you are arseholes, dear." For a woman born close to the beginning of the century, she was extremely liberal with her vocabulary, and proud of it too. She once said that she could make a sailor blush with the number of expletives she knew.

"So, who did this to you, Peter?" Terry takes the seat next to him at the kitchen table. Dot joins them, providing each of them with a bowl of stew and a cup of tea.

"Chris." He says, flatly.

"Chris? Why on earth are you going around speaking to him in the first place, dear? You know he's four ants short of a picnic, especially when tensions are so high."

"I just thought he was on our side, that's all." He concedes.

"Sides? What sides are you on about, lad?" Probes Terry.

"I guess I should start from the beginning."

Before he continues, he takes a mouthful of the warm, homemade chicken stew. His mouth explodes with flavours he hasn't experienced in years. A tear escapes and trickles down his face.

"What's the matter, dear?" Dot strokes his arm.

"Nothing. It's just that this is the first act of kindness I've had since... well..." There's no need to finish the thought, and, try as he might, he couldn't, the tears and hitching sobs wouldn't permit it. For the next few, long, moments, the room is filled with just the sound of the three people slurping their stew.

"How's the stew?" Terry continues, "Didn't I tell you she was a good cook. I've been the luckiest man to be able to eat her food for all of my adult life."

Dot smiles at him, reaching her hand across the table to hold her husbands in hers. They have stood the test of time and come out the other side stronger than ever, each and every time. Looking at them together, Peter realised that he had never had that with his wife. He wondered if many people were lucky enough to have what the Smith's had, he felt truly honoured to be in their company.

"The stew is perfect, as is the hospitality." Peter takes another mouthful. "Anyway, before I go any further, what was your honest assessment of the meeting tonight?"

Terry and Dot exchange a brief look, and then speak in unison.

"Eerie."

Which, Peter thought, was eerie in itself.

Peter is about to ask them to elaborate when Dot proceeds. "The way most of them just lapped it all up, and don't you worry, you weren't the only one to notice that not everyone was enthralled by our new Mayor. We were fortunate to also notice something else. Some of the people who were standing and cheering, well, I'm not too sure how to put it-"

"-They looked as if they were hypnotised." Terry finished.

Peter's heart dropped. He knew that there was something... well, *off*, with the new Mayor, and perhaps even thought, deep down, that there was something not quite right with the reception they had received, but to have his fears vocalised by someone else, changed the game. This just made it all too real for him.

"By the look on your face, you thought the same thing too. Tell me, dear, did you have any interaction with them before this evening?"

"Yes…"

"Did anything happen to you, either during or after your meeting with them?" Dot continues.

Peter thinks for a moment, then it hits him. If he said what he was about to say to anyone else, first of all, they wouldn't listen, but secondly, they'd think he had gone mad. He felt safe from any of that here.

"Now that I think about it, and it might sound a little odd, but I couldn't stop laughing."

Peter saw the look in Terry's eyes. "That's what happened to Dot here too. Not two minutes had gone by when he left us, that she fell down and burst into hysterics. I thought she was going to laugh to death, she bleedin' might have too, if she didn't start choking."

"The same happened to me."

"And you don't think this is a coincidence?"
"No." Peter and Dot said in unison.
"I was afraid you'd say that."

They finished the rest of their meal in relative silence, and, once they were all done, Terry asked, "Peter, where do you normally sleep at night?"

"Well, for the past few weeks I've been sleeping in the doorway of the Kent's old residence. I make sure I'm no bother, and it's boarded up anyway. I've never stole anything fro-"

"Hush dear. Remember, we're not here to judge you. As you yourself put it, I think we're on the same side... Whatever that is. Anyway, you shan't be staying in any doorway from now. Terry and I will make up the spare room upstairs for you, well, as long as you don't mind a few cobwebs here and there. Tez and I haven't been up there in goodness knows how long."

"No, no, this is too much. There is no way I could ever repay you for this, and besides, I'm happy sleeping outside, it gives me the chance to gaze at the stars."

"Nonsense!" Dot cuts in, "If you're worried about repaying us, you can help Terry with the store, and all the maintenance jobs he's piled up over the years." She shoots him a look and Terry feigns innocence. "If what those *strangers* say becomes true, and Kerwall town does become a flourishing town again, then we'll need the help anyway. Oh, and there's a skylight window for you to gaze at the stars. I won't have you trying to bleedin' say otherwise. I don't trust those strangers, not one bit, I don't know why, I just don't, and I'd rather have like-minded people around Terry and I, for safety as much as anything, I guess." She lets out a huge sigh. The two men could tell that she had been wanting to let this out

Kerwall Town

for quite some time, vocalising, once again, what they were thinking.

"I guess there's no arguing with the new arrangement then?"

"I wouldn't even bother," Terry smiled, "I've never won a single argument in all our married life."

"You bet your arse you haven't!" Dot said, seemingly still pent up with adrenaline.

"What I suggest we all do now, is go into the living room, and talk about what we all know so far. It's early days, but never too early to get a plan of action together. This is *our* town after all, not theirs, so if they think they can just take it from under our noses, well, they've got another thing coming!" Terry slams his fist down on the kitchen table, hard, his face had turned a deep red, and a thick vein is sticking out prominently from his neck.

Dot pats Terry on the back. "Before you burst a blood vessel, dear, fetch us a pen and paper from the draw. We'll be needing to write things down. Especially us, you know how forgetful we both are these days."

It was a fact of life that neither of them liked to admit; as they were getting up in years, their capacity for remembering was growing smaller. It wasn't yet at the stage where they would need to be in a home, but Dot harboured secret fears that Terry might be heading there. She didn't know how her heart would cope without him, it was the kind of thought which no matter how often she pushed to the very back of her mind, it kept creeping forward.

Once they were all settled in the living room, and Terry had handed over a pen and some paper to the man with the reshaped nose, it was Peter who spoke first.

"Ok, I guess the first step will be to ask: who else do you think distrusts them?"

Terry and Dot mull this over for a moment, before Dot gives an answer, "Ricky Turner. Definitely him. He didn't stand up once. He looked downright furious to be there in the first place." Terry nodded in agreement, and Peter writes his name on the paper.

Ricky was the proprietor of the town's only petrol station. He was a middle-aged bachelor, with an ever-growing beer belly, impossible to miss around town with his unmistakable long, ginger beard. It was so long at one point, that it was rumoured he could tuck it into his belt. It now falls at a more conservative length, just in the middle of his chest. His hair was almost the same length. He kept himself to himself and was very mild-mannered, so, to see him in such a state that evening was baffling.

"Denise Carter too." Terry suggests. "Although, she looked more solemn than usual. Poor girl. Terrible what happened to her, it really was." Then, as if remembering that in his present company was a man haunted by his own sorrow, added, "and you too, it was awful what happened to you too."

Peter waves away the words with his hand.

"It's all in the past." He says, writing Denise Carter down on the list.

Denise rarely left her house since her little girl was killed by the carelessness of a hit and run driver three years ago. Her marriage was buried alongside her child. Her ex-husband, Dave Skinner, now lives out of town, blissfully unaware of how Denise spends her days. Her now dull existence is limited to remaining cooped up in the house, barely eating or drinking. The once-

Kerwall Town

glamorous lady of Kerwall, now cuts a forlorn figure wandering the halls of her bare home. Upon arrival at the town meeting, at first, no one had recognised her at all. She kept to herself at the back of the hall, and when the meeting started, took the seat right next to Terry and Dot in the centre of the crowd. It was probably her attempt to blend in, but with a history as dark as Denise's, she didn't have that luxury. There had been a great deal of gossip spread about her since the incident, people would rather invent their own stories so they had something to talk about when they were starved from the truth. Most seemed to care very little for reality at all because their lies fed their appetites like no truth ever could. Denise used to run a book club in her spare time, and her Tupperware parties were the talk of the town in her heyday. Her parties were so good that women would come from towns over, just to experience her hospitality. Nobody knows exactly quite how much she and her husband were earning, but it must have been an enviable amount. Their house cast the longest shadow on their street, and when the tragedy of their daughter blackened their door, rumours swirled that they received a significant payout. Money can never replace the loss of a child though, and shortly after that, Dave left her; now she roams the shell of her empty, spacious home, alone. The curtains are always drawn, and the front and back gardens are wild with weeds and knee-high grass. The once pristine house, that had been painted a perfect white, is now falling into a dilapidated state, the paint flakes off at the corners, shingles on the roof have smashed to the ground, and ivy has started the race to the house's heights, stretching over windows that lie upon its path. Perhaps the worst part though is the shattered windowpanes. Some of the Kerwall youth had struck a few of the windows one Halloween, as some kind of prank, or dare, or whatever they do when they're high on whatever drug they're taking. It was Chris Kempo who was asked to board them up with some old wood, not for Denise's benefit though. It was done so that the town didn't look too unattractive. Compared to the rest of the town's falling buildings, Denise's house should have been the least of their worries.

"Can we be sure that she's one of us though, and wasn't just going through the motions? I mean, I don't even remember the last time I saw her outside. The look you saw on her face could just have been the shock of mixing with so many people, after hiding away for years." Peter asked, doubtfully.

Terry and Dot mulled this over before Dot vocalised their thoughts. "Perhaps you're right. I don't even know what to think, and I don't truly know why I don't trust those ... those *strangers!* Terry and I have been in this town long enough, and Terry has seen plenty of the world, we've never felt like we did when we met *him*".

"Certainly haven't... And I've seen the worst of humanity."

Dot manoeuvres herself up and out of the orange, velvet, corner sofa with a soft grunt. "Before we continue with this, anyone else want another hot drink?"

Both Terry and Peter opted for another round of tea. They all found the cold evening was starting to seep into their bones.

As she makes her way back into the mustard yellow and orange tiled kitchen, the men spoke amongst themselves. She put fresh water into the flower-patterned kettle, the water forming waves against the cold metal sides. The lights in the kitchen snap off, Dot's blood runs cold as she feels a presence standing directly behind her. The unmistakable warmth of breath touches her ear, rippling over her skin, and a long hand touches her neck.

"No sugar in mine this time, please Dot!" Shouts Peter from the living room. The lights come back on as quickly as they had turned off, and Dot looks out of the window just in time to see a large black bat. She was sure that was it, fly past the window. Perhaps that was the thing that was causing the scurrying sounds in the storage loft she thought, and then, as if compelled to, she forgot about ever seeing such a thing.

"I thought we could all do with some biscuits." Says Dot, entering the living room again. She places the *Victoria* assorted biscuit tin on the velvet sofa's conjoined table. Peter and Terry both dig in as soon as it's placed, filling their mouths immediately. "Feeding time at the zoo is it, dears? It's as if you've all been starved for a month." The company she was in dawned on her. "Sorry, Peter, dear. You carry on. It was mostly aimed at this gannet here." Shooting a look at Terry. Peter insists there's no harm done, while he munches greedily on a custard cream. Terry tries to plead his innocence, with a chocolate bourbon stuffed into his mouth. Dot gives him another look, a softer one this time, she can never stay mad at him for too long, and heads back into the kitchen to collect the now perfectly brewed teas. Moments later, she's back in the living room, stepping onto the loud floral floor to re-enter the embrace of its comforting stained wood panels, balancing the three cups of tea on a tray. She puts the tray on the wooden coffee table and sinks back into the sofa.

"Right then, dears. Where were we? Did you think of any more people who we could talk to about this... Whatever this is?"

The men look at each other sheepishly.

"We got side-tracked." Concedes Terry.

Dot tuts. "Football talk? Honestly, you can't leave men alone for two minutes without them resorting to talking about bleedin' football."

Peter and Terry apologise in unison.

While Terry, Dot, and Peter were discussing the goings-on of the town meeting and trying to establish who to trust, Denise was getting ready for bed. She was in her nightclothes, which in reality she wore in the day too, and heading up to bed when she heard a light knock on the door. Her hand froze on the bannister as she contemplated answering. The only people to ever knock were out of town salesmen. The rest of the town knew not to bother her. Some of them, due to the lies that had been spun about her, had even grown afraid.

She only knew of the town meeting courtesy of her single remaining friend from the community, Mike Rose, the town's resident postman. He would always ensure that he stopped and chatted to her at her front door whilst delivering her post. It took a few weeks for him to gain her trust, and once he had, all the lies he had heard about her seemed so ridiculous. When he told her about the mandatory town meeting this morning she was perturbed, to say the least. It had been Mike's idea for her to stand at the back of the hall, and then make her way to the middle to sit and listen.

The door knocked again, bringing her crashing back to reality. She gripped the bannister tighter, digging her nails in enough to draw a little blood. Over the past three years, she had taken to self-harming, the scars zigzagging up and down her arms were a testament to that, which is why, on the rare occasion that she did go out, she was sure to cover up. She swept her unwashed hair from her face smearing blood from her fingers across her forehead. The door knocked once more, with increasing urgency.

"Alright, I'm coming! Give me a chance!" She shouted as she walked back down the stairs, pulling her dressing gown tight to her chest.

Denise opened the door, just a crack, and saw a smiling face beaming through it. The face staring back at her was impossibly beautiful, with flawless pale white skin and a dark green highlight in her infinitely black hair. It was the woman from the meeting, she thought, and hugged her dressing gown even tighter to her.

"Good evening. I am so sorry to bother you… Denise, right?"

Denise nodded.

"I thought so. I know it's late, but I was wondering if I could trouble you for a small pot of milk? You see, we've just moved in across the road from you, and in all our haste we forgot to buy milk. I can't seem to settle without my evening cup of tea, and I saw a light on through the crack in your curtains and assumed you must be a night owl, like me."

Victoria gives her a pleasant smile, revealing perfect teeth.

"Oh. Let me just go and check. I might have a bit left for you."

"Thank you so much." Victoria's eyes are darting between the bloodstain on Denise's forehead and the blood on her fingertips, only breaking away when Denise walks down the hallway to the kitchen.

Halfway down the hallway, she turns to look at Victoria standing in the decrepit doorway.

"Would you like to come in for a moment?" She doesn't know why she says it.

"That would be... *wonderful.*" She replies, almost salivating, and closed the door behind her.

Elsewhere in Kerwall town, Ricky was manning the petrol station. In the '50s, when Kerwall was in the *boom period*, there were at least six other petrol stations. Turner's Service Station was now all that remained. There were only three pumps, all in beige with a thick red strip down the side and a large plastic dome on top, not only acting as a means of advertising for Shell but as a source of light too. There was also a small shop set a little way back from the forecourt. It's big windows, that needed a good clean, stretched the length of the single-story building. The roof sagged in the right-hand corner, and the door, which required replacing since the late '60s, needed to be opened with force.

Since most of his customers were regulars, he had become accustomed to their vehicles. So, when a long black car pulled up, at around the same time that Victoria was invited into Denise's home, and Peter, Terry, and Dot were discussing who to trust, Ricky rose from his chair, with the imprint of his ass, by the counter and walked out to greet them. Regardless that his custom was exclusively from locals these days, he didn't trust them to fill their own petrol tanks, and he was damn sure not going to let an out of towner do it.

Kerwall Town

"How much do you want me to put in?" Ricky asks the man as he gets out of the car.

"Fill her up, please. It's been a long journey and an even longer day. It's the first chance I've had." His voice was as smooth as velvet. He straightened his oil green tie and stuck out his leather-clad hand. Ricky looked at it and then shook it, not wanting to seem rude, even though his every instinct told him not to take it. Even before the meeting this evening, he didn't like the man now stood on his property. He especially didn't like the woman, and just like those few others in the town, he didn't know why.

Ricky filled up Mr Chatman's car and when he was done the new Mayor paid him, with a generous tip.

"I like you, Ricky."

The hair on the nape of Ricky's neck stood to attention. "How do you know my name?" His voice quivered.

"Why it's on your overalls, right there." Replies the Mayor, pointing to a spot just above Ricky's heart. Frances is giving him a smile full of teeth.

Ricky looks down at the leather-coated finger that is pressing into his chest. 'It's a long finger', was his initial thought.

"Oh yeah." He felt rather foolish. Maybe his mum was right, maybe all the years of smoking dope *did* rot his brain, he thought.

"I'm sure we'll be seeing much more of each other over the coming weeks, Ricky. You would like that, wouldn't you?" The Mayor's hand is now on Ricky's back, and he gives it a hearty smack as if they were in on a big secret together.

"I would like that, yes."

"Resplendent."

S.D. Reed

With that, the new Mayor got back in his car and drove away.

Ricky looked down at his chest, where the Mayor had laid his finger. There was nothing there, but a few moments ago he would have sworn on his own life that his name was stitched in oil green on his navy overalls in that very place. He couldn't remember if his name had been there before this evening, but was sure that he had seen it.

A giggle escapes his lips. Then another. And another. Within a few moments, he was doubled over in hysterics, and turning blue in the face. His eyes were bulging out of his ginger framed face. He clawed at his throat, desperate to somehow stop the laughing, his nails digging deep into the soft tissue under his beard, it only made him laugh harder. The straining caused the blood vessels in his throat to rupture, even still, he couldn't stop laughing. He collapsed onto his back in the middle of the petrol station's forecourt. There was no laughter coming from him now, just a single death rattle. His eyes milky white in the ambient glow of the *Shell* light.

While Ricky was struggling to remain, not only in Kerwall town but the world itself, Mike Rose, the town's postman and Denise's only friend, was still sorting letters in his ramshackle, cosy sized office. His only company was the creaking sound of the sign above the door whenever the September breeze outside got a hold of it.

Like most business owners in the town, Mike's place of work was also his residence. He was sat in his floral wallpapered living room, listening to *Pink Floyd*. This evening, he was chomping on a special variety of

Kerwall Town

mushroom. Earlier on, he had been adamant that the petals surrounding him were so vibrant, so close, that he could smell them. They got bigger still and as *Time* drifted by, they threatened to consume the whole room. A giant bird, or something resembling one, had circled him and bitten his neck. Instead of crying out in pain, Mike had said a simple thank you. That must have been around two hours ago, although, in Mike's current state, time was an extremely loose concept. Luckily for Mike, being the postman of a *very* small town, there were few letters to be sorted. However, he thought it best to stop the work for the evening, and get something to eat, as he was starving. He was dressed just in shorts, leaving his hairy, athletic chest exposed. The fridge cast a brilliant light across the kitchen floor when he opened it. At first it was too bright, forcing him to shield his eyes with his free hand. The hand holding the door was also helping him maintain balance as the room seemingly divided itself onto different levels. The black and white checkered floor playing havoc, making him question what was real, and what wasn't.

"Get a grip!" He said to himself, shaking his head. This seemed to make things better, albeit for just a moment. From the fridge, he grabbed a carton of near stale milk and drank straight from it. He placed it on the side counter, almost missing and spilling the liquid onto the floor, and hunted through the cupboards for something to fill his rumbling stomach. He found a tin of spam hidden away and opted to use only his hands to force the food into his mouth. 'Who needs cutlery when you're high as fuck?', he thought. When it became impossible to shovel anymore out, he used his tongue to consume the remaining morsels. After ensuring that the tin was entirely empty, he left it on the kitchen side to clean up in the morning and went to the bathroom to take a leak. As he was leaving, he caught a glimpse of himself in the mirror, his brown eyes stared back at him as normal. He didn't look like a man in his 40's at all, he was in great shape thanks to his workout of the daily postal route. There was something else in his reflection too, something that wasn't there before. It looked like two small bite marks halfway up his neck. He laid his hand over the holes, expecting it to elicit pain, but there was none. It felt smooth as if something with great precision had done it with immense care. He didn't feel intoxicated anymore either, in fact, he didn't feel the need to eat those funky mushrooms ever again. What he was feeling was energised and an absolute need to go out into the cold September air. It felt like it was the single most important thing in the world, and he embraced the need as though embracing an old friend. What he failed to notice was that the reflection that stared back at him was almost translucent, he had been preoccupied with the two additions to his neck and his insatiable appetite.

He ran downstairs with a renewed vigour and threw open the door to the night's air. The cold on his cheeks was a sensation of pure ecstasy, he felt as if he could run for miles, better yet, he felt like he could fly. He planted his feet on the ground outside his home, bent his knees, and jumped. To his absolute surprise, as he was jumping, his body morphed into a small bat. He flapped his new, tiny wings for all they were worth and rose into the night sky. Flying came as natural to him as breathing. It was as if he had known how to do it all of his life but never dared try. For the first time, he felt whole.

Death was tugging at Ricky's soul, who was still crumpled under the luminous light of the *Shell* sign. He could almost feel Death itself standing just a few feet away from him, silently stalking him, waiting for the last rattling breath to escape from his pale white lips. He could even hear the flapping of Grim's cloak around its heels as it approached his nearly lifeless body. Ricky would have bet everything he owned that these were his last few seconds on earth and that Death was standing right above him, ready to claim his being.

"Breathe normally and stop choking." The silky tone reverberated in Ricky's ice-cold ear.

All of a sudden, Ricky's chest began to rise and fall at a steadying pace and after a few moments had passed he realised that he was able to sit up. He looked around at Lloyd-Chatman, who was knelt beside him, watching carefully with his piercing eyes.

"Where am I?" Ricky's wafer-thin voice is barely audible.

"Don't worry, you're safe here, with me." Lloyd-Chatman speaks carefully, stroking Ricky's ginger mane. "Now listen, I can't have you out on the cold street like this."

"No, you can't." Replied Ricky, still in his new thin voice. He was staring into the Mayor's eyes with deep concentration, filled with the fear that if he didn't, he would sink right through the ground beneath him. He found a little strength when he clutched onto Francis too, it was a radiance of power and he tried to hold onto it. Frances looked down at Ricky's dirty hands on his suit in disdain. He looked like a beggar on the streets, begging to stay alive.

"I want you to go back to your home," says the Mayor, still in his velvet voice, "and I want you to turn on your oven. Turn it up as high as it will go and then I want you to do something very special for me, can you do that?"

Ricky was nodding his head eagerly, he looked pathetic, almost like a dog waiting for his master to throw the stick he so desperately wanted.

"I want you to climb inside it and shut the door. If you can't fit, *make* yourself fit. It is very important that you do this. You are ever so useless to this town. Nobody needs you anyway." He punctuated his words with his cruel, chilling cackle.

"Nobody needs me anyway." Replied Ricky, flatly.

"So, what are you going to do about it?" The Mayor asked, shrugging his shoulders mockingly and pouting his lips.

"I'm going to turn the oven on at full heat, make myself fit inside, and close the door."

"Exactly, that's a good boy."

The Mayor helps Ricky to his feet and hold him by his shoulders for a moment. He then turns him around, so that he is facing the door to the petrol station, and gives him a gentle push. He picks up his handkerchief and shakes the dust off it, he then wipes the parts of his body that Ricky touched. He felt the touch of a peasant was most repulsive.

"Go then, there is no time like the present. You will be doing a valuable service to this town. your sacrifice will not be in vain and will be for Kerwall."

"It won't be in vain." Ricky repeats as he strides towards his own demise.

Kerwall Town

Ricky walks into his house with legs that didn't know what they were doing. His eyes fully fixated on the small white oven in the centre of his kitchen. The grill was at the top, four hobs lay below, and under that was an oven, where he'd normally put his meat on a Sunday. It would be a different kind of meat going in there today though, and he had promised that he would fit in no matter what.

The hobs were coated in months of old grease and crumbs, along with burn stains, and the odd dead fly singed onto the surface. The grill was a mess too. It appeared as though it had its own colony forming amongst the charred remains of Ricky's every meal.

He turns the oven on to its highest temperature and opens the door, it creaks in anticipation. He bends down, takes out the shelves and places them onto the kitchen table with a *clink*, the sound hangs in the air, unregistered. He pulls the door wider, this time hot air billows into his face instantly. He puts his head directly in, followed by his shoulders, that's all that fits. He tries to turn his head into the top corner of the oven, the flames now licking at his neck and clothes. His ginger hair singes away as the flames grab at it greedily. He still can't fit all the way in. His skin is starting to blister and bubble, blood flowing freely from the scorches. He pushes himself out of the fire pit, evidently not feeling an ounce of the immense pain.

"Must fit. For Kerwall." He says to himself in a now hoarse voice. He walks over to the draw, the flames now melting his clothes into his skin, and selects a butcher's knife from the tray. He keeps the impossibly sharp knife, exactly that, sharp. The lethality of this weapon had always provided Ricky with a sense of security, it was his protection. The steely blade is glistening now in the evening moonlight shining in through the window, he brings it down on his left thigh, showering the floor with blood. He hacks at it again, and again, his hands quickly becoming a crimson mess. The knife strikes into the bone and for a brief moment, it gets stuck, not wanting to be pulled free despite Ricky's best efforts. He uses both of his hands to grip the handle and tendons tear away as the knife pulls free from his femur. He hacks away with more intensity now, focused on the same spot. Dark red blood pools around him and when he strikes the leg a final time it falls in a wet thud as it meets with the blood-stained floor.

His left leg is now in two separate pieces. The top of his thigh is gushing a red fountain, the formerly black and white floor now a dark, sticky red. He proceeds to do the same to his right thigh, more blood, more slashing at gristle. The butcher's utensil is slicing through the tendons as if they were butter, now that he had refined the art. When the knife gets stuck in his bone yet again, he yanks it out once more with all of his force, sinews and blood cling to the knife as it pulls free from the marrow. Combating this, he decides to put the blade above the open flame in the oven for a few moments, attempting to make cutting through his own body even easier. All the while he is still on fire, the flames thrashing insatiably at every patch of his skin, and what's more, he's smiling, humming even. He wants to fly; he doesn't fear the Reaper. His eyes are fixated on the job at hand, not seeming to feel any pain. He is laughing so hard that tears are rolling down his face, leaving tracks on his blood-stained cheeks.

Where his legs once were, remains nothing but bloody stumps, he opens the oven door for a final time, throws his separated limbs in first and then proceeds to awkwardly shuffle his body closer to the entrance of his fiery coffin. He hops in like a deformed bunny. The flames caress the bloodied limbs making them clot and blister. His beer belly is almost fully stuffed inside the oven, but it needs a little more persuading if it's to fit in with the rest of his maimed body. So, reaching for the blade, still half consumed by the oven, flames licking freely at his exposed flesh, Ricky cuts away at his stomach. His intestines fall into a heap at the foot of the oven, popping from the heat after mere seconds. His arms are his next problem, easily solved with further blade work, his left arm is now a separate limb and, using his right, he stuffs it into the small hole already made in his open stomach. Lastly comes his head. The once long ginger beard and hair now reduced to nothing. He is now completely inside the oven and he shuts the door with his remaining hand, and all remaining effort, cooking himself alive for Kerwall.

As the sun was rising to start a new dewy September morning, Ricky's corpse echoed a charred piece of meat left overnight on a BBQ grill.

4

The Factory

The town still held one operational factory and of the 915 residents, over two hundred worked at the Kerwall Toy Factory, of which most were women. It produced animatronic dolls in corn yellow dresses and with sunflower hair. The plasticine heads were sculpted by the men and the rest of the body was assembled on the shop floor by the women. Once the dolls were built, they were sent to another part of the plant, where they stitched in a label reading '*Made in Beautiful Kerwall*'. No one who owned one really knew if the town existed or not, regardless, up and down England many wished they could visit. A few people had stumbled upon it recently but none had stayed, and what was most peculiar was that non-locals who entered the town had no recollection of ever visiting once they left.

Finally, a man would insert a tape recording into the back. If the toy's owner, usually a little girl, pushed the doll's tummy it would say a few select phrases, such as "*A good lady looks after her man*", and "*I want to grow up to be a housewife*". There was another layer to the voice too. It was one you could barely hear, even if you were listening intently for it. It was the voice of a man saying "Kerwall town does not exist." It was a recent addition and the man's voice, unbeknownst to the everyone, was none other than that of Frances Lloyd-Chatman. He and his business associate had been laying down the foundations of their plan for this humble town for many months, possibly years, watching it fall onto its knees, whilst subconsciously suggesting to the most powerful and able townsfolk to either become submissive or leave. That was the true reason why Jennifer and Scott Ramsey had left town overnight. Many believed it was due to their ever-growing Tupperware parties, but the truth was that Frances and Victoria didn't like how powerful they were becoming, making them a threat. There had been talk that Scott was going to run for Mayor in the next term, and he most certainly would have won. The couple were invited to dinner at an out of town restaurant by Frances and Victoria. They were led to believe they had been chosen to be the recipients of a *Tupperware Lifetime Achievement Award*, but to accept it, they must move to a grander and more prestigious part of the country. They didn't even allow themselves the thought that they were being set up. Their only thought was, 'it's too good *not* to be true'. Jennifer and Scott couldn't believe their luck and were convinced to pack up and leave that very evening, which is exactly what they did. They were also asked to completely forget that Frances and Victoria existed, forgetting about the town too. As soon as they left the restaurant and packed up their things, they had no recollection of living anywhere but their new home on the coast, which was a great deal smaller than their former home in Kerwall.

The factory was a long brick building, the windows in the roof serving as the only natural light source in the otherwise dingy workplace. It was the largest building in the town by a long way and the only one that produced enough money, and jobs, to keep the town alive; which it was barely doing.

The shape of the factory was akin to a large 'L' and was set out over two tumbling floors. The shop floor itself was split into a further five sections. The body moulding block was the first station, where the shape of the doll was formed in a variety of skin tones. Second came the head assembly, where the lifelike heads were produced and attached to the small bodies. It was also where the eerie, convincing eyes were popped into their sockets by the workers. Little did anyone know that the reason they were so realistic was because that's exactly what they were. Lifelike. It had been another initiative by the now town owners, put into action many months back. The eyes had been gathered from their countless victims, serving them no purpose anymore. Many were eyes that belonged to former enemies of Victoria herself. It was also where the lips were spray-painted in a fire truck red. There was then 'The Salon', where the women would give the blonde doll its iconic fashionable locks, often beehives or a bouffant. Fourth came the 'Sweat Shop', where hand-made and up to the minute fashions were stitched and then draped over the doll's fragile frames. Finally, came 'Quality and Packaging', where dolls were thoroughly checked over, ensuring that there were no imperfections, and packed to a pristine standard. To make a single doll from start to finish would take just three hours. The factory remained open twenty-four hours a day from Monday - Thursday and closed at 5 p.m. sharp on a Friday. No dolls were made on the weekends, and on Sundays, most of the town attended Church.

Kerwall Town

"Good weekend, Kitty?" Asked Patty. They were walking down the street with Linda and Mable, who were, as ever, falling a few paces behind.

"Same as always: cooking, cleaning, ironing and of course, church yesterday."

Patty recalls the floral print dress, with the denim hem, which Kitty had been wearing the previous day. "Oh, I loved your dress! You'll have to give me the pattern for it!"

"Pop by later on and I'll give it to you."

Patty was a comfortable way through her fortieth years. When she wasn't at work, she had curlers tightly wrapped in her fading brown hair. Today she had on a white bonnet scarf and a fag was balanced in her thin lips. The ash at the end of her cigarette was threatening to topple to the floor at any moment. Linda was also smoking, flicking her ash away as fast as it was forming. It was a nervous tick of hers. Patty and Linda had grown up together and had always lived next door to one another. They had trodden an almost identical path, the only difference being that Patty is a widow and Linda is divorced.

Mable is clutching her tin lunchbox tightly to her grey work smock and walking a few paces faster now, desperate to keep up, her long auburn hair flowing in the day's morning breeze. She lived with her ginger cat, Tinkey, at her parents' home. She was one of the most beautiful women in all of Kerwall, but she was so shy and reserved that she didn't notice all the men falling at her feet on a weekly basis. "What did you think of the Vicar's speech?"

"Load of shite, as always! We already know that we have to be good to one another, so why don't that useless cow, Shelly! If I had just three minutes alone with her, I'd knock her front teeth out and shove a pencil up her arse in the hope it comes through the newly formed gap in her mouth, that way she can draw herself a new personality." Retorts Linda.

The women laugh harmoniously. They all knew of the long-standing rivalry between Linda and Shelly. A few years ago, Shelly had been in their friendship group, but the consensus was that she had *'arse-licked'* her way to the top, as Linda put it. Other rumours were that she had slept with the Managing Director, Paul Danson, to get to her position as Team Leader. A position that didn't exist until Shelly had taken it on. She now spends the majority of her shift walking up and down the factory floor, bellowing orders, before sitting down chatting to Paul for the remainder of the afternoon.

Linda would never say any of this outside of the friendship group, nor to Shelly's face; the one-time she did it backfired when Shelly went straight to the higher-ups. So now, whenever they were near each other, there was an undeniable tension. Shelly could sense it too; she wasn't that dumb after all. When Shelly had been promoted, she made sure that Linda didn't have the same break slot as the rest of her friends.

"I quite liked the message." Kitty tried to get back to the topic at hand.

"It's a good job the good Vicar is handsome, I'll say that much, because he drones on endlessly." Continues Linda.

"You're only saying that because he didn't want to go on a date with you!" Patty laughed.

"Oh, hush you! It's only, *only,* because he's a man of the cloth. If he wasn't, he would be husband number two by now, I can guarantee it!"

Kerwall Town

"Don't be so sure about that, I think he's sweet on our Mable!" Linda grinned.

Mable goes a deep shade of red. "Oh, don't be so silly, and as you say, he's a man of the cloth." She clutches her lunchbox even tighter and puts her head down so they can't see how red she's become.

"Well, all men have needs, and it's the '70s, darling, the decade of sexual liberation, and trust me, I'll be the one to liberate him!"

The women tell her to move on, laughing at the prospect.

The group now joined the drones of others lining up to stamp their clocking in card. The line was a-hum with not only church the night before, but also the town meeting. There was no talk on the subject of Ricky, who by now had flies nesting in his eye sockets.

Once the clock-in procedure was complete, the women put their lunchboxes into their lockers and sat in the break room waiting for the work whistle to signal them to go onto the shop floor.

Paul Danson was already at his desk, chatting to Shelly who was perched in front of him. She was twiddling her fingers in her long blond hair, trying, and failing, to look sexy. His hand was massaging the inside of her thigh.

"Stop! Someone might be looking?" Whistled Shelly. Unfortunately for her, her lisp had always created issues, so introducing herself was always a source of minor embarrassment. That was her only flaw, or noticeable one anyway.

"They won't." He replied, moving up slowly to her crotch. She didn't for one second try to stop him. She instead continued to twirl her locks with her elegant index finger, while staring at him with her ice-blue eyes. She was as beautiful as he was ugly. He was a small, well-fed man with a receding hairline, swiftly approaching his sixties. He was also the laziest man in Kerwall, by other residents' judgement. He was extremely lucky to be in such a high powered, and higher-paid position. The only person in town fond of him was Shelly, and that was perhaps because they were both as useless as each other, and shared a mean streak a mile long. It was mostly just playground antics they resorted to, but to those they were inconveniencing, the daily tirade was unbearable.

The work whistle ripped through the air and, moments later, Shelly was standing next to the work board in front of her diligent staff.

"Right everyone. We were all at the town meeting, and I hope you all took heed of what was said. This is a new era, for not only Kerwall but the factory too. So, start pulling your weight!" Her sounds tripped over each other as she struggled to keep up with her S's.

"She's one to talk." Whispered Linda to Patty, who had to put her hand to her mouth in an attempt to mute her laughter.

"Care to share the joke, Linda?" Asked Shelly.

"Not really." She retorted languidly.

Shelly's low grunt expresses the extent of her frustration. "Get to work. Oh… and enjoy your day."

That was something she always said. It was so insincere that it was laughable.

Today, all of the gang were on 'eye-popping' duty. The eyes were so lifelike, that some even thought they were human eyes, it was a common observation,

Kerwall Town

regularly dismissed as fiction. They came in an assortment of colours, no two dolls exactly the same, but the most sought-after colour was sky blue.

The almost complete dolls would come down the conveyor belt and the women would push in the eyes. They each only had around a minute to insert them before the next four toys dropped down simultaneously. Patty and Linda sat next to each other, as did Kitty and Mable adjacent to them. To pop the eyes in properly, they had to lie the doll completely flat on the 'jig', and then press a button. From there, two eyes would shoot down from the narrow silver pipes which formed part of the 'jig'. It was always accompanied by a '*flum*' sound as the eyes came hurtling down the pipe at speed, and stuck themselves into the head of the doll.

The task was as mundane as can be, all they did was push a button and make sure that the doll was lined up properly. If it wasn't, the eye would end up in the cheek or the forehead and it would have to go into the rejection pile. Too many of those in one day, and it would be docked from their pay-packet at the end of the week. It did, however, give them plenty of time to chat and the pay was good, so it was almost a win-win situation. They had all been doing the job for so long, that they could do it with their eyes closed.

Normally, the workers wouldn't be put on the same job more than twice in a week. The group were facing their tenth time in two and a half weeks. They didn't care though, although it was repetitive, it was better than some of the other jobs at the factory. They were also lucky to be on a machine, they could have been allocated to cleaning duty, which was the most boring job the factory could bestow. It was often seen as a punishment, which is why, although Shelly was a pain in the ass, it was good practice to keep on the right side of her.

The first four dolls came down the conveyor at 9:15 a.m. It took a while for the machines to whirr into action and for the first parts of the doll to be made; the women, while they were waiting, absentmindedly pushed a broom around and spoke about Tupperware. It wasn't until the third set of dolls came down that they started to talk about the events of the town meeting. Patty Beaux ignited the flame.

"What did you make of the town hall meeting? You know, that *bunny,* Victoria, was it? wanting to take Kerwall to the max?"

"I didn't take in much of what she was saying, all my attention was on that fox, Frances!" Chimes in Kitty. "Don't be telling my husband I said that by the way, especially you, Linda, I know what you're like!" She jokes.

"What's that supposed to mean?" Linda replies a little defensively.

"Hey, don't have a cow, I'm just jonesing with you."

This seems to simmer some of the minor tension that could have brewed between the two of them. Kitty and Linda have a somewhat fractious relationship at times, although it never turns to malice. A lot of the women's vernacular comes from the American films that have invaded Kerwall's cinema and, of course, Kitty, via her American husband.

"I think what they were saying could only be a good thing for the town. It might finally put us back on the map!" Mable was growing excited, she was aiming for casual, but overshot.

Kerwall Town

"I don't want to be on a map. I like this town as it is now. Shitty." Linda continues. "As soon as you put this town on a map, we no longer have our freedom. We'll have to conform to '*the man*' and, bitch, this woman ain't bowing down to any man anytime soon. I'll tell you that for free!"

"So, you're saying that you didn't dig what they were saying?" Asks Patty.

"Oh, don't get me mixed up, I'm all for the investment. There're only so many times I can look at the piss pot ramshackle streets and be ok with it. I just don't want the *people* to come with it. I'm happy with our small town."

"Maybe a new man will swing by and sweep you off your feet?" Said Mable.

"I already got rid of one man; I don't want another anytime soon… Unless it's the Vicar of course… Or that Frances, but he'll have to get rid of Victoria first. I ain't into that freaky three-way sex, no thank you!"

"I don't think they're together, they're just business partners." Patty mused.

"Are you kidding me, two impossibly beautiful and *young* people like that are made for each other. They are definitely going steady." Replied Kitty.

"I hope this conversation is about work." Shelly probed, knowing the answer. As soon as the women heard her stilted speech, eyes rolled and the happiness seemed to have been instantly sucked away. She had that effect on all of the workforce. She was a little bit of an enigma, some days she could be mostly ok to talk to and then others she would be utterly vindictive. Whenever she came over to talk though, she would spend at least 10 minutes, and if care wasn't taken, mistakes would be made whilst attempting to entertain her fickle personality. If she wasn't given a worker's full attention, her whining and complaining would be taken directly to Paul. However, if her subject permitted a single mistake, they would be deemed incompetent and, again, reported to Paul Danson... It was the cycle of the factory. Every decision made, resulted in negative consequences, regardless of how much desperate effort was made to prevent it. Ultimately, no matter what, it was always the operators who took the blame. They were seen as wholly unintelligent and disposable these days. They had been indispensable before, during the boom period there would be a dozen or so new workers each week.

"We were just talking about the town meeting." Explained Mable.

"Hardly about work now, is it?"

"Of course, it is! You even said at the clock earlier it was." Linda was finding it harder each day to not lose her cool with Shelly. She was even starting to wonder if the whole stupid act that she put on, was even an act at all, but questioned herself, no one can be *that* stupid, *that* often, Linda thought.

"I know that, I wouldn't have said it at the clock otherwise now, would I? Silly thing. I meant that we're at work now, so we can keep talking to a minimum, can't we?" The women had to focus on every word to understand her clearly. Shelly smiled in such a condescending way that it made Linda want to put her head on the conveyor belt, under the pipe and pop new eyes into her skull. But Linda was a good, Christian girl, so she refrained. By this time, she had two dolls on her side of the conveyor, so, when Shelly wasn't looking, she stashed the most recent one under the table. She'd catch up with it later.

"I think what we're all trying to say is that changes are coming, and we're excited for them." Said Mable, calmly. She was often the peacekeeper. She hated confrontation of any kind, and even at the faintest whiff of an argument, she would try to quell it or sink into herself. While she was talking, and when she wasn't tending to her doll, of course, she was busy twirling her fingers into knots. There was a child-like innocence about her that some people found endearing, but a few of the townsfolk just found it to be annoying, or thought that she was a *'little bit simple'*. She wasn't. She was one of the smartest people in the whole of Kerwall. The fact that she lived at home with her parents, was another reason why some people found her odd. She never noticed the funny looks she got in the streets sometimes, if she did, she never paid them any mind. Mable had it all, looks and brains. She just refused to flaunt them. The job at the factory was to tide her over until she could do what she wanted, to become a writer. She would sit in her room for hours on end, creating new words. She had never shown anyone her work, she was too scared to, but she didn't fool herself into thinking they weren't good. Other than Tinkey, it was the thing she adored most in the world. Her favourite stories to write were horror. It completely juxtaposed her personality, but that is what she finds so alluring about it. It was her chance to try on a different mask, and she liked the way the horror one fit.

Shelly decided not to continue the conversation. She was lost in it before it even got going if truth be told.

"Don't you go falling behind. I know what you four are like when you're put together. You should thank your lucky stars I was kind enough to put you all here." She said and left. It was her way of making them feel small, she flaunted supposed power over them, and the favour she gave them, in allowing them to work together. It didn't matter that they were the four best operators in the factory, they didn't make mistakes, and it was Paul Danson who arranged the job wall. Shelly didn't have much say in it at all, but liked to think that she did.

Linda lit up a fag and started to smoke. The other women, except for Mable, followed suit.

"I tell you, one day, that woman is going to regret talking to us like that." Patty huffed.

"I bet she couldn't do our job, even if she tried with all the little brain cells in that pretty little head of hers." Snapped Kitty.

"She's a dumb cow, there's no way she'd be able to pop the eyes in right, let alone keep up with the machine." Replied Linda. The little corner they occupied was quickly becoming engulfed in plumes of smoke. Mable was the only one of the gang who didn't smoke. She had tried it, very briefly, behind the bike sheds when she was at school. It was in the pouring rain no less, after half a drag she felt as though she was coughing her guts up. For the briefest of moments, she thought she was the coolest woman alive … Until she couldn't stop coughing that is. She had stubbed the smoke out on the concrete floor in such a hurry that she stepped in a puddle deep enough to soak her bell-bottoms up to her ankle, it had weighed her down for the rest of the afternoon.

The only other time she had tried smoking was the first time she had seen the women at work do it, it ended much the same way, a coughing fit after just one drag. She surmised that she just wasn't built to smoke, and she was ok with it. After all, she had heard a crazy rumour that smoking was bad for the health anyway. There was no way she thought that it was true, but it made her feel a little better that she *couldn't* smoke, just in case it turned out to be a fact.

Despite the extreme volume within the factory walls, courtesy of the screaming machines and constant hubbub of talking, the workers were not provided ear protection. Whilst after a while, operators learnt to tune out the sounds, the damage caused could never be undone. Some of the older workers were almost deaf as a doorpost after working there since it opened in the early '50s.

"What do you think the new Mayor will do for the factory?" Asked Mable through the ever-thickening smoke.

"I'd like to think he'd pay us more, that would be far out" Kitty dreamed. They were already paid a decent wage, but Kitty especially wanted to earn more, enough to get out of Kerwall.

"Maybe they'll let more women be supervisors and bosses..." Patty continued her thought.

"...But actual useful ones, like *us*." Chimed in Linda, "Reality is, they won't though. We're the ones who pretty much run this place. Why would they promote their top performers? No one else will fill our shoes."

"Well, with new townspeople, they might. You never know, there could be dozens of women out there who want a job like this." Said Mable, her naivety shining through the words.

"Oh, I'm sure there are plenty of women, men too, just queueing outside the town line right now, just *dying* to work in a place like this!" Retorted Linda.

"*In a town like this!*" Sniggered Patty.

"I'll live in hope. It's what my parents and *God* taught me." Mable declared, for the first time showing a little bit of moxie, the women appreciate it. Not that they'd ever directly tell her that.

"Shit in one hand, hope in the other. No prizes for guessing which one fills up quicker." Grunted Linda, who had, by now, caught up on the doll Shelly made her fall behind on earlier.

Adam McCallum, Kitty's husband, walked past the women and blew his wife a kiss, she caught it gleefully. He was impressively tall at 6ft 3, he had deep blue eyes, and a buzz cut. He was too young to have served in the Second World War, but his father had, and he had always insisted that he kept his hair short.

Kitty and her husband were the youngest couple in town, both in age and length of their marriage. They had met at a work's day out one lazy Saturday afternoon, five years ago. Every six months, the factory organises a BBQ in an attempt to boost the workers' morale, but it had been dressed up as the owner being a caring philanthropist. Regardless of its intent, it was the highlight of the worker's calendar. The BBQ was held every summer in Kerwall Town Park, the only place in town that wasn't falling into disrepair. The flowers were still maintained and the grass was manicured regularly. The fountain in the middle of the small lake still functioned too. It was almost as if the park and the town were two completely separate worlds. Every resident was on a rota to keep it looking it's best and there were punishments if it wasn't upheld. No one knew what those punishments were, no one wanted to find out either.

Kerwall Town

At around 4:30 p.m., just as dusk was falling outside, the monotony of factory life came to a screeching halt. On the surveillance balcony stood Frances Lloyd-Chatman. He was smiling ear to ear and looked dashing in an oil green tartan suit and crisp white shirt.

"Good afternoon everyone." He laughed, with a cheeriness akin to a game show host. "Please, turn off the machines for all of five minutes."

The men who were in charge of the machines did as they were asked without a word. Now that the machines were off it was as quiet as a graveyard in the countryside. The women stubbed out their eighth fag of the day on the singed side of the machine. Linda and Patty were busy watching the rest of the factory looking up in amazement, they didn't catch the Mayor's gaze. There was an uneasy feeling in their stomachs.

"Thank you." He said when all of the machines had fallen silent. "Gather round, all of you. I want to be able to see all of you fantastic workers. *You* are the *lifeblood* of this town."

They were all now gathered in the centre of the factory floor, looking up at their new overnight Mayor. They clung onto his every word.

"As you are all aware, I am your new Mayor. What you may not know, is that I am also the new owner of this factory." His maniacal laugh punctuated each point.

Spontaneous applause broke out, no one was sure who had started it, but after a few seconds, everyone joined in. Mable looked around, hands clapping, and realised that the *whole* factory was here, everyone, from every site, all crammed in and listening intently to this stranger. She felt fortunate being able to listen to this man, she thought she would do anything for him if he asked. It was a feeling shared by most of the people in the factory.

"Thank you. You may stop clapping." He ordered, and instantly they did. It was as if they weren't even clapping just milliseconds before. "Now, in a few short days, the size of this factory workforce will swell. In a few months, it will be as big, no, bigger, than it ever was. There will be jobs for everyone, but we must all make sacrifices to make it work. Does that sound agreeable?"

The workforce agreed immediately, without the slightest bit of resistance.

"Fantastic. The sacrifices will be worth it, I promise you. You will all be required to work an extra Saturday shift, but not here, in the mines. Starting this week. Remember, you are all the life*blood* of this town, so you must lead by example. Do you all understand?"

"Understood", they all echoed back to the new Mayor.

"Good. That is all for now. Carry on with your day. I will be watching."

With that, he was gone. The crowd dispersed back to their assigned sections and the women finished up their last couple of dolls for the day. When the work whistle signalled the end of their shift and the beginning of the next one, they left without uttering another word until they had gotten halfway down the street. They weren't the only ones. When the Mayor left, the only noise came from the machines.

"More work and a new owner. I knew he was going to change things for the better!" Said Kitty, breaking the silence while Patty lit a fag.

"I've never worked down the mines... I don't even know what to do, let alone *mine!* Oh dear, I hope we get trained." Mable could get herself worked up over anything, her anxiety overtaking her shyness.

"Relax. There'll be nothing to it. If the men could do it back in the day, us women can do it just as well." Said Patty.

"Better, don't you mean." Teased Linda.

"Did anyone hear him say we'll be paid more for the extra shift?" Kitty queried.

"No, but he can't expect us to work more hours for the same amount of money, even if we *are* the … what did he call us…?" Probed Patty.

"The life*blood,* or something like that." Said Linda, hesitantly.

"I knew things were going to change, but I didn't expect it to happen so soon. These really *are* exciting times to be living in Kerwall!" Mable was regaining her optimism now.

"Where are they going to get all the extra workers from? That's what I want to know." Said Kitty.

"I'm sure they have their ways. They seem to get things done; I'll give them that." Assured Linda.

After a few moments, they came to the fork in the road where Patty and Linda split from Kitty and Mable. There was a quick exchange of goodbyes and promises were made to call each other later, after dinner, to see if anyone has heard anything worth reporting.

When Patty and Linda are alone, they walked down the street in silence, both quietly reflecting the events of the day. Later on, they told each other that they had an uneasy feeling about the Mayor and Mayoress. Neither of them could explain why. They later made a pact to keep this from their friends too, no matter what. They hadn't seen what the two of them had on the factory floor, because they had been blinded by the stranger and his promises. Patty and Linda thought it best to play along as well as they could. They felt their life depended on it.

5

A Rectory Dysfunction

Elsewhere in Kerwall that evening, the Vicar, Henry Blackburn, was tending to his church garden. It was erected many moons before the town itself had come to exist in the '50s, but no one can recall exactly when. There is some argument that it predated several of the world wonders. The most confusing aspect of the mystery was that it still stood in tremendous condition. The church rose to an imposing 312ft over the town. On top of the ornately decorated gothic steeple was a warped, slender spire reaching its way towards the heavens. Legend has it that the crook formed when God and Lucifer battled for supremacy, the final moments of the crusade taking place atop the iron spire. The weight of the two behemoths, was almost too much for the holy structure to bear, eventually granting God the advantage; Lucifer lost his footing, allowing God to claim victory with a final finishing blow. However, history is written by the victors. A darker rumour envelops these events: Lucifer permitted God to win, laying claim to pockets of the world without God's knowledge. Kerwall was one such place. A place where evil could roam free without the watchful eye of earths creator. But those are just stories, the truth, in this case, is much, much worse.

The church stood on the top of the only hill in Kerwall, looking over the towns every street, like watchful eyes over the residents. At the base of the hill lay the home of Kerwall's deceased inhabitants. Whilst it was impossible to remember what had come before, there could be no clearer indicator than those headstones, some now too weathered to read. The ones that were legible were dated as far back as 950 A.D. The accuracy of these were often called into question, regularly becoming something of a talking point at Tupperware parties.

"You'll overwater them if you carry on like that!" Bellowed Kerwall's other Vicar, Reginald Dundon. He was as old as time itself. What little hair he had left, was white, and thin, and scraped back over his flaky scalp, making his deep brown eyes perpetually bulge. He was known by most of his clergy as *'The Sinister Minister.'* He no longer had time for pleasantries, preferring to spend his sermon time rehashing the same verses on repeat; people had stopped listening to him, so he stopped giving much effort back. The ones that had stayed only did so out of respect for God, not him. In the '60s he had a somewhat cult following, but his worshipers have now either passed on or attended church on the days Henry led the sermons.

Henry was the exact opposite. He was tall and slender, always perfectly clean shaven with oversized black rimmed glasses and piercing blue eyes. His face was framed by almost shoulder length slick brown hair. Henry also had the patience to deal with anyone, at any time, especially dear old Reggie. Only Henry could use that moniker for the elder minister. Someone else had once tried the name affectionately and had received a back hand across the face, followed by scores of abuse and claims of blasphemy in response. The person in question had ran away clutching their scorching cheek. The following week, upon returning to the service, the imprint of the distinctive ring was still brightly etched into his face.

The flowers around them were an assortment of tulips in every colour, pansies and snap dragons, there was also a collection of daffodils and freesias in every hue. The garden was a passion project that the both of them wholeheartedly doted on.

"I'm sorry, dear Reggie." Henry said, calmly. He put the tin watering can down on the floor.

"Don't be sorry. Just learn from your stupidity." That was Reggie's way of saying no problem, Henry had surmised, and learnt to accept. "Here, put some of those flowers in this and finish the cleaning chores." He handed Henry an ornate vase and picked a variety of flowers to display within it. Moments later they were standing outside the large, wooden church door. A voice stopped Henry in his tracks before opening it.

"Gentleman!"

The two holy men turned around to face the undeniably gorgeous Victoria. This evening she was wearing oil green flares and an understated black blouse. Her long black hair, with the trademark streak, was flowing freely around her in the light breeze.

It was Reginald Dundon who offered his hand to her, giving a slight bow in the process. When recounting this incident later, he would have no recollection of ever doing so. She took his hand gracefully in hers, a long, white glove preventing direct contact.

"It's a pleasure to meet you both." She inhaled the scent of the flowers in the vase, acting as if they were the most beautiful thing that she had ever had the pleasure of smelling. "Oh, those are absolutely wonderful! What is your secret to such a strong-smelling array of flowers?"

Before Henry could answer, Reginald interjected. His eyes never leaving hers for a second. "A family secret going back generations. I'd have to kill you if I told you." He laughs, sounding almost gleeful.

"Or I could kill *you.*" She replies with a sardonic smile. The two men weren't at first sure whether or not she was joking, and then her face broke into what they assumed was a genuine smile.

"Would you like to come in for a cup of tea?" Asked Reginald.

The smile from Victoria's face evaporated faster than it had risen and a small burning began in her stomach.

"No!" She said, and then, trying to regain her composure, "No, thank you. Churches and I don't get on I'm afraid. I was raised by the most evil nuns and just the *thought* of a church sends me back to when I was a child, being beaten by those loathsome creatures... No offence."

"None taken." Henry gently bowed his head. "I'm sorry for your terrible ordeal." He added.

"To what do we owe the pleasure of your visit?"

"Well, as new Mayoress, I just want to keep a close eye on our residents. I don't want any stone left unturned and I want to meet *every* resident personally.

Kerwall Town

After all, how can I run a town successfully if I don't know what the townspeople want?"

"I thought Frances was the new Mayor?" Quizzed Henry.

"Oh, silly!" Victoria laughs. "Behind every successful man is a woman with conviction and brains. You could say I keep his *blood* pumping, and pretty soon, I'll be doing the same to the whole of the town. So, my question to you is simple: how can I help you both?"

The two men look at each other for a brief moment. They really had everything they needed.

"We want for nothing; truth be told to shame the devil." Henry responded. "We have the most loyal flock of followers. God has truly blessed us and we are eternally thankful for Him." Henry absentmindedly touched the handmade cross which adorned his neck. Victoria, in turn, gave a small hiss that remained unregistered by either of the men.

"So very privileged of you both. How many members of your *flock* would you say you have on a regular basis?" She asked.

The two men thought for a moment before Reginald advised, "Anywhere between 25 to 40 when I do the sermons, and you can triple that when *he* does them." His ending words were uttered with a slight scorn in his voice that was only picked up by Victoria. She was getting all the information that she needed, without them knowing. She didn't care in the slightest about their answers, she only cared for *how* they answered and interacted with one another. It was fractured, to say the least.

"Tripled? Why would you say that is?" She probed, knowing that it would ruffle the feathers of the old man.

"Because he panders to them and feeds them '*hippie love.*'" He said, using mocking air quotes.

"Interesting."

Henry was still tightly holding his cross against his chest. The atmosphere had turned thick ever since she had arrived, and he wasn't sure why. He was on high guard though, trying his hardest to not let it register on his face. He didn't trust this woman in the slightest. It was almost as if God himself was telling him that this woman was pure evil. Reginald either didn't get the message, or chose to ignore it, still hopelessly transfixed by the mysterious woman.

"What days do you do your sermons, gentleman?"

"I perform the ones on Tuesday, Wednesday and Sunday." Henry responds.

"Monday and Friday are mine." Reginald finishes.

"And at what time?"

"6 p.m." They both answer simultaneously.

Victoria noticed that Reginald was receptive and Henry was trying not to be. This was interesting, she would be sure to pass it onto Frances later on. She knew from the weeks prior that they had a somewhat difficult relationship, but it was heaven sent that it was this bad. It would make it ever so much easier to turn them against one another, when the time came. To her, and Frances, this was a sport and they were the best in the game.

"I shan't keep you lovely gentleman much longer, I promise, just one more question. What time do your congregation leave the church?"

This time they didn't answer in unison and their facial expressions was the direct antithesis of one another. Reggie was all too eager to answer, almost trying to please the woman in some strange way,

Kerwall Town

whereas Henry, hand still on his cross, dipped his head into his chest and furrowed his brow, in an attempt to look as if he was in deep thought.

"Well, that depends on a sermon to sermon basis, but usually no one stays longer than 7:45 p.m."

Of course, Victoria knew this too. Once again, she was purely interested in the way they conversed with not just her, but with each other too, continuously monitoring if they were to lower their guard.

"Thank you, gentleman, you have been most helpful. I shall bid you both a fine evening." She made to turn and leave, but Reggie called after her.

"Here, take this flower." He passed her a white tulip.

"How very kind of you." She replied, sniffing the bud in an overly extravagant way.

"I do hope we'll see you in our church one day, and extinguish the demons of the past for you."

Victoria laughed. "I like my demons. They keep me company."

Before they could say another word, she left.

"That was strange." Henry stood stock still.

"Don't be so stupid, there was nothing strange whatsoever."

Henry shrugged, but couldn't quite shake the feeling of unease which had washed over him as she spoke to them. There was something rising underneath the surface too, something he didn't want to admit to himself yet, but felt it clear as day. He felt a strong sense of lust for her.

Reggie took charge of watering the rest of the flowers, and Henry went inside the church, continuing as before the interruption by the new Mayoress. That's what he told Reggie anyway, but instead of continuing down the nave, he marched directly into his office, and closed the door. It was a small, pokey room that smelt of tobacco and liquor. The two sins he allowed himself. Adorning the wood panelled walls was a portrait of the Supreme Pontiff, standing in profile, in a gold leaf frame. He bowed graciously as he walked past and opened his desk draw, retrieving a long mahogany box. He opened it gently and held the item tentatively in his hands before carefully placing it back down. He took off his black shirt, and white collar, and picked up the item from the box once more, before walking over to the portrait. He knelt down in front of it and held the item out in his palms.

"Please forgive me." He spoke directly to the portrait, moving the item cautiously into one hand. It consisted of many strands and was made of the finest leather. In some circles to have the Cat -o- nine tails used on him would have cost him a pretty penny. In Henry's office, he was alone. He raked the whip across his back. The crack reverberating round the hollow room. As the whip drew blood instantly on already wounded skin, he didn't shed a tear. He begged for forgiveness a further nine times, each time it was followed by a hard crack across his back. Once his self-punishment was complete, he stood up and wiped some blood from his back with his index finger, then smeared it onto the lips of the portrait before kissing it with his own.

He washed himself in the adjoining shower room, cleansing his skin of blood with warm water and soap. He'd lost count of how many times he had done this to himself, but each time he did so, he felt himself edging closer to God. He felt he was becoming purer in the process, and that was all he ever wanted.

Meanwhile, Reggie had finished watering the plants and was busy riffling through old sermons. He had decided to insert some variation, and add in a whole new homily, one from his very first few weeks of being a vicar in Kerwall. Everything else is changing, he thought, so why couldn't he.

6

Town Detectives

Nora Roberts was awoken by the dispatch radio by her bed at 6:00 a.m. the following morning. By 6:30 a.m. she had combed her brunette bob cut hair and was putting police tape across Ricky's petrol station.

"What have we got today?" Damien Gold paced over to her. Many people had speculated as to whether that was his real name. When some townsfolk had asked him first hand he had shrugged his shoulders, and that was that. He and Nora were the only full-time detectives that Kerwall had to offer.

"Not sure yet. John just said it was bad and that he needed us both here right away." She explained. Police Chief, John Hunt, was a proud Kerwall resident, even though he only transferred to the town ten years prior, and was counting down the days to his retirement. He had hoped that Kerwall would ease him off into the sunset, and up until now, it mostly had.

Damien and Nora's cars were the only ones sat on the forecourt, and the sun wasn't going to fill the sky for a little while yet. Damien helped Nora tape up the rest of what was now a crime scene under the ambient glow of the petrol station lights. Just as they were about

Kerwall Town

finished, John pulled up. He was a tall man, with cotton coloured curls.

"Have you...seen it yet?" He asked, striding up to them.

"Not yet, we thought it best to tape up first and wait for you."

"Good."

"Who called it in?" Enquired Damien.

"Chris Kempo. You know, the janitor... or whatever the fuck he does around here. Anyway, he said he saw the lights on in the place at around 5 a.m. this morning, and thought it was strange, so he went to have a look..."

"Why was he up that early walking round the town?" Nora was suspicious of everyone and everything.

"Fuck knows, I don't even know what he does most of the time anyway." John said absently.

"What did he see exactly?" As she asked it, she was a little afraid of the answer.

"Go see for yourselves, but brace yourselves." He gestured with his hand to the door of the petrol station. Nora and Damien exchanged a look, daring each other to step forwards. After a moment, it was Nora who decided to go in first.

The smell hit her instantly. She thought she smelt burnt meat... or flesh, but there was no fire. Her eyes scanned the room, seemingly not wanting her to see the horror that lay in the corner of the kitchen. Damien was just a beat behind her, but he saw it first. His scream shattered the silence of the early morning. It also broke Nora's temporary blindness. Hanging out of the oven was the upturned face of the former resident, Ricky Turner... what was left of it anyway. His lips had been burnt away, most of his nose was melted to the side of his cheek, exposing the bones that formed his skull. One of his eyes lay open, watching them from its new position by his chin. The other was unidentifiable, what was left of it having melted into every surface after exploding. There was blood everywhere, and severed limbs too. Nora ran out of the room and threw up over the concrete. Damien, falling right behind her, wasn't as good at aiming, and regurgitated last night's meal down the front of his uniform. Strands of sickly spit hung from his lips and his eyes were full of strained tears as he continued to dry heave.

"Lasted longer than me, I'll give you that." John turned to Nora.

"What... the... *fuck!*" Was all she could respond.

John shook his head.

All three of them thinking the same thing, and all felt bound from speaking. Eventually, Damien managed to articulate it first, still with dangling sick strands falling from his lip. He was now sat on the floor, back against the wall, his head firmly in his hands.

"Does this mean the Skin Snatcher is *here!? Please* let this be some ungodly coincidence."

"We don't have enough evidence to confirm nor deny it yet. We should know by the end of the week. The fact that you had the same gut feeling as I did, and I'm sure Nora too, says a lot though."

The Skin Snatcher was the name given to the notorious serial killer who had plagued John's last few years of service. They had gone quiet around three years ago, and up until now hadn't made an appearance in Kerwall.

"Do we know the time of death yet?" Nora attempted to remain professional.

The sick on the pavement was still steaming in the morning air. The smell could almost have been described as pleasant in comparison to the pungent aroma filling the kitchen. 'Poor Ricky', she thought.

"Not yet. Only us and Chris even know about it. But rest assured, by mid-morning, everyone in Kerwall will know. That Chris' mouth is bigger than a whore's vagina."

"And as dirty as one."

It could have been the image his co-workers had so eloquently described, the sudden remembrance of the sight in the kitchen, or perhaps an amalgamation of both, that made Damien sick up on himself again. Whatever it was, John had seen enough.

"Pull yourself together, for fuck's sake! I need you both on the case, so stop puking your guts up. Go back home, put your uniform in the wash, and get a clean set of clothes. Meet us both at the station in an hour. Don't be late." John's words were enough to snap Damien out of the state that had befallen him. He sulked his way to his car and drove to his house as demanded.

"I'm not getting in that car until it has been deep cleaned. And I mean *deep cleaned!*" Laughed Nora.

"I still won't. Smells like that linger long after. Come on, let's get a coffee at the station while we're waiting for pukes-a-lot. "

By the time Damien had changed into a fresh uniform and made his way back to the station, forty-five minutes had passed. In that time, Nora and John had drank their first coffee and were starting on their second. He had tried, to no avail, to get the taste of sick out of his mouth by brushing his teeth excessively. He tried to clean his tongue, but that had just made him sick again, so gave up after the first attempt. Damien had a weak stomach for such things, if he had to look at vomit, he would be sick all over again.

"Nice of you to show up." John joked.

"Any more information on Ricky yet?" The memory resurfaced and sick threatened to break past his lips.

"Not yet. I've sent Bill over there to greet Doctor Sharpe. They should have the body here by 11 a.m."

"In how many bags?" Asked Nora, only half-joking.

"Are you sure that ol' Billy-Boy can handle the... the sih..." Damien puts his hand to his mouth as fresh chunks of sick tumble out of his muzzle.

"For fuck's sake, Dame, get a hold of yourself. It's just a cut up, crispy, cadaver." Teased Nora.

"Oh, don't take the piss, Nora, you can see what it's doing to the poor sod." He hands him a handkerchief from his suit pocket. "Here, you can keep that one."

Damien takes it gratefully and wipes his mouth free of the sick that had built up in his bushy beard.

"Thank you." He says, starting to sound a little more like himself now.

"You need to get a hold of yourself, we need all of our staff on this one."

"What do you mean, *all*, it's only us two anyway, well, I guess you could count Bill to *some* degree."

"Bill? He's three ants short of a picnic!" Laughed Damien.

"Now you leave Bill alone. He might be a little slower on the uptake... some may even say a little simple, but he's got an inquisitive mind... more that you pair anyway and doesn't miss a trick. I'm hoping he can spot something we missed. And besides, with all those horror films and comic books he reads, he should be used to the gore." John had a soft spot for William

Kerwall Town

'Bill' Thornton, always had. He went against everyone's wishes when he had hired him four years ago. His mum had approached John, pleaded in fact, to give him a filling job. According to her, he was a whizz at it and loved the police too, it was all he could talk about. John had owed her a favour, and duly obliged, he hasn't looked back since. He's even helped out on a few cases here and there, mostly petty crime, but John has come to rely on Bill's keen eye for detail.

"Well, I hope he lasts in there longer than we did!"

"Come to think of it, I'm not worried about him puking his guts up at the sight of poor Ricky. I'm more worried about him being stuck in a room with *PrickfaceMcgee*, Sorry, *Doctor Prickface.*" Nora spat the words out, scorn filling her voice.

She had loathed Doctor Brian Sharpe ever since he tried to make a move on her the night of her husband's funeral. At the time, he was still with his wife. He had cornered Nora as the evening drew to a close. He was extremely drunk, as was she, in the games room of the function hall. He was slurring his words and breathing all over her. The next thing she knew, his body was pressed up against hers as he shoved her up the wall. His hand gripped her then long, layered hair. He was breathing heavily in her ear, sweat pouring down his face. Her arms were stuck behind her, pressed into the cool concrete. He pulled her hair even tighter, forcing her into sobriety. Nora was now fully aware of what was going on, and what he was trying to do. His other hand was clumsily unbuckling his belt. A moment later, she could feel him rubbing against her thigh. She was trying to pull away, but he pulled tighter still on her hair, bringing tears to her eyes. He had managed to work his way up her skirt and forced himself into her knickers, trying to guide his dick with his hand. He would have succeeded if she hadn't wrestled her arms free and slapped him across the face with all of her strength. The force of the slap drew blood from his bottom lip. He let go of her hair instantly and she punched him square in his eye, leaving a dark shadow that would only last him two weeks. With a swift knee for good measure, she ran from the room as if hell itself was chasing her. She didn't look back. If she had, she would have seen him gasping for air on the floor, clinging to his flaccid pride. No one knew, and Nora would take it to the grave. Prison was too good for him. She vowed that she would one day get her full revenge on him, she just had to bide her time.

What she didn't know, was that he had tried it on with other women over the years too, and he was often successful in his advances. Mostly, he prayed on the vulnerable women who came into his office, once or twice assaulting young adult males too. Since the town has gotten smaller and smaller over the years, his targets have become scarcer. It doesn't stop him though. He simply goes further afield when he's desperate to fulfil his lust. His most recent targets reside in the neighbouring town. He skulks in dingy alleyways at the dead of night, waiting for working mum's with armfuls of shopping to walk past, grabbing at them and forcing them to succumb. There is no telling how many women he has impregnated over the years, let alone how many he has mentally scarred. Upon his re-entry into Kerwall, he always felt a sense of sickness in the pit of his stomach, he put it down to his conscience, but the truth ran a little deeper. One thing was for sure, he hated that

Kerwall Town

feeling, and because of it, he was making less and less trips out of town.

"So, are we sure it's the Skin Snatcher's M.O.?" Damien breaks Nora away from her hate filled memories.

"We're not sure of anything right now, apart from the fact we have one less townsperson."

"He's a pretty integral one too. I mean, I know you don't need a degree to pump petrol, but who's gonna take over the store now?" Nora switches back.

"Well, I reckon that will be something for the new Mayor of the town to decide, don't you? A week hasn't even gone by and we've already got a shit show on our hands." John murmured, and took another swig of his coffee.

"Funny how the moment we get a new Mayor we get a murder on our hands."

"That's just a coincidence." Retorts Nora. "This Town has been rotten for some time. He's just shaking the tree, so the shit falls out."

"I've got to agree with Nora here, sorry Damien. But come on now, you've been in this game long enough, and this town even longer, to know that a lot of the people here are shitty. They've got to be, to have been able to survive this long. The government don't care about us, hell, I'd bet they've downright forgotten about us, wiped us off the map. Human nature is about survival. That goes double for the humans who inhabit our fare Kerwall town."

"I'm glad you've finally saw the light about how shit this town is, John." Said Nora.

"Oh, I've always known, but love is blind, and I'm still foolishly in love with the place. That doesn't mean I don't see what goes on here though. Foolishness is not the same as stupidness."

While they had been talking, Damien had poured himself a coffee and had mostly finished it when the ringing of the phone sliced through their lulled voices. John picked it up on the second ring.

Neither Damien or Nora could hear what was being said on the other end, but they both knew it was Doctor Prickface Sharpe. His nasal tone echoed through the receiver, exacerbating his already grating voice. John tried his best to calm him down, but to no avail. Mere moments later and he hung up.

"I'm pretty sure the good doctor has now been scarred for life." Said John, after a heavy sigh.

"How about Bill?"

"He never mentioned him, but if I know Bill as well as I think I do, then he'll be fine."

Nora didn't bother vocalising what she thought of the next instalment in the selfishness of Prickface. She decided the men wouldn't understand anyway. She might have believed she was their equal, maybe even their *sister,* but when it came to matters of sexual assault, Nora thought they might side with the man. Besides, it was her who wanted to take him out, and she would take great pleasure in doing so. Maybe even torture him while she's at it.

She had countless dreams, starting at his fingernails. She would tie him up in a chair, and place a rusty nail just under his finger. Then, slowly walk over to the other side of the room, her shoes clack clacking on the stone floor, and pick up a hammer. She would put a gloved finger to his lips when he started to scream, and then wail, as she brought the hammer crashing down.

Kerwall Town

The metal nail would crack the keratin on his index finger. She would do it over and over on each finger, eventually graduating to taking the hammer to his knuckles. She would revel in the fact that he couldn't do anything about it, with his hands bound behind his back. He would be powerless, just as he had done to her.

Nora broke away from her thoughts once again, it was a little harder this time as fantasising about torturing the "good" doctor was one of her favourite pastimes. She even thought that, other than her daughter, it was one of the only things that gave her life joy.

"Where is Ricky now?" She was beginning to find it harder, and harder, to keep a grip on reality. Most of her time was now consumed with dreaming of torture methods. It kept her awake throughout the night and she was terrified of what she was becoming.

"Well, he was meant to be coming here at 11 a.m., as discussed, since we have the town's only morgue, but I think it'll be longer. From what I could hear in the background, he has left Bill to put the pieces of Ricky into the bags, so could one of you come with me to help him out?" John aimed the question at both of them, but knew before speaking that Damien would never agree.

"I'll come with you." Nora got the message.

"While you're both there, I'll pull the files up on the Skin Snatcher case. Maybe we can learn something from it." Damien proposed, desperately trying to sound helpful. There was no way he could go back to the haunting sight of the petrol station. Those images will

92

torment his nightmares for as long as he's walking on God's green earth.

As Nora and John left the station. Damien lit a smoke and poured himself another coffee.

It didn't take long for the pair to arrive at the petrol station. Nora wasn't at all surprised to see that while Bill was doing his best efforts putting Ricky's pieces into bags, Sharpe was shirking all responsibility. Well, in reality, he was in the middle of seeing his breakfast for the second time that morning. It was miraculous that he didn't choke on his chunder, Nora thought to herself, fighting hard not to slip into her dark place again.

"I see you had omelette and… carrots for breakfast." John laughed despite the situation.

Dr Sharpe didn't respond, he couldn't respond. He was now dry heaving, hunched over in his expensive corduroy suit and black leather shoes, having narrowly avoided staining the ridiculous spats. Why a man would wear those things was beyond John, especially seeing as they went out of style alongside the great depression. Decades later and obviously the Doctor hadn't got the memo. One of the great things about living in Kerwall, it seemed, was that they weren't slaves to fashion nor style. However, on the flip side, there was no outside help. There was no outside *anything*.

"What's your diagnosis?" Nora was trying to sound professional, and trying even harder not to add *Prickface* at the end of her question.

A trail of saliva hung from the Doctors thin lips connecting, at the other end, to the concrete. Pools of water were congregating in his dark brown eyes. He put the heel of his hand to his mouth, wiping the saliva away, and stood up.

Kerwall Town

"Pretty obvious what's happened here, don't you think?" He said, in a condescending tone. Dr Sharpe had a penchant for being rude, but, seeing as he was the only Doctor in town, people had to deal with it. He knew he was unanimously hated by the townsfolk, he seemed to revel in it. His ex-wife, Abigail Trent, used to be his receptionist. Following the divorce, she moved to work at the town's only Supermarket, it was family owned and the pay was better. 'There's no way she's earning a living wage, I'm not having a woman try and emasculate me!' He would often roar during their disputes, which usually led to at least half of the kitchen being thrown at one another. More often than not, the physical abuse hadn't bothered her, however, when he said in all seriousness that he should have scraped out the inconveniences while she was asleep, it stung her deeply. Then, she saw red, and attacked him with all the fury of a woman scorned. In the town of Kerwall you can't file for divorce, not legally anyway, there isn't the resources, but for all intents and purposes they were estranged. Their children, Evan, 15, and Trevor, 16, both lived with their mother and had always taken her side. Evan had always hated his father, whereas Trevor tried to keep the peace.

"Why don't you try and enlighten me, buttercup?" Smirked Nora, tipping him a wink which boiled the Doctors' piss, she loved to watch him squirm.

"I don't expect someone with *your* intelligence to understand this, but when a *professional* sees a cadaver in that kind of state, with absolutely no sign of breaking or entering, then it can be reasonably assumed that the person has committed the ultimate sin, suicide." Replied the Doctor, firmly planted on his high horse with a stick up his arse for good measure.

"It's a twenty-four-hour petrol station, dip-shit, of course there'd be no sign of breaking or entering... any *professional* would know that." She venomously retorted.

John, who was watching this disastrous back and forth unfold, decided to intervene before it got out of hand. Nora had a reputation for running her mouth when it wasn't warranted, and John knew that a lot of the men around here didn't take too kindly to a woman telling them what to do. Especially in a tone drenched in sass.

"So, what you're saying is this was self-inflicted." Said John to the Doctor. Turning to Nora he added, "And you're saying otherwise. Well, I've got to tell you both, there is no surprise that you're on opposing sides of an argument. I'm sure we'll know more when we get the body back to the station."

"It's Ricky." Nora said, flatly.

"What is?" Enquired the Doctor.

"The *body* that you're both referring to. His name is... was, Ricky. And it sure as fuck didn't take you both long to forget that. He was a resident here all his life. You would both speak to him at least once a week, and as soon as he dies, he loses his name and becomes a *body,* or a *cadaver,* for you both to prod and probe. He's dead. And I can assure you that he didn't kill himself. Someone cut him up, and stuffed him in that oven, and turned on the flames to cook him alive." She neglected the fact that she too had referred to him as a cadaver earlier on, but that was in jest, to wind Damien up.

Both men winced at her cutting depiction, and it was exactly the kind of reaction that she wanted from them.

"You're right." John spoke after a sobering moment. "I'll call him by his name, Ricky, if that's what would please you?"

Kerwall Town

Nora didn't reply, simply giving a nod in the affirmative.

"I got all the parts in the bags, Chief!"

They turned around in unison to see the cheery voiced Bill. His formerly white gloves were now stained red, along with most of his uniform, but it didn't seem to bother him in the slightest, if anything, he looked more alive. John ruffled his black hair, managing to find the only spot that didn't have any of the body's... Ricky's, blood on it.

"Good job, Bill. I knew we could count on you."

Bill flushed red with pride and gave them a smile from ear to ear. His green eyes were a stark contrast to the deep red filling his cheeks and covering his newly stained uniform.

"I don't know how you're going to sort this one out, Doc, I really don't."

"Why don't you start with the two puncture wounds on his neck." Bill interjected.

The three of them looked at him in utter confusion.

"What do you mean *puncture wounds?*" Nora turned squarely to Bill.

"The ones on his neck. I just told you, silly. His body looks liked it has been sucked dry too, you can tell by his lips. They're all wrinkly, especially by his philtrum, it looks like the face you make when you're sucking on lemons."

John felt a sense of pride stir within him. Once again, his instincts with Bill had been right. He seems to be able to see past the surface, further than the others.

What none of them knew was the truth.

Frances Lloyd-Chatman had, at some point, decided to drain the blood from Ricky's veins, but, for whatever reason, he had stopped. Perhaps his blood wasn't pure enough, or perhaps he wanted to give the police in this town something to ponder, a red herring of sorts.

7

Dotty

While the detectives of Kerwall were examining Ricky's body in the Police morgue, Dotty was serving breakfast for herself, Peter, and Terry. She was wearing a psychedelic, rainbow dressing gown, and her pink curlers were tightly supporting her hair. Terry was in his pyjamas still too, a crisp white vest and rainbow striped cotton loungers. Their smoke-free skin still framed them youthfully.

"Peter!" Called Dot from the kitchen door. "Breakfast!"

"I'll be down in a moment."

She turns back to the pan and sings quietly to herself.

"Soul dancing, you and I
We were just two souls under the glow of the moon
And I wish we were like this every-night
But now all I have is a picture frame
To kiss good-night."

"I don't recognise that song, where did you hear it from?" He had entered the room, unnoticed by either of them, and was leaning on the kitchen doorframe, transfixed by her soothing voice.

"Hear it from?" Terry chortled. "She *wrote it!*" He said, beaming with pride.

"You should record it and put it on the radio! Honestly, it'll sell like sliced bread!" Peter was so enthused, that for a moment, he forgot the previous night's events; they all had, and it was a welcomed distraction.

"She did, back in the 60s', but the country, well the *world,* was swept up in *Beatlemania*, so it didn't even get into the charts."

"I wouldn't have wanted all that fuss and bother anyway." Said Dotty, dismissively, placing the breakfasts under their noses in an effort to change the subject.

"This looks delicious, thank you!"

"You are certainly welcome Peter, now hush up and dig in before it gets cold. We got a big day ahead of us."

Terry and Peter were two gentlemen who didn't need to be told twice to eat a well-cooked breakfast, and Dotty was an exceptional cook. They had both cleaned their plates within twenty-five minutes. Peter could have eaten it in half the time, he was still famished from his nights out on the cold streets. If he wasn't in such polite company, then he would have wolfed it down and chased it with a strong coffee.

"I'm still so grateful for what you're both doing for me." Peter says as he wipes his mouth clean with the heel of his hand. Dotty mocks disgust at the sight.

"You can be more grateful by not being a dirty pig and wiping your mouth with your hand. It's a good way to start an infection." She hands him a handkerchief from the draw by the sink. "Here, use this. Keep it up your sleeve and save your thank yous. You're doing us just as much of a favour, don't forget."

Kerwall Town

"What time do you open?"

Terry looked at his beige faced *Tissot* wrist watch, that he had carried with him for almost twenty years. The display read 7:45 a.m.

"On most days, around 8:30, but we don't tend to get our first customer until -"

"-Three months later!" Dotty laughed.

"Behave yourself woman, we had young Trevor come in not three days ago buying some things."

"That was two and a half months ago, maybe more, Tez. I swear, you're so full of shit sometimes you make the toilet jealous."

"Well, whenever it was, we still get customers - that's my point. *And* not that I believe what our new Mayor says for one second, but if he *is* right about putting us back on the map, I'm sure we'll have people buying holiday homes here soon enough, and wanting to start their DIY jobs."

"Ter, sweetie, I've always admired your optimism. It's one of the first things I fell in love with. So, if you want to believe it, then go ahead. While you two boys are playing shopkeeper, I'll head to the supermarket, and by the time you finish, you'll have a lovely meal to come back to."

"Well, you be careful out there. We still don't know the lay of the land in these uncertain times... And make sure you write a list too." The last part he almost didn't add, he felt ashamed to, but it passed his lips through necessity. He *was* worried about her. He had noticed that she was becoming more and more forgetful. It was just his way of trying to help, though hindsight is a wonderful thing, and perhaps he should have saved it for when Peter wasn't in earshot, he thought.

"*Write…A…List?*'" She spat the words out, insulted to her core.

"I just meant, in case you forgot, that's all."

"I know the purpose of a list, Terry Smith! I have been doing the shopping for goodness knows how many years."

Peter shrank into his chair, hoping to fade into the fabric.

"I was only trying to help."

Dot laughs, and laughs hard, forgoing her previous dour demeanour.

"Am I missing something?" A confused Peter enquired.

"I'm just winding Tez up, that's all. Got you good this time, didn't I?" She says, still laughing. It was Terry's turn to be nonplussed. She continues, "When you've been married for as long as we have, Peter, you find new ways to piss each other off, and it's funny as hell!"

Now Terry was laughing too, and Peter, still looking a little confused, let two nervous laughs escape.

"Right, young man!" Terry gets up from the table. "We better get dressed and ready for work."

"Going to be a busy day for you both, that's for sure. I can feel it in my bones!" She laughs again, and leaves the kitchen to head upstairs. When Terry thought the coast was clear, he spoke in a hushed, conspiratorial tone to Peter, "Truth is, I was being serous about the list."

"You were?"

"I've been noticing she's become a little more forgetful as of late."

"How do you mean?"

Kerwall Town

"Just little things so far. Like this morning, I came down before her, and I noticed that the remote control was in the fridge. And I've started to notice her hiding food over the house too."

It was like a weight had been lifted off of his chest. For months he had wanted to talk to someone about Dotty, but his only friend *was* Dotty, and there was no way he could talk to her about it. Well, he did try to once, but she just shrugged it off, and tried to blame him. He didn't know what to do if things got worse, but one thing was for sure, his life *was* Dotty. If anything happened to her his life would crumble into a million pieces.

Peter, not knowing what to say, or how to comfort Terry, stood up and placed a hand over his bony shoulder.

"C'mon, let's get ready, like Dotty said, we got a big day ahead of us… I gotta tell you though, I haven't had a job for a long time."

"There's nothing to it. All you've got to do is keep the shelves free of dust, and, on the absolute rare occasion, help the residents with some maintenance work around their home."

Peter gives him a reassuring smile.

"Dotty's already put some clothes for you to wear on your bed, we're roughly the same size, and if you don't fancy wearing the tie, there's an orange ascot." Explains Terry, then adds, "It was Dot's idea to always dress smart. She says it's for the customers, but I do it for her. There isn't anything I wouldn't do for her." He was starting to get teary again, so he excused himself from the table and went upstairs to get ready. Peter did the same.

By the time Terry entered the bedroom, Dotty was already dressed. Her age was impossible to identify through her timeless fashion, other women her age would clad themselves in bedizen garments, but inside Dotty was a young and free spirit. This morning she was looking resplendent in corn yellow flares, accompanied by a striped shirt, with a pink neck scarf, setting off her snow-white hair. She was a woman whom others thought was made up from the moment she opened her eyes each morning. She had never felt the need to take time to apply makeup. Dotty stood tall, meeting Terry at their even 6ft. Her high cheekbones glinted in the morning sunlight.

Although they rarely interacted with many people from the town, many of the woman privately wished to look even half as good when they reached Dotty's age. Terry and Dot have been married for eons, yet he was still enchanted by her, and every day he felt like the luckiest man alive. When his eyes fully captured her beauty, all he could mutter was, "Wow!"

She gives him a warm smile. "Who are you 'wowing' at mister?"

"How do you get more beautiful each day?"

Instead of answering him, she kisses his forehead. He gets changed slowly, and, unbeknownst to him, she watches with interest. As always, she helps him fix his braces and tie his ascot. Today she had selected one in cornfield blue. Initially, she had considered the green one, but remembered the streaks and shades of Frances and Victoria and didn't want to appear as the same team as them, at least not yet anyway. Once she was done helping him get dressed, she planted another kiss on his forehead.

"I won't be gone too long, alright."

Terry stands up, pale blue eyes staring back into his own. Once again, he had an intense feeling wash over him. He hadn't been able to fully shake it since the meeting.

"Just be safe, ok?"

She looks at him, slightly concerned. "Be safe… At the supermarket? I know you don't go there much, Tez, but two things: one, Kerwall is the safest place to be, and two, if you stand outside our door and squint, you can see the supermarket. I'll be fine. Honestly, what's gotten into you?" She gave his hand a reassuring squeeze.

"I'm not sure, bad dream I guess." That's all he could say, and really, all he knew *what* to say. Right now, his dread was just a seedling, and there was no telling if it was going to sprout into a fully-fledged anxiety tree. Just then, the kitchen telephone rang, making them both jump a little. It rarely rang, and when it did, it was mostly the former Mayor wanting to discuss town meetings.

"I'll get it." Dotty welcomed the change of subject. She picks up the receiver just before it cuts off.

"Hello…Smith residence, Dotty speaking…Jack! … You are? … both of you?"

Terry has made his way into the kitchen after her and asks who it is. She puts a hand to the receiver and mouths 'Jack and Donna'. The smile on his face is as big as Dot's. Moments later, Peter returns to the kitchen to join them. The two men could be twins in their matching uniforms, save for the different coloured ascots. He offers them each another coffee, and Terry accepts, explaining that he'll take it to the shop floor. It doesn't take long, and before Dot ends the call, both he and Terry are holding a fresh cup of coffee in their hands.

Dot hangs up, still smiling.

"Jack and Donna are coming over!" She bursts out excitedly.

"When?" Terry asks, still unable to shake the unease, despite this good news.

"They were calling from a petrol station about 100 miles away. Somewhere called... *Wowick?* I couldn't quite catch the name. Anyway, they're coming down to see us and have a catch up with Eve and Abe. They said it'll only be a flying visit..." She was going at a hundred miles an hour, cleaning the sides in the kitchen as she spoke. "...Before you both start work, would you mind getting the spare bedding from the loft? I asked him if they wanted the mattress, but he said the sofas were just fine."

"Sure, we'll get on that, won't we Pete?"

Peter nods, then adds. "Who's Jack and Donna? I recognise the names, but can't place them."

"They're our grandchildren. Oh, we haven't seen them in so long!"

Realisation dawns on Pete's face. "Ohhh, I remember now. They hung around with the detective's daughter, Eve, is it? and Krystal's son, Abe."

"That's right, the Kerwall JADEs." Dot says, affectionately.

She kisses Terry on the lips, a wave of excitement and familiarity washes over her, and said her goodbyes, leaving the two smartly dressed men to open up the shop. As they were making their way down, Terry decided that it was a good idea to start with taking an inventory. When Peter enquired when it had last been done, Terry shrugged his shoulders, audibly deflated. It was one of the many things on his to do list which he hadn't gotten around to doing.

The JADEs, as they were always referred to, were third-generation teens which the whole town had pinned their hopes on, some still did. They were championed to succeed for Kerwall, dragging the town out of the darkness. That was until Jack and Donna's parents moved away in search of greener pastures. Generally, parents would be seen to pressure their teens to prosper, which could be bad enough. For the Kerwall JADEs, the pressure was insurmountable; as if they were ants on a cracked pavement in the blisteringly sun, the entire town holding magnifying glasses which were trained on them. Jack and Donna's parents got them out before it wreaked havoc with their mental health, they finished college in another town, and haven't looked back since. Abe and Eve, although still in the town, have managed to find their own success.

It was almost as though as soon as half of the JADEs left, so did the pressure. On the rare occasions when the group were back together, it was a moment of bliss for the town. The one year a street party was supposedly thrown in their honour. In actuality, the former Mayor, Richard Percy, had excess funds and thought that a party was the perfect excuse, he viewed it as kismet. That day, the town danced in the streets long into the night, and there were many a sore head the following morning. On that day, everyone forgot about the dilapidated buildings and the potholes in the road; Patty had forgotten about them so much that she had fallen into one. She managed to keep hold of her drink in one hand and pulled herself back up with the aid of the other. They forgot about the other things that made the town almost unbearable to live in too; like the poverty, and the isolation. On that day, they became a family. All of them, together. It took two full days for the town to return to normal, and get the streets clean again. Now, there are more derelict buildings, more poverty, and a hell of a lot more potholes.

8

Kerwall Town

Many of the town's residents believed that there was a strange undercurrent to Kerwall. Some cosmic force compelling them to stay, despite all its flaws. After all, most of them had been there all their lives, where else could they go.

In some ways, the town could be classified as a cult.

Some townsfolk could feel the cosmic force, they say it beats to the rhythm of their own heartbeat. Other Kerwall residents go as far as to say that they often feel watched… not by other people, but by the town itself. "The Town is *alive!*" Chris Kempo had once declared; many years before he rearranged the facial features of Peter Wright. At first, everyone had laughed him off, but it couldn't be ignored in the dead of night, as they sat alone in the pitch black of their isolated houses.

Former resident, Graham Turner, had been found dead in his home three years ago. He was a likeable person, he lived alone, and there was small talk around town that he was homosexual. He had started to complain about being watched in his home. Privately, he thought it was homophobia from some of the residents. He assumed that the flamboyant cat was out of the bag, and some didn't take too kindly to it. The case was, in reality, much more unsettling.

On one occasion, he had been watching a late-night programme on his old, black and white television, set into its brown and yellow frame, and balanced precariously on its frail built-in legs in his bedroom. It had been a relic when he bought it years before. All of a sudden, a bitter cold consumed the room. He knew that he wasn't imagining it, as his teeth started to uncontrollably chatter, his breath visible in the air. Then, before he knew it, the power to the television cut out. Leaving him solitary, and cloaked in darkness. He forced his eyes closed, trying to shut out whatever was happening around him. He heard footsteps encroaching from the hallway. As they reached the door, it creaked open. He told himself it was nothing, that he was making things worse by having his eyes closed, so he opened them. There was a small boy sat cross-legged at the foot of his bed. Graham screamed, and pulled the duvet over his head. "No! No! No! GO AWAY!" He pleaded. After an agonisingly long time, he slowly pulled the duvet off of his head to find the boy was no longer there. The television snapped back on, and the room filled with warmth once again. When he found the courage to break free of his fear, he darted towards the light switch and turned it on. He had tried to rationalise it all, telling himself that he went cold because the window was open. He closed it tightly before he got back into bed, where he lay awake all night. The next day, he spoke to Andy Cooper, whom he rented the house off of. "Oh, never mind our Steve. He's always lived there." If Andy had been hoping to calm Graham down, he had the opposite effect.

After that incident, he had acquired an obsessive habit, making sure the curtains were fully drawn at night, not permitting the slightest glimmer of light through. He also made sure that the windows were firmly shut. Just the thought of the slightest opening in the curtains gave him restless nights. Deep inside his mind, a voice said it was wholly irrational, that nothing will get him, regardless of how the curtains were drawn. That was never the voice that spoke the loudest through the darkness. The clearest voice determined that, if he didn't, anything would be able to get in. His fear was justified one night, he could have sworn on his own mother that he saw an eye, it was peering through a crack in the curtain.

For the next few weeks, when Graham was seen doing his shopping in town, he was constantly muttering to himself, and avoiding reflections in shopfront windows, or in the stores. He kept people at least two metres away at all times. He started to wear gloves, thinking his fear could be transmitted to others through touch alone. He would randomly shout out in the middle of the street, and then laugh it off maniacally. He felt as though someone was constantly watching him. The worst, however, was when he was at home, blinded by the constant lights. He felt someone sitting right next to him, felt the warm sensation of breath in his ear, only to turn around, and find no one there. Ordinarily, the sight of an open door, especially at night, would be a little unsettling, but not to Graham. Open doors felt safe, except, of course, the front door. That was kept securely locked. Within Kerwall he became a pariah, although he was glad about that. No one understood what he was going through.

He also began conversing with himself, responding in a different tone. When people saw him do this, they would cross to the other side of the street, or walk back up the aisle in the supermarket. He took no notice. His life became consumed by avoiding all reflections, and answering his own questions in a deep register.

When he needed to go to the loo in the dead of night, he would move as fast as he could, evading the bathroom mirror. There was something about it that he didn't like. It was just a regular looking mirror, but his mind had begun to play tricks on him. Sometimes, he would convince himself that the reflection staring back at him wasn't his own. Something else made him uneasy too, it was as if something was watching him through it, through his own eyes. His last night alive, it was a sweltering hot evening, so he allowed himself to have the window open. He had awoken from an extremely vivid dream. It was about a woman; she had wanted to enter his home. Graham had decided to put his fear to bed once and for all. So, when he got up that night to go to the loo, he made sure to stare at the mirror. But something *did* stare back at him. Before he could scream, he had pissed himself. He was found dead two days later; his eyes scratched out, the mirror smashed, and two small puncture wounds in his neck. The house has been derelict ever since. It became known as 'The Mad House'. Local superstition dictated that no one could ever cross its threshold, and, in passing the steel gates, inhabitants must bless themselves, or sign the cross. Whilst not official laws, they were strictly abided by. Reports say that should legend be ignored, the perpetrator would either lose their minds, or receive eternal bad luck. No one is able to verify these claims, because everyone has upheld the superstition.

There were other cases too, far too many to be dismissed. The citizens knew that Kerwall was haunted, they believed they were being watched, but seldom few said it out loud for fear of judgement. Just because it was a shared belief, didn't mean it could be discussed. The common misconception is that people are scared of the unknown, and whilst that may be true, what's more terrifying is the known. The knowledge that safe places are not safe, but speaking it aloud would shatter the illusion of the discoverer, pushing them to insanity. Which is precisely what the town wants. It feeds off of insanity, requires the warped reflections, the drawn curtains, the checks under the bed. Kerwall town has been controlling its residence since its creation.

There is a folktale which runs through the blood of Kerwall, passed down to each generation. The origin, and truth, remain unknown. The tale has changed over time, but is always routed in the concept of a power within the deep depths of the town. Some residents think that Kerwall is too new to have folktales, believing that it was fabricated to give the town character. Others argue that the town is older than is known, a government project that has been running since early civilisation. The only thing that was accepted, but, again, never spoken about, was that the town was in complete lockdown. There has never been a new resident recorded, but, occasionally, a handful appear together – always young, and always in couples. It was widely speculated that this was to prevent gene pool cross contamination.

No one can remember when the last residents entered, but they can remember who, Stacy and Jason

Baker. At the time, they were newlyweds filled with ambition. Stacy quickly fell pregnant, but lost the baby at just a few months old due to cot death. However, some believe that foul play was to blame. She suffered from a lapse in sanity when her baby died. Stacy, not wanting Jason to know of the loss of their only child, kept it bundled in blankets and made out that it was still alive. She was seen out with them around the town, cooing and lulling, as all new mothers would. One afternoon, while in the line at Cooper's Supermarket, Abigail Trent had asked to see the bundle of joy. As she reached out her arms to receive the baby, Stacy's eyes went wild, she clutched the baby firmly to her chest, and screamed. The blankets had become dishevelled, revealing the purple lips and sunken face of the newborn to Abigail, and others in the line. Stacy screamed louder as a chorus of shrieks rang through the store. She collapsed to the floor grasping her baby, wailing and sobbing. When attempts were made to help her to her feet, or to take the baby from her, she had launched herself at them with a clawed hand. It had taken Nora, Damien, John, and Jason to calm her. To this day, she has no recollection of that incident, or of having a baby. Whatever had happened to her when she was removed from her home, still worked to this day. Dark shadowy circles remain on her temples, leading to speculation of electroshock therapy. No one discussed the matter; not even Jason, who stayed loyally by her side. When he had said his vows, he had meant every word. To look at her now, her traumatic history had faded, the last evidence covered by her hair. She works at Cooper's now, having given up on a dream that she never knew that she had. Jason works there too, on occasion, alongside picking up the odd shift at the local pub run

Kerwall Town

by Daniel Knowles. He wasn't proud of working for Daniel, but he paid well, and it was certainly better to be working *for* him, than against. Jason and Stacy were now entering into midlife, both were happy and active members of the town. Kerwall was all they had known for the better part of their lives, and the prospect of going elsewhere was simply unthinkable.

On some nights, when everyone was sleeping, Stacy would lie awake, her hands resting on her stomach, holding it as if there was growth inside. Sometimes, she could feel something too, repetitive like a heartbeat. The next morning, she would have no recollection of anything.

Daniel Knowles was an intimidating man. He was second in command to former Mayor, Richard Percy, and was livid when he discovered that he had been overlooked to be the new town leader. He stood at 6ft 4' and had a barrel of a chest. Before he spoke, he would often brush his hands through his thick black goatee, before running them back into his crisp black hair. All the while, deliberately making his subject wait, making them stare into his dark brown, almost black, soulless eyes.

Despite being the proprietor of Kerwall's only bar, Daniels primary income was from his role as a loan shark. His greatest joys in life, however, included his love for killing people, his prey was mostly out of towners, or those who fell behind on their loans, and his coke addiction. He refused to give up either of them. The Kerwall police are scared of him but, just to be sure, he has them in his back pocket anyway. In some towns this would make them dirty cops, in Kerwall it makes them smart ones. Even though he was indignant at being overlooked, Daniel was already planning ways to regain his power. That was all he had ever wanted. Power. Ever since he was young, he had used his intimidating frame to get what he wanted, by any means necessary.

He was raised by his Mum alone, after his Dad died of alcohol poisoning when Daniel was eight. His Mum was abusive. Often, she would stub cigarettes out onto his bare skin, and once or twice on his lip. When he was around 15, she was found bludgeoned to death in the kitchen. At the time, John was still new to the town, and he will never forget what he saw: a young man, standing over his already cold Mum, her blood staining his shirt. On the floor, was an iron. It had been used to cave her skull in, and there were bits of her brain clinging on, alongside blood and hair. When John asked what had happened, Daniel replied with the utmost of calm, "She fell." John winced whilst Daniel smiled. He was proud of his work. From that day forth, whenever John looked at Daniel, he was sent back to that day. It scared the shit out of him. At one point, John had him nailed as The Skin Snatcher, but while Daniel was serving time in prison, the killer had struck again, just outside of Kerwall.

Some people, like John and Daniel, did leave the town but never for very long. They would soon get a strange sick feeling after leaving the perimeters. John, who had always said he was transferred here, wasn't telling the whole truth, although, he didn't know that. He had been drawn here subconsciously by the strange *hum*. In his own town, the missing person's report filed on him is still active. Although, after 10 years, the case has gone cold. The day that he left his own town, he

Kerwall Town

also left his family. His loving wife, two kids, and one grandchild. They haven't given up looking for him. He has no recollection that they exist, let alone that he's missing. He belonged to the town now, and that was all that mattered. Everything that came before was insignificant.

Other Kerwall residents had very little desire to leave town. They were fooled into thinking they had everything they wanted, in some ways they did, because the town made them think that way. It drove their low ambition, not questioning the things outside the parameters of their own existence. Of course, a wild animal poked in its cage for long enough is bound to bite back. Kerwall's secrets are dying to be let out, even if their discoverer might not be able to handle it. People were beginning to hear the heartbeat of the town echo in their skulls at night, reverberating through their entire bodies.

Kerwall was waking up from a deep slumber; it was alive and well.

Part Two

9

The Kerwall JADEs

It was Donna's turn to take over the driving for the final leg of their journey. Her brother, Jack, was sprawled in the passenger seat with his feet up on the dashboard, singing *Elton John's* 'Goodbye Brick Road'. Whenever the two of them came back and forth to Kerwall, they were strangely unaffected by the town's withdrawal symptoms. Given that no one spoke about them, or could remember them, the pair didn't know it existed. Donna was a year older than Jack, and liked to remind him of it whenever possible. They both enjoyed having fun from time to time, but Donna was most certainly the more serious of the two. They would both argue who was the smarter, like most siblings. She was wearing a bright pink floral bandana to keep her long, blond curly hair out of her face. There were no street signs in Kerwall, the only way to know it was there was if you have been a resident. It felt like auto pilot was switched on... something was guiding residents homeward.

"Shouldn't be too much longer now." Donna flicked the indicator left, turning into an old dirt road.

The sun was glinting on the chrome grill of their faded, rusting mint green *Ford Cortina*. It was a reliable car, which they had gone halves on. Donna had devised a system for how the car sharing would work, and it did, most of the time. She drove over a hidden dirt pothole, and the wheel kicked up dust plumes, which drifted into the open passenger window. Donna manoeuvred the wheel so she wouldn't cause damage. She forgot that it was there each time, and over the years it had grown in size; just another sign that the country had forgotten Kerwall, and that both parties wanted it that way.

Jack coughed on the dust and shot her a look to slow down.

"I know how to drive." She said, unexpectedly querulously. She absolutely despised being criticised, especially by her brother. Moreover, she hated being proved wrong, as she was most of the time right… In her head at least.

"Chillax, Donna-Do. I was just messin' with ya! Take a chill pill."

"Oh, fuck you." She laughs in spite of herself. "And take your dirty shoes off the dash, I've just cleaned this car."

He gives her a look, but moves anyway, slouching deeper in the passenger seat and drumming his hands on his chest.

"I wonder how much has changed in our little town since we were last here?" Jack pondered.

"Kerwall, change? Don't be so silly. The only thing that changes is more buildings become empty. You know Richard hates change."

"Ha, good point. The only change he knows about is the kind you get from Cooper's." Jack, evidently pleased with his joke, laughs himself into a coughing fit.

"See, that's what happens when you make stupid jokes. Your body tries to reject them."

"You're a reject."

Donna exhales exasperatedly. She knew that when he was in a goofball mood, there was no way of getting any sense out of him, and she knew that he was doing it to try and wind her up. Younger siblings seemed to have a knack of that, she had observed, but it was still wholly frustrating.

As their *Cortina* drove them passed the distressed 'Welcome to Kerwall Town' sign, they could barely see it, ivy had clambered over the wooden frame. In a few days, the sign won't be visible at all. Not that it mattered, with only the residents knowing the town even existed. To others on the road passing by, it didn't even register. Just another trick which the town played, only letting people in and out when and *if* it wanted to.

When they reached the centre of the town, they were amazed at how many more buildings were in a state of ruin. It couldn't have been longer than eleven months since they were last here. Or, maybe it was closer to thirteen months. When not in the town itself, time started to feel like treacle as they tried to remember their last visit. The high street remained a mishmash of decades, the only thing stores had in common was the stark dilapidation.

"What's Chris up to?" Asked Jack.

Donna had slowed the car down, trying to take it all in. The roads were mostly empty, so it didn't matter if she was going at 15 miles an hour, or 30, no one would have cared. She turned her head to look at Chris who was busy constructing something on the town green. It looked like some sort of platform. There was green bunting on the floor surrounding it too.

"I'm not sure, but at least they're finally building something new." She honked her horn and shouted his name. He turned around, startled. When he realised it was Donna, he smiled and waved. They returned his salutation.

Less than five minutes later, they were pulling up outside their grandparent's house and place of work, the fabled hardware store. Jack grabbed the rucksack out of the boot and held it loosely in his hand. At this time of day, they knew there would be no one in the house itself, so entered through the work door.

Terry was stood at the bottom of the ladder, passing things to Peter, when the bell above the door chimed. He rushed over the second he saw who it was and embraced them in a warm hug.

"Did you have a safe journey?" He asked.

"Sure did, G'pa. The roads are pretty groovy this time of day." Smiled Jack, setting his bag down by the counter.

"And you made sure you changed drivers every so often, right?"

"Just like you taught us." Donna replied, planting a kiss on his cheek.

It was then that they noticed Peter. He was making his way down from the ladder, trying not to intrude on the moment. Jack cocked his head in his direction and spoke barley above a whisper. "You do know he's in your store, and on your ladder, don't you?"

Terry laughs. "I haven't lost my marbles yet you know! Peter, my grandkids want to make sure I know you're in the store."

Donna and Jack flush red up to their hairlines.

Donna squirmed, trying to extricate herself from the embarrassment by protesting that it was Jack who wanted to know, not her, but it fell on deaf ears.

"I should hope you know I was here, otherwise all the stocktaking we've done this morning would be a little confusing for you when you next check."

He walks over to the confused grandchildren and holds out a hand. The last time they had seen that hand, it was clad in tatty fingerless gloves, poking out of the dirty blanket which had covered his body. Whilst he was unaware that this was the last time that they had seen him, it registered on their faces. They took his hand and shook it regardless. It was undoubtedly cleaner than the last time.

"Let me formerly introduce myself." Offered Peter after he shook both their hands. "I'm Peter, as I'm sure you both know, and your grandparents have kindly allowed me to stay here for a while and, in exchange, I help around the store."

"Oh, so it's like a charity thing?" Asked Jack.

"No. It's the *right* thing." Corrected Terry.

"Hey, do either of you know what Chris is doing on the green?" Interjected Donna. The sound of Chris' name formed a knot in Peter's stomach. It wasn't that he was now afraid of Chris, but what Peter felt capable of doing to him.

"Sorry, can't say I know. Haven't left the store all morning." Shrugged Terry. "What did it look like?" He continued.

"Hard to tell, but if I was a guessing man, some sort of platform." Proposed Jack.

"You both seem a little uneasy... Is everything ok?" Asked Donna, sensing the room.

"We were going to wait till Dotty got back, but I guess we can fill them in now, right Peter?"

Peter shrugs, as if to say why not. "We can just give them the CliffsNotes for now, and fill them in properly when she gets here, I'm sure Dot won't be too much longer." He says.

Jack and Donna exchange a worried look. "Is everything... okay?" Asked Donna, gently.

"You're not sick are you, G'pa!? or is G'ma sick?!" Worry stricken, Jack jumps in.

Terry gives him a grave look and says. "Worse."

"Fuck! How could anything be worse than that?" Jack protested.

Donna sharply elbows him in the rib, reminding Jack to watch his language.

"Gather round for a moment, and we'll have a little chat. But just a small one, this is a long story, and it's already getting longer and, dare I say, more dangerous. And don't bother interrupting me until I'm done, so if you've got a question, keep a lid on it. I'm getting up there in years, and my retention for things isn't as sharp as it used to be. Luckily, we've got Peter here, so if I forget anything, he'll be apt to set me straight. Get used to seeing him around, he's a good man, and we're in short supply of good men these days. Especially in Kerwall, and if our suspicions are correct, which I think they are, we're going to have to rely on him pretty heavily. Now, park your keisters on the counter." They swiftly obliged. It pulled them back to a time when they

Kerwall Town

were both little dots, and he would tell them stories, while they listened in awe sat on the counter.

He briefed them; telling them about the new Mayor and Mayoress, the laughing fits after meeting them, and that the reason for Peter's temporary disfigurement was the fist of Chris Kempo. An awful lot had happened in a short 24 hours, and with the news of Chris' building, things were escalating further. When he was done, his grandchildren looked at him amazed. Here they were, not forty-five minutes ago saying that nothing much happens in Kerwall, and their Grandpa comes along and smashes their little paradigm.

"So, what do you think's going on, G'pa?" Jack asked when he was sure the story was finished.

Terry ran a shaky hand through his snowy hair. "I haven't the foggiest of ideas. I was kind of hoping you two would know. You're both *clued up cats* as they say."

"Choice words, G'pa! Give me some skin for that one!" He shows him his palm, hoping Terry would reciprocate, and after a slight prompt from Donna, he does.

While Terry was filling in his grandchildren on fair Kerwall, Dotty was getting an update of her own at Cooper's. The supermarket in question was more akin to a large general store, than an actual supermarket. It had the basic food needs, and a couple of none food items; like mops, rubber gloves and batteries. There was a rule when Kerwall first opened, no store could sell the same items as another. It was a rule which had been warmly accepted by all the residents, and was one of the few that instilled some harmony. There was no undercutting of prices and no dodgy deals. However, despite the rule being put into place to stop business going bust, it happened anyway. Many of the high street stores sat abandoned, or were in need of desperate repair.

Andy Cooper, the long-time proprietor of Cooper's obtained most of his stock from long standing trade deals. He would leave in his lorry with a few of his staff on a Sunday morning and get his shipment from the neighbouring town, that queasy feeling never leaving their stomachs. It was mostly non-perishable items, like tinned food, that he could bulk buy and some fresh dairy items too.

He glided over to Dotty as soon as he saw her enter and hasn't stopped talking to her since. That was fifteen minutes ago. Andy was often the first person to get the gossip of the town, and he liked to make sure Terry and Dot were second. He was somewhere towards the end of his 60's and was a Kerwall original. His once jet-black hair was now a steel grey, and was styled in such a way that made his great blue eyes pop.

"What do you mean, *dead!*" She asked, flabbergasted.

"Oh, honey, I mean dead as in his ticket has been punched. He's gone to the great light show in the sky. Need I go on?" Andy's sass was legendary in town, and rubbed many people the wrong way, but not Dot, she upped and gave it right back, and he loved her all the more for it.

"I'm quite aware of how dying works, you dozy a 'peth. I *mean*, I only saw him last night, what on earth happened to him?" She was fond of Ricky, had known him all his life and now that life has been cut short.

"Not *what* happened to him, ask yourself *who* happened to him?" He said coyly.

"Ok, fine, I'll bite, *who* happened to him?"

They were in the middle of the store, and some of the other shoppers were starting to gather around their conversation. Andy didn't mind, he loved the spotlight.

"I haven't got a clue! Buuut, I *do* know how he died, and it's quite the gruesome story, so if you've had your breakfast, I'll save you the details."

"Oh, away with your pandering, just say what's happened to poor Ricky."

"What's that about Ricky?" Asked Adam McCallum, he wasn't one of the original earwigger's, but at the sound of Ricky's name his ears pricked up. He was on friendly terms with Ricky and they would often grab a beer or two together at Daniel's pub, The Crow's Nest.

"He was found dead this morning at his residence." Muttered a voice from the growing crowd.

"Alright, alright! It's my news and I'm the one who's going to tell it." Boomed Andy. One hand was on his hip and the other was cocked by his side campily. He had never hidden the fact that he was gay, but didn't need to either. Kerwall, for all its faults was generally an accepting place. Graham would have said otherwise.

"Simmer down, queen, don't get your lingerie in a twist!" Mocked Shelly. She might be incompetent at most things, but barbed comments were her specialty.

"Actually, darling, they're thongs today, and I pull them off better than you ever will." He pursed his lips at her, making her think twice about interrupting him again.

"How do we know you're not bullshitting us, Andy?" Kitty McCallum challenged. The couple were out doing their weekly shop. They enjoyed spending their time together, and neither one of them considered any job in their marriage a *'masculine or feminine'* one. It was just shared.

"Well, you can go and ask Ricky yourself if you want, darling, but I hear he's in multiple locations at the moment."

"What's that supposed to mean?"

"Stop asking questions and I'll tell you all." He waited for silence. He now held almost the whole store captivated, and he loved every second. Ordinarily, he would have been a little vexed that Dotty wasn't told first, but, in a roundabout way, she was. She was in attendance, and that's what counted. When he played this scene back in his memory in years to come, he would picture himself like Jesus delivering the *'sermon on the mount.'*

"Now that I've got everybody's attention, it saddens me to have to tell you that our resident and friend, Ricky Turner, owner of the petrol station here in beautifully shit Kerwall, was found dead this morning."

Someone in the congregation moved their lips to speak, but Andy put a single finger to his own and continued. "I have it on good authority that he was brutally *murdered.* Although, the official word is that it was suicide. When all this comes out though, there is no way you'll accept anything other than the fact he was murdered. He was found in his oven, burned and chopped to pieces."

Gasps echoed throughout the store. There hasn't been a murder in Kerwall for quite some time, that the residents know about anyway.

"Why are you peddling this murder theory if the official word is suicide?" Asked Shelly curtly. "That's highly unprofess…Unprofesh…wrong of you, and you should be ashamed of yourself."

Kerwall Town

"Why do you always suck dick in the workplace, that's highly 'unprofessional' of you!" Clapped back Andy.

"Oh, fuck off you dirty fag. That's all you are. I pray for you each night to see the error of your ways, so you will be accepted into the kingdom of heaven, and not rot in eternal damnation, and this is the thanks I get!?" She was red in the face now, with a vein sticking out of her forehead.

"You know what I pray for each night, Shelly pie, I pray that you get a decent haircut, and sort out that little lisp of yours, but it turns out God can't perform miracles. Now, unless you're gonna quiet your hate speeches, get the fuck out of my store, m'kay?"

Shelly went a deeper shade of red. She knew she was beaten in this exchange, and shrunk into the background, twiddling her hair nervously.

"Who told you about this?" Asked Dot, trying to get back on track with the news.

He held her hand in both of his. "Dotty, I can't reveal my sources, but would I lie to you? The rest of these bitches, maybe, but never you."

Some of the crowd laughed a little at this, some were still too taken aback by the shock of his news.

"Does it have something to do with what Chris is building out on the green?" Adam probed.

"I didn't know, Chris *was* building anything on the green. What does it look like?" For once Andy wasn't the one with the answers.

"He's been out there all morning, hammering away, woke me up too! I shouted out my window for him to cool it, but he stuck his finger up at me, damn piece of shit. Looks like he's building some kind of platform, but I'm not too sure. I'm hoping the new Mayor or

Mayoress will fill us in when they get the chance later today."

The topic of discussion was similar in the Roberts household. Nora and her daughter, Eve, were sat at the kitchen table. Nora had made a habit to, when possible, always have breakfast with her daughter. It was hard to make happen, being an on-call officer in the town, but she made it work. Breakfast was *their* time, and it didn't matter if it was morning, noon, or night when they ate, it would be breakfast. It was their little thing.

"So, you don't think he killed himself?" Asked Eve, once she was sure that her mum had finished recounting the story. This was another ritual that they shared, Nora would recount her police work, leaving in all the grizzly details. She had decided that Eve was old enough to handle it at 19. Eve was hoping to follow in her mum's footsteps and one day become a police officer, anywhere but Kerwall. Her dreams rested further afield.

"Not with the evidence that's been put in front of us, no. Of course, Prickface is saying it can't be murder … that'll mean more paperwork his end, or something like that."

She had passed her hatred of the 'good' doctor onto her daughter, but has never told her *why*.

"I think it's murder too. There's no way you can chop yourself up into pieces and then shove yourself in an oven. And then there's the two bites… or holes in his neck, that Billy discovered. Is it a calling card or some sort of sick cult thing? There are so many questions, but not enough answers!" Eve lived for the thrill of these cases, and it's what made Nora think she was made to become a great detective. Ever since she was little, she had an inquisitive mind and it was starting to pay dividend.

Nora looked at the clock, and sighed.

"That's all we got time for this morning, kiddo. I'll be back later. Got any plans yourself for the day?" She asked as she was putting on her coat.

"Sure do! Jack and Donna are coming down, and we're gonna meet up with Abe!"

"Just like old times then! Don't go looking for trouble, I know what you're all like once you get together."

Eve gives her mum a look of mock offence, Nora kissed her on the cheek, and left. Eve finished up her cereal and then washed up both bowls, before getting ready for the day.

The last of the Kerwall JADEs was Abe, and this morning, like every morning since his dad had died, he started his day by looking at the black framed picture on his bedside table. It was the last photo that they took together. It was just the two of them, in the back garden. Abe's mum, Krystal, had caught them in a perfect candid moment, arms around each other, smiling away. Abe remembers that moment perfectly. It had been etched in his mind and stored away in his 'perfect moments.' He had just scored a great goal past his Dad, and they were roughhousing playfully.

To look at Abe, and then to his late Dad, Colin, they looked identical. Same pale skin and light freckles on the bridge of their nose, same thick black hair and deep blue eyes. Colin was a miner before they closed them down, leaving Colin without a job, like many of the town's workers. He spiralled into a dark depression and was found one morning in the bath tub with his wrists and neck slit. That was five years ago. It was Abe who had found his Dad. He's kept awake most nights by the image, and they infect his dreams. They formed nightmares, startling him awake, screaming and drenched in sweat. In his sleep he tries to save his Dad, but is always just a second too late. His Dad always cuts that fatal artery moments before he reaches him. What haunts Abe the most, is that whilst his mum's hairdressing scissors hack away at the veins, his dad is looking directly at him, smiling. As if to say 'it's ok, son, it's only blood.' His eyes are as big as saucers, and there's something about them, it's almost as if they're inviting him to join in. Abe would do anything to trade places with his Dad, unless there was a way to bring him back. He would take that chance at any cost.

He loved his mum, there was no denying that, but he couldn't help shake the nagging feeling that, even though he knew his mum loved him, she would love him more if he was a girl. Krystal had lost a girl in childbirth, the year before Abe was born. Often, before her husband died, it was all that she would talk about. Focusing on what she didn't have, and neglecting what she did. Krystal is the town's only hairdresser, one of the few luxury shops Kerwall has to offer. Surprisingly, it stands in good condition, as it ought to, given that she spends most of her time there chatting to customers, and when there aren't any, she's busy cleaning and sanitising, scrubbing away. If Andy didn't get the gossip of the town first, then Krystal surely would. Secrets were spilt while hair was being cut. It was probably the relaxed state and rare sense of trust, the world's perception rested on every snip of those scissors.

Kerwall Town

Abe was determined to follow in his father's footsteps, and now that the mines were open again, he was able to do just that. His mum wanted him to follow in *her* footsteps, and take over her business when she retired, but he had no interest in cutting hair. He didn't want to touch, or see, another pair of scissors in his lifetime. The way they glint in the light makes his stomach churn, transporting him back to that moment. No, there was absolutely no chance in hell that he would pick up a pair of scissors. He would work with his hands, that was for certain, but it would be down in the mines, like his Dad used to. He was determined to make him proud.

Of the JADEs, Abe was unquestionably the most complex. His calm demeanour was juxtaposed by a million emotions bubbling away on the inside. There were times, more than he would like to admit, where he felt out of place when he was with his friends. He felt that they had never had to struggle for anything in their lives, never had to go to bed hungry, never had to work for anything, because every *goddamn* thing was handed to them. There were times where he resented them, and their happy lives, where they've never had to feel anything, never had to grieve for anyone, and it was slowly starting to eat away at him. There were still parts of him that loved them though, and he tried desperately to cling onto that love. The darker side of him spoke in a luring, velvet voice, it told him that he could be anything he pleased, if he was willing to take matters into his own hands. He was looking forward to meeting up with them, despite it all they had been friends since nursery, and it had been a while. They would call every so often, checking how he was, but he couldn't shake the feeling that they called Eve more. Abe hated feeling like this, but once the dark cloud surrounded him, there was little that he could do. Abe got himself ready, and headed out to the Shake Shack, where the rest of the gang was planning to meet.

Abe and Eve were having a catch up of their own outside the Shake Shack, and joking about Jack and Donna being late again. It was a running theme. The siblings always blamed their tardiness on each other, but they were both to blame. Neither have a handle on time management. No matter how much they tried to be early, they would end up being late, it was almost as if they were constantly running in treacle.

Elsewhere, Dotty had rushed back with the news that she had heard at Cooper's. The others listened with unbelieving ears. There was just no way that Ricky was dead, Peter had said. Jack and Donna instantly dismissed the theory of suicide, not with how Dot had described his death, it wasn't possible.

"If you ask me, our new Mayor and Mayoress have a lot to answer for!" Declared Terry.

"You think they had something to do with it?" Donna puzzled.

"Seems pretty convenient, as soon as they walk into town, someone winds up dead. And I don't think it's a coincidence that we thought that Ricky was on our side either. He saw right through their cockamamy bullshit like we did." Added Dot.

"What do you mean *our side*?" Asked Jack.

"We think something bad is happening, but we really don't know what... yet, anyway. We've all had this strange feeling, like we're..." Peter looks over to Terry and Dot for assistance.

"Being brainwashed."

"And you say not everyone in the town *feels* like you three do?" Donna was trying to make sense of it all.

"Well, we're not sure. We've made a list of people who we *think* could be on our side, but we haven't approached them yet." Dot explains.

"Can we see it?"

"Later dear, we're not finished with it yet, and truth be told, we really shouldn't be bothering you with all of this." Dot said squeezing Jacks hand.

"Bothering us? Not a chance, if there's something fishy going on here, we're going to help you fix it. No one upsets *our* G'pa and G'ma and gets away with it!" Said Jack defiantly.

Donna looks at the clock on the wall, and is alarmed to see that they're late for their meet up.

"We gotta go. We'll be back soon. If you need us, we're only at the Shake Shack." She blurts out, rushing through the door with Jack.

The Shake Shack sits at the top of the high street, on the corner. The owner, Jeremy Williams, is Kerwall original. He's in his mid-50's and took over the family business after his father's stroke in the dawn of Jeremy's twenties. He has a heart of gold and never fails to make people laugh with his zany charisma. There is never a dark room when he's around. His crisp white shirt and bubble-gum pink bow tie looked resplendent against his thick brown beard and hazel eyes. When his father had owned the Shake Shack, it sold only milkshakes, but Jeremy extended the menu to desserts and sweets. It was another of the few places which remained well looked after. All the items on the menu were homemade, something that Jeremy took pride in, and it was the reason as to why so many people used it as a meeting point. He was a great host too, never forgetting an order, nor a face. He sourced his ingredients from a neighbouring town, much the same way as Cooper did with his groceries, so they occasionally travelled together. Andy had once taken a liking to Jeremy and with all the delicacy in the world Jeremy explained that he wasn't gay, but if he was, then he would be honoured and flattered by Andy's advances.

The radio was on in the background of the Shake Shack, a pop song was resonating though the seating. Abe and Eve entered and took one of the booths by the window. It was decorated to look like a 60s' American diner; red leather booths, cream piping, and chrome stools with cheery red seats. The floor was a traditional chessboard of black and white linoleum. In contrast to the rest of Kerwall, the building appeared somehow futuristic, even as an echo to a previous decade.

Jeremy was clearing the plates off of another table when he spotted Abe and Eve. "Good to see you both!" He beams at them.

"You too, Mr Williams!" Said Eve.

"Having your usual today?" He asks.

"Not today! Jack and Donna are on their way, so we're going for a little change."

"Jack and Donna? How groovy! When will they get here-?" Before he can finish, they burst through the door. Jeremy hugs them both whilst Jack and Donna were still trying to catch their breath, having raced from the hardware store in record time.

"My, my, it's been a little while since I've seen you two!"

Kerwall Town

"Man, I've missed this awesome place! You don't know how many times I've told people in our new town about you guys and this place... and *those* shakes!" Jack begins to salivate.

"Oooookay, sorry about him." Donna rolls her eyes.

"No harm done." Jeremy says, laughing. "So, shall I leave you all for a minute to see what you want?"

"Sure thing, but I think we can all do with a coffee anyway? Right guys?" Says Eve.

They all agree, so Jeremy turns and leaves them be. The song on the radio switches to a Ben. E. King number, the group unconsciously tap to the familiar emotional music.

"The more things change, the more they stay the same, eh, Eve?" Abe outwardly jokes.

"Huh?"

"Those two." He exhaled dismissively. It was becoming harder to tell if he was now having them on or not. He was, after all, the prankster of the group, alongside Jack.

"We have some major news-!" Exclaimed Donna.

"-It's killer!" Interrupted Jack, garnering a rueful look from his sister.

"What do you mean, *killer?* As in literally?" Eve raised her eyebrows.

"Literally!" Confirmed Jack.

"Who?" Asked Abe.

"You know Ricky, the petrol station guy?" Donna began.

"Yeah." Said Eve and Abe in unison.

"Him!" Said Jack.

"No way!" Eve and Abe said, once more in unison.

"Yes way!" Vowed Donna.

"When? How? And who told you?" Questioned Eve.

"I *love* how you two are back in town for less than two minutes, and you already know what's going on more than us." Abe whined, almost petulantly.

"It's been five minutes *actually*." Joked Jack.

"Back on topic here, people!" Called Eve.

"Right!" Said Donna. "Ricky was found dead this morning. The police call it suicide... but..." She stops.

"But what!?" Asks Eve, leaning over the table.

Before Donna could continue, Jeremy places their coffees on the table.

"Here you are, Kerwall JADEs!" He says, grinning.

"Aww, man! People still aren't calling us that, are they?" Asked Jack, sounding embarrassed.

"Sure are." Said Eve meekly.

"The town is proud of you all, that's why." Confesses Jeremy.

Meanwhile, Donna is scanning the Shake Shack, she discovers that there is no one else around.

"Hey, Mr Williams, is anyone in the restrooms?"

"No Ma'am! It's just you four and me."

"Good. Pull up a pew." Says Donna.

"Let me just get my coffee too then. Wow, this really is like old times."

They would always involve Jeremy Williams in their discussions. He was someone they could trust wholeheartedly, one of the few *good* adults in the town; although, in the blink of an eye, they have found themselves becoming adults too. Jeremy came back and pulled up a stool, after lowering it so it didn't look ridiculously tall.

Kerwall Town

Donna quickly filled him in on what was said, so when she next spoke, everyone had the same information.

"So, why don't you think he did himself in?" Asked Eve.

"Can you not say it like that, please?" Abe retorted.

"Oh! Shit! I'm sorry, Abe!" She says with genuine concern, putting a hand on his shoulder. He doesn't shrink away so her apology has been accepted, at least, in her eyes.

Donna relays how Ricky was found to the audience in front of her again, this time in a little more detail.

"But that's not the strangest part." Added Jack.

"There's more?" Jeremy raised an eyebrow.

"Yup! He was also found with two strange holes, or *bite* marks on his neck!" Said Jack.

"Bite marks?" Eve repeated, confused.

"Yup! *BITE* marks" Said Jack again.

"So, what do you all think?" Asked Donna.

"He was obviously murdered. There's no question about that." Jeremy responded.

"But by *what?*" Asked Abe.

Eve didn't tell them that her mum had already told her everything this morning, she acted just as surprised as the rest of them. What her mum told her about her cases was their little secret.

"Just to be clear" Jeremy scanned the Shake Shack before he continued, checking no one had snuck in. He leaned in closer. "Are we talking about, Vampires?" Now that the question was out of his mouth, he thought he sounded stupid. There was no such thing as them, they were only in books, he thought.

"Don't be so stupid." Said Abe. "Obviously, it's some sort of red herring. *Or*, the loon who killed Ricky

138

was just a bit horny, that's all. They bit him as some sort of fetish. Nothing more, nothing less."

"Come on, Abe! Where's your sense of adventure?" Asked Jack.

"Sense of adventure? Someone gets killed and you think it's an adventure? This isn't kids' stuff, and we're not kids anymore!" Retorted Abe.

"Wow, who died and made you the moron king?"

"The fuck you just say?" Shouted Abe.

"Hey, hey, cool it!" Jeremy stood up, arms outstretched, trying to separate the two of them. When he looked over to Abe, he saw that he was laughing, Jack was too.

"Am I missing something?" Jeremy asked, as perplexed as Peter the day that Dot and Terry had the faux argument in front of him.

"Just two goofballs, being dimwits!" Eve rolled her eyes.

"You gotta admit, we had you going for a minute then!" Said Jack. He high-fives Abe.

"Yeaaaah, you really got us." Mocked Donna.

"How long have we been dreaming of something cool happening to Kerwall?" Asked Jack. "And now Vampires!"

"*If* it's vampires." Said Eve.

"Look at the evidence!" Replied Jack, excitedly.

"I have. And I'm not sure yet. First of all, *why* would vampires attack Kerwall, and why only Ricky?"

"That we know of!" Said Jack.

"You think there have been more attacks?" Asked Abe.

"Well, I don't know, but I think it's probably wise to write a list about what we know about vampires first.

Mr Williams, can we get a pad and a pen?" Asks Donna.

He pulls them out of his apron and passes them over to Donna.

"I think, if you're serious about this that is, keep a log on who comes out in the day too, because you know vampires are synonymous with the night time. So, you can sort of make a rough guess of who might be infected already that way." Said Jeremy.

"Dude! That's a great idea!" Says Jack, excitedly.

"Ok." Says Donna. "We know they come out at night; we know they bite people -"

"-And that *when* they bite, it may or may not turn them into a vampire." Said Jack.

"Wait, that's not true, is it?" Implored Abe.

"Of course, it is! How do you think you get the different types?" Jack demanded.

"There are different types?" Asked Eve.

"Of course!"

"A moment ago, we didn't even know that vampires were real, and now they're in our back garden!" Said Jeremy almost in disbelief.

"Is there a book with this sort of thing on?" Donna asked.

"I'm sure the library will have something on it." Eve responded.

"Well then, let's go!" Said Jack, excitedly.

They all got up to leave.

"Are you coming too, Mr Williams?" Donna asked, noticing that he was still sat on his stool.

"I guess I could close the Shack down for an hour. The breakfast rush is over anyway."

"Great!" Eve smiled.

"Are you sure you want an old codger like me tagging along, cramping your style?" Asked Jeremy.

"Man, you're the silent 'J' in front of the un-silent 'J' in JADEs. You're one of us, now grab your keys, we won't be long." Jack always found a way to make people feel special. It was his real talent. Jeremy was touched by his kindness. He liked the four of them, and there truly was something special about them.

10

Secrets Unearthed

Kerwall Library had doubled as a community hall and gathering place when it first opened. It is now one of the most dilapidated buildings in all of Kerwall. Loose bricks and shingles tumbled from its exterior and the peeling paper inside extended its decay. It was the least funded amity in the town and only remained open following requests from a strong contingent of the residents, spearheaded by the JADEs.

It was run by Debbie Gibbons. She's an owlish looking woman, with hair that looks like an old Brillo Pad. She lives alone with her two cockatoos. Small, mouse-brown eyes are hidden behind her thick framed glasses. She was behind her desk, as always, when the group rushed in.

"Ms Gibbons!" Jack panted on her desk.

"Shh! This is a library, not a race track!" She scolded in her nasal voice.

"Sorry about him." Donna apologised. Then, in hushed tones added "Do you have any books on vampires or mythology?"

"Well, which?"

"No, not *witches! Vampires.*" Chimed Jack.

"I know what your sister asked. I asked which was it, Vampires *or* mythology. There is quite the difference." Debbie Gibbons was quite the aficionado on monsters, and she took it entirely seriously.

"Both then." Donna answered.

Debbie pointed them in the direction of the books they had requested, there were several on the subject.

They made their way to the back of the library, and found the books gathering dust on the bottom shelf. There were eight altogether, but Debbie said that only one of them was worth their time, it was called the *'Book of Strigoi'*. Donna found it instantly. It was a thick, leather-bound book with golden writing spiralled over the front.

"Strangest book I've ever seen." Murmured Abe.

"Strangest I've ever *felt.*" Said Donna.

Jack, taking the book off Donna, opens it in the middle and breathes it in.

"Ew! Jack!" Donna took the book back off him.

"Strangest I've ever sniffed." Laughed Jack.

"Hey! Be careful with that book!"

Jack considered telling Debbie to shush, but thought better of it, this time. Instead, he whispered a sorry in her direction.

They each had a vampiric book in their hands. Donna was still scouring the *'Book of Strigoi,* she found it fascinating. It went into great detail about Romanian vampires, including an extended family tree of the vampire line.

"Hey, look at this!" Jack called.

They all look up from their books.

"What have you found?" Jeremy had swapped his book on vampires for *'Kerwall Through the Years'.*

Kerwall Town

"This book tells you about the different vampire types! See, I knew it was real!" He says, feeling vindicated.

"Well, go on then, what are the types?" Eve probes.

"It says there are four different types. It's like a hierarchy structure. This is crazy!" Jack was captivated by what he was reading.

"Ok, then share the knowledge!" Demanded Abe.

"Alright, alright, calm down." He clears his throat, and reads directly from the text.

"'*Vampire types:*

Type A, also known as the Alpha Vampire. Type A are immortal and the ancient vampire. Within legend they are defined as the root of the pure line, or original line, of all vampiric creatures. Type A are also classified as endangered-'"

"-Endangered, the fuck they are!" Abe sneered.

"Shh!" Whispered Eve, shooting him a look that could have killed.

Jack, waiting a beat for any more interruptions, decides to continue reading from the text. He follows the words on the ancient book with his index finger so he doesn't miss a single line, knowing that the information could save their lives.

"'*They have the ability to turn humans into Type B Vampires, but are too pure to produce Type C Vampires. The only known ways to kill a Type A Vampire is with the assistance of another Type A, decapitation, or a silver steak directly through the heart. Warning. Type A Vampires are extremely dangerous. Under NO CIRCUMSTANCES must you EVER engage with one. If you suspect an individual of being a Type A Vampire, DO NOT approach. If possible, remove yourself from the vicinity in which they reside. DO NOT make them aware of your knowledge. All Vampires, regardless of type, cannot withstand sunlight (unknown duration, further research is required) and must receive explicit permission to enter any premises. They cannot enter churches, regardless of invitation. Once they have obtained authorisation to enter your place of residence, they are able to ingress and egress as they desire. CAUTION: Type A Vampires have exceptional mind control abilities. They WILL attempt to control your thoughts and movements, should they be provided the opportunity. DO NOT engage in direct eye contact. Type A Vampires possess the ability to transform into bats in an instant. They have exceptional hearing and speed.'"*

"So, basically, we're all screwed." Scoffs Eve.

"That's what it's implying, yeah." Conceded Jack.

"Having vampires as residents just took a morbid turn, eh, Jack?" Donna couldn't resist a dig at him.

"What else does it say? Does it tell you about the other types?" Asked Jeremy.

"Yeah… Should I continue?" Jack was deflated.

"Might as well arm ourselves with knowledge, it is our best weapon after all."

"Ok then…

Type B Vampires. They are created by the original Type A's. They possess all the powers of a Type A, however have reduced strength. They are also not immortal, although they can live for many hundreds of years. They are able to fly, through transformation into a bat, but take the form of a much smaller species of bat. They can also be controlled by Type A's. They, in turn, can control Type C's, Type F's and humans. They are similarly extremely deadly to humans. As previously, DO NOT ENGAGE. They are ruthless, cunning and malevolent creatures. They kill for enjoyment, not requirement, and in some cultures folklore states that they hunt humans as a form of sport.'"

Jack gives a quick glance up from the book to see if they are all still following, and finds that they are hanging on his every word, as if their lives were dependant on it.

"Type C Vampires can ONLY be created by Type B's. The Vampire gene is present within them, at a reduced quantity than either the A or B types. They fly through transformation into bats, but are, again, a smaller bat variant and cannot maintain this form for long durations. Doing so results in chronic fatigue which may last a few days; therefore, Type C's rarely fly unless it is deemed absolutely necessary. They are able use other powers, but only on humans, and only after a great deal of practice. They are not immortal. They cannot make other Type C's but do create Type F's."

"Ok, so, what you're saying is, these fuckers can make more, -" Abe interjected.

"-But each time it's watered down." Interrupted Eve. "Sorry, carry on, Jack."

"Within Type F's, the Vampire gene is almost untraceable. They are mostly human. They lack almost all vampire powers, and are often unaware that they have the gene at all. If they ARE aware, then they can control and strengthen their power to be that of a Type C. If they are not aware, the gene lays dormant inside them. They have the power to cause lethargy and depression, but it is unbeknownst to either party. Eventually, the dormant Vampire gene acts as if a virus and tries to kill all the human traits within the host, leaving an empty shell. Extremely submissive."

"Does it say anything else on them?" Asked Donna.

"Not really about the types, it just says that you can kill them all the same way as a 'Type A'. This is bad!"

"Wait, let's not jump the gun here, we still don't know if we *are* dealing with vampires. One bitten neck doesn't mean we have a flock... right?" Eve doubted her words as she spoke them.

"Why take the risk? From this point, we need to act as though this town has vampires." Jack responded.

"Who do we trust with this information?" Jeremy's question was on all of their minds. With a town as corrupt as Kerwall, it was hard to find people to trust.

"Well, I know we can trust our grandparents, and they seem to be able to trust Peter, -" said Donna.

"Peter? The town drunk! I'm sorry, but *I* can't trust him!" Abe retorts.

"Why, because your social standing tells you not to? My grandparents have a great barometer, and they know who's an asshole, and who isn't. If they trust Peter, we all should too. And from what I saw of him today, he looked sober." Jack scowls.

Abe put his palms up in submission.

"You can trust me!" Debbie made them all jump.

"Jesus fucking Christ!" Jack clutched his chest.

"Language, young man!" She scolds.

"How long have you been listening in?" Asks Donna a little suspiciously.

"I didn't need to listen in, your brother's voice carries like a fog horn over water. Now, I'm assuming you're talking about Victoria and Frances, correct?" She asks, rhetorically.

They all nod in the affirmative. Debbie was one shrewd cookie, Donna thought, and wondered how much she could be trusted. She made a mental note to run in by her grandparents later.

"Yeah…" Says Jeremy. "… How long have you suspected?"

"Oh, from the moment I saw them! Well, *HER* in particular." She says.

"What do you mean by that?" Asks Eve.

Debbie goes over to one of the few remaining books they hadn't pilfered through on the shelve, opens it up about a quarter way through, and puts it on the table. Her pale hand points to a woman in a family portrait. She is positioned in the centre, flanked by a man and a woman with a hand on each of her shoulders. There was another three people in the painting too, two women and a man. All with the same stoic expression. All with deep black hair and impossibly white skin. Even though the photo of the painting was in black and white, their abnormally pale skin seemed to glow.

Jack leans for a closer look, he can smell Debbie's perfume hanging off of her cardigan, the fumes of dusty books filled his nostrils. Her faded and chipped maroon nails pinned open the pages.

"Who does that look like to you… Not you or Jack, you obviously wouldn't get the reference." She said to Donna.

"That's impossible!" Abe exclaimed.

"When was this portrait taken?" Asked Jeremy.

Debbie points her finger to the date and reads it out. "Painting of the Viridi family, taken circa 1812."

"Wasn't that when us and the Americans fought over maritime rights?" Jack asked.

"Ha, nerd!" Laughed Abe.

"We're *all* nerds, you dingus!" Said Donna.

"Yes, I believe it was… What does that have to do with anything?" Asked Debbie, confused.

"Nothing, just sharing information." Jack replies.

Debbie gives him a respectful look. She had known him to be smart, but didn't quite know to what extent. He continually surprised her. *Maybe he wasn't just a coasting prankster* she mused.

"Getting back on topic, you really think this is that Victoria woman, our new Mayoress?" Donna probes.

"I do. And I will stand by that." Debbie say defiantly.

"No need to. I think I can safely say, we all believe you." Replied Donna.

"Yeah, with evidence this strong, how can we not. I mean, we can argue the case of a doppelgänger, but I think it's pretty pointless, don't you think?" Said Jack.

"So, our take home from this is: stay home, stay alert and don't let anyone in, no matter what?" Abe checked them off on his hand as he spoke.

"Well, we could fight." Proposed Jack.

"Oh yeah, of course, I forgot that option. How stupid of me. Oh, wait not stupid of me, stupid of *you!* Come on, Jack. There is no way we can stop this!" Abe mocked.

"Well, not with that attitude we can't. And not alone either. We'll need all the good people of Kerwall to help us. My G'pa and G'ma are already writing a list, but I think we should all get together tonight and discuss it with them, see who else we can add." Said Jack.

"Good idea." Agreed Eve.

"What I'd like to know is what are they doing here?" Asked Donna.

"Well, Kerwall is primed and ready for the taking. They can fuck us dry without any lube. Most of the town are old and won't put up a fight." Said Jack.

Donna elbows him. "Do you have to be so vulgar all the time?" She complains.

"I don't have to be, but I like to be." He shrugs.

"Well, at least tone it down a bit." She begs.

"Sorry, can't." He replies.

"Honestly, you're unbearable at times!" She whines.

The rest of them look on. Debbie was new to this sideshow, but to the others, it was just an everyday facet, and a fact of life. Donna and Jack argued as sure as the sun would rise in the morning and be taken over by the moon at night.

Jeremy has drifted away from the main group and is pawing away at the book he found earlier, cross referencing it with another on mythology and folktales.

"This is all well and awful, but it doesn't explain *why* they're here. Sure, we might be an easy target, but there's got to be plenty of towns like us, right?" Queried Eve.

"Well, the book said that they like to hunt us as a kind of sport." Responded Abe.

"Basically, they are the hunters and we are the foxes." Said Donna.

"That's one way to put it." Said Jack, flatly.

"Maybe they need to replenish their vampire stock?" Asked Debbie. "Who knows when the last time they, I'm going to say 'bred' was. It's common knowledge that they are family creatures too." She concludes.

"They are?!" Asks Eve, confused.

"Oh yeah, because I always hunt and suck the blood or random dudes on my family vacations." Jack joked.

"You suck off random dudes?" Laughed Abe.

"Not as much as your mum does!" Retorted Jack.

This prompts playful pushing and roughhousing.

"This is a library, not a Wrestling ring!" Bemoans Debbie.

"Urm… You're gonna want to look at this!" Theres a shaky undertone to Jeremy's voice, cutting Jack and Abe's play fighting to a halt.

They all look over, and see that he has turned a pasty white.

"Are you ok?" Asked Donna, as they make their way over to him.

"I think I found why they're here." Said Jeremy meekly.

They gather around him, looking over his shoulder at the book, but can't initially see what has shaken him. Sweat glistened on his philtrum, and he licked at it absently.

"Well, what is it?" Abe sounded a little impatient.

"According to this, Kerwall has been around a hell of a lot longer than we've been led to believe. And more importantly, I think I've found what they're after."

On one of the pages is a painting of an ancient sceptre. It was about three foot in height and made out of what looked like faience or bone. The paining was so realistic it looked as though it could be picked up off of the page. Jeremy wondered who had painted it and how they got so close enough to be able to replicate the detail. It was coal coloured and had evidently seen damage; chips were dotted over its edges. On top of the sceptre was what looked like a bats head surrounded by sharp thorns.

"They're after a stick?" Asked Abe, confused.

"A stick? No, no, it's a lot more than that." Said Jeremy, stunned by what he has just read.

"There's no way Kerwall has been around long enough to have something like this hidden here. My mum always told me it opened its doors, or whatever, in like the 50's." Eve, like the rest of them, had always been told that Kerwall is a relatively new town.

Within the space of twenty or so minutes, what they knew about the world, and Kerwall, had been shattered into a million tiny fragments.

Kerwall Town

"Wait, wait, that can't be possible!" Exclaimed Debbie, taking the book from the table and thrusting it up to her eyes. She starts pacing the library like a caged animal in a poorly maintained zoo.

"What is it now!?" Demanded Jack, who's concern was growing exponentially quicker than the rest of the gang.

"This!" Debbie says. Her wiry hair stood on end, as if she had been electrocuted by some *cosmic force.*

"Again, what!?" Said Jack, growing more concerned still.

Debbie slams the book on the table and points to the date under the sceptre.

"3150B.C.!? What the hell!" Donna shouted.

"Wasn't that Ancient Egyptian times? Like with the Pharos and Anubis, and all that?" Asked Jack.

"Yes! But why is it here?" Questioned Debbie.

"More to the point, what does it do!?" Asked Eve.

Debbie read directly from the book, like Jack had done moments prior.

"*'The ancient sceptre, known to be called 'Sceptru Intuneric Zei' (or Sceptre of the Dark Gods, in its closest English translation) is believed to grant the holder unlimited power. It accentuates the power that the holder already possesses. Therefore, is mostly used by those with unquestionable strength to begin with. Such as Vampires. The sceptre would provide Vampires greater control over an unprecedented amount of people at any given time. When held, it can also alter the user's transformation, increasing the power of their new form, such as a more ferocious form of bat. It is also believed that if a Type A Vampire holds it, their chance of creating not only stronger vampires in general, but creating more Type A's, is increased. Reports through the ages also suggest that if a human holds the sceptre it will make them immune to*

Vampire powers, though it is not known for how long the effects will last.'"

"So, it's not just a stick?" Asked Abe, in awe.

"Groovy." Jack says, emotionless.

"No, Jack. Not groovy. Far from it in fact. This could be. No, no, not could *IS* extremely dangerous!" Said Debbie, her voice registering a new pitch.

"So, correct me if I'm wrong here, but our little town is home to an ancient Vampiric artefact. A town that now has Vampires in it, we're all assuming Type A's. *And* they know this thing is here and they want to use it to create some sort of what? Army?" Urged Donna.

"Groovy." Said Jack, once more with no conviction. It was almost as if that was the only word he could say, trapped by his shock. He's turned the colour of chalk.

"Urm, Jack, are you ok?" Asked Jeremy, growing worried.

"Yeah… Everything is fine. Just my greatest dream, in reality is actually a horrible nightmare. I've got to be dreaming. Somebody pinch me!" Pleaded Jack.

Instead of pinching him, Donna punches her brother in his left bicep with all the power she could muster. The searing pain is instant, and the force of the punch makes the top of his arm numb. He clutches it meekly with his other hand.

"OW! I said *pinch* not *punch!* You dickwad!" Tears threaten to spill from his eyes.

"Sorry. That's why you should enunciate. Learning is fun." Emphasised Donna, with not a breadcrumb of remorse. She was practically gleeful and trying to stop a round of giggles.

"What's so funny?" Asked Eve, once more confused.

The question sends Donna into laughter.

"I think she's broken too." Said Abe.

After a few moments, her laughter subsides, and so does the pain in Jack's arm, but he continues to rub it while staring daggers at his sister.

"We're all fucked. Aren't we?" Said Donna after her laughter falls to a small giggle, forgetting to mind her own language. Debbie tuts at her, which was felt absurd considering the circumstances.

"I don't get what's so funny about that." Said Jeremy, who was still trying, unsuccessfully, to hide his concern.

"We don't have to be." Said Jack confidently.

"What?" Implored Eve.

"I said we don't have to be." He repeated.

"Oh, so you know a way to stop a vampire race then?" Abe spat in a sarcastic tone that Jack thought was uncalled for.

"As a matter of fact, I do. And so do you all. You just read how to stop them, and you just read what they're after. We have the element of surprise. Not them. If we're smart, we can, and will, stop this." He had risen to his feet, impassioned.

"What if we don't want to stop them?" Murmured Abe.

"What do you mean!? We *have* to stop them!" Said Donna with a touch of crazy in her eyes and her hair taking on a dishevelled look.

"Well, I dunno about you, but I think being an immortal, a vampire no less, sounds pretty tubular to me!" Abe babbled.

"You've completely lost it, haven't you!" Sighed Eve in disbelief.

"Actually no. The more I think about it, the better I think it is." Abe defended his view with conviction.

"So, you're telling me, you'll be ok with watching your loved ones die while you pass through the years, never being able to meet them again in the afterlife? … If there is one… God I hope there is!" Jeremy pleaded with him.

"I don't believe that there is a lord above, so I make my heaven here." Retorted Abe.

"This is the part where you tell us you're kidding right… right?" Begged Donna.

"No. honestly. I've thought about this for a long time." Abe continues.

"You mean a long time as in since you found out about the existence of them ten minutes ago?" Mocked Jack.

"Don't be so naive, Jack. We've said for years about this kind of thing, and how rad it would be if vampires were real." Said Abe.

"Yeah, but that was all make-believe stuff, man. C'mon, you gotta see that wanting something like this is pretty scary. It's not a joke. Lives *will* be in danger." Continued Jack.

"Who's laughing?" Asked Abe, rhetorically. "Look, I'm not saying I'm not going to help you all. I just want to be straight up about how I feel about it."

"Well, it's been duly noted." Said Debbie dryly.

"I think we need to tell my grandparents about this right away. We should all go, so we *all* know what's being said and we can all have an input on who to put on our safe list." Said Donna.

They all agree that it's a good idea.

"I can't stay too long though; the Shake Shack normally has a mini rush at 12pm." Stated Jeremy.

A quick look at the oversized library clock told them that it was quarter to 11.

"I normally close the library for lunch from 11:30-12:30 anyway, so it could work out fine with me." Said Debbie.

"Ok, so we're all in agreement?" Confirmed Donna.

They nod in accordance and moments later they are out the door. It was a cloudy and dull mid-morning, with a light breeze. The sun was hidden in the clouds somewhere, playing amongst the thick vapours.

As they all clambered into the Hardware store, they stopped in their tracks. The room fell silent. Frances Lloyd-Chatman greeted them with a smile that stretched the width of his face.

11

The Meeting of the Minds

The groups hearts were beating so loudly in their chests that Frances Lloyd-Chatman could hear them. It was music to his ears, reminding him of *Ludwig Van Beethoven's 5th symphony,* in C minor. The thought of blood pumping around their mortal bodies was enough to make his mouth water, he did his best to control himself.

"Hello everyone. Nice of you to join us." He says, smooth as silk. His punctuating laugh took those who were meeting him for the first time by surprise.

"What's going on?" Asks Jack. The words didn't sound as if they belonged to him, or even came from him; but instead, from a distant land, a million miles from here.

"It's ok, dear." Said Dot.

"The Mayor, -" Started Terry.

"-Please, remember it's just Frances."

"Right, yes,"

Jack noticed they were all struggling against the pull of Frances' eyes. His voice was smooth, like jazz emanating from a gramophone, luring them in.

Kerwall Town

"Frances here, was just telling us about the mandatory meeting tonight on the green." Peter continued from Terry.

"I have just realised, that I'm in the presence of the *infamous*, Kerwall JADEs. My, my, what an honour and a privilege. Charmed in fact." His black leather clad hand juts towards the ensemble. They all reluctantly take turns shaking it, first Debbie, then Jeremy, followed by Eve, Donna and Jack. Abe is last to take it, but when he does, he meets the snake like eyes of the Mayor, and a hint of a smile is mirrored in their faces. It's unregistered by anyone else. Frances gives Abe's hand a subtle squeeze of acknowledgement.

"I should hope to see you all there at 7:30pm, *dead* on." He concludes.

"We'll be there alright." Terry almost rushed him out the door with his words.

"May I ask you something?" Asked Jack, a little meekly. His friends shot him a look, all of but Abe. It was only a quick one, and it was out of surprise more than anything. Frances, who was almost out the door, turned back and smiled at him.

"Why of course you can, young Jack. Ask away. I'm an open book."

Alarm bells sprung to life in Jack's head at the word *book*. Did Frances know about their research already? He registered the panic in the other's eyes too, and tried his best to conceal his own. After all, wasn't mind reading one of the Vampiric powers? He couldn't remember. It all seemed to be fading away from him. He tried to shake it off as best as he could and asked the question regardless.

"Where's Victoria? I mean, Ms Viridi?" He had tried to sound strong, but the words whimpered out of him at just below a whisper.

Frances placed his hand on Jack's shoulder in a friendly manner, but the touch was repulsive, it felt cold. Jack attempted to conceal his emotion.

"She has, *other* business to attend to. But rest assured, she'll be at the meeting with us later on this evening." With that, Frances Lloyd-Chatman left. A strange sense of unease remained in the hardware store after him. The eerie silence was broken moments later, by Dot's uncontrollable laughter. It was an unnatural and unsettling sound, like chinks of metal rattling round in a tin can.

"What's so funny?" Asked Abe.

Terry didn't answer. He rushes into the kitchen and comes back seconds later with a glass of cold water. The others are now stood beside her, trying to ask if she is ok, to get any response at all. Her face is turning a strange purple as she chokes on her own laughter.

"What's wrong with her!" Donna screams.

"Out of my way!" Shouts Terry. They all scatter like ants at the sound of his voice. He throws the icy water in her face, hoping that it will stop her. It doesn't. In desperation he shakes her by the shoulders, shouting her name into her face. Still nothing. He is forced to do the thing he swore he would never do. He slaps her across the face. The sound echoes through the hardware store and sharp intakes of breath follow. Tears sting Terry's eyes, but mercifully it's worked. The laughing, and choking, stop. He leads her over to the chair behind the counter and sits her carefully down. As he kneels beside her, he ignores the firecracker pop of his knees and kisses her hand. Taking her delicate,

Kerwall Town

shaking hands into his own, he covers the harsh slap with a gentle kiss.

"Someone get me a tea towel and a cup of tea, three sugars, for the shock. Quickly." Terry speaks urgently to the room. Jack scrambles out of the room.

"Are you ok, gran?" Donna kneels on her other side. Dot gives her a smile that isn't as reassuring as she might have been aiming for.

"Yes, dear. I'll be right as rain again in a moment. Nasty bastard, isn't he?" She says, now with a more natural smile.

"Who?"

"Why that Frances, of course. Our new and esteemed Mayor. He did this to me the first time too." She explains, feeling more like herself with every passing moment.

"I take it Debbie and Jeremy here are on our side?" Asks Terry.

"We sure are." Jeremy holds out his hand for Terry to shake. He duly obliged from his kneeling position by his wife's side.

"It would seem so." Says Debbie. She was still wrestling internally with the facts laid out before her.

Jack re-enters the room with the tea towel and sweetened tea, along with a few biscuits on a brown floral tray.

"Tea for the lady, and biscuits for all." He sets them down on the counter. They all gratefully take one.

"How are you feeling now, G'ma?" Jack asks.

"Back to normal. I tell you, it's a funny… excuse the pun, situation. Thank you, Tez. That's the second time in two days you've saved my life from *him*."

"You save my life everyday just by being in it." Terry kisses her on the lips once again.

S.D. Reed

"Alright, get a room, lovebirds!" Jack jokes.

Terry gestures with his arms as if to say, *this is my house,* and they all laugh. A genuine one, not a life threatening one.

"I think we all need to talk." Donna says, after a moment.

"Wise idea." Replies Terry.

"Still got that list, G'ma?"

Dot retrieves it from her pocket and puts it on the counter, next to the tray. They all gather around it and murmur in agreement.

"You can add my mum to the list." Said Abe.

"Mine too, and probably her partner, and maybe even the whole department." Eve adds.

Dot writes them all on the list, along with Debbie and Jeremy.

"Guess I can cross his name off. Poor guy." Dot says, pointing to Ricky.

"Do you think that's everyone in the town who we can trust?" Asks Peter.

"I can't think of anyone else for now, but I'm sure we'll get a better measure tonight. That's how we added the others." Terry explains.

They all looked at the list. It really did amount to all the people in the whole of Kerwall that they could trust. Even then, they still weren't convinced with Denise.

"I'm sure Andy Cooper will be on our side too actually." Dot says, adding him to the list. Twelve people. There are twelve people they can trust in the whole town. The irony wasn't lost on her that she was using a red pen. At the time, it was all she had to hand.

~~Ricky Turner~~
Denise Carter?
Peter Wright

Terry and Dotty Smith
The Kerwall JADEs
Jeremy Williams
Debbie Gibbons
Nora Roberts
Krystal Jackson
Andy Cooper

"So, when do we start asking the others to join our 'team'?" Jack ponders.

"I think the safest way is to wait until after the meeting. We can confront them, and anyone else, in twos, and tell them to meet us… God knows where. Definitely not here." Says Terry.

"What about the park?" Dotty suggests.

"No!" They all shout in unison, making Dot and Terry jump a little bit.

"Why?" Peter asks, confused.

"We have a little more information about our Mayor and Mayoress." Donna begins.

"CliffsNotes, they're VAMPIRES!" Interrupts Jack.

"What do you mean, Vampires?"

"They're not real." Peter utters, more disrespectfully than he had intended.

"And how would you know, have you seen one?" Asks Dot.

"Well, no." He replies, confused.

"And do you believe in God?" She continues.

"Of course, I do, I mean, he hasn't given me the best cards to deal with as of late, but I'm still a believer, of course." This was the first time he had opened up about his faith, and it was a weight off his shoulders in some way.

"And have you seen him, this *God?*" She pushes further.

"Well, no." He says.

"Yet you believe in his existence?"

"Absolutely." Replies Peter.

"I see. Yet, you haven't seen him. You haven't seen Vampires either, yet you've dismissed the existence of them instantly, funny that." Dot says, leaving Peter utterly perplexed.

"There's books on God though, and about him too." Peter is desperately trying to win the argument. He refuses to believe that the two subject matters can be compared.

"And I can assure you there are books on Vampires too."

"Yes but, -"

"Believe with your eyes, not with your mind, Peter."

Peter doesn't say anything back, he can't say anything. His world view may have just been changed forever.

"So, Vampires you say?" Terry tries to get back on track.

"Right! And the worst kind too!" Jack seemed almost excited again.

"There are different types?" Asks Terry, trying to hide his sudden fear.

"Sure are!" Replies Jack.

Jack, Donna, and the others fill Peter, Dot and Terry in on their discovery at the library, giving them all the details. Jack drew a picture of the Sceptre, as close as he could recall, but Donna soon ripped it up. 'Just to be safe.' She had said. They also told them about vampiric powers, and speculated on more they might possess, like mind reading.

Kerwall Town

"And you are absolutely sure, that they're... they're... *Vampires?*" Peter finally asks.

"Well, we are *absolutely* sure they are not human. Just look at what he did to Grandma earlier."

"That could have just of been a coincidence? ... Right?" Peter's voice lacked conviction. He didn't even have to look deep down; the truth was right there on the surface.

"Don't shit on my ice cream and call it sprinkles." Donna retorts, surprising herself. "Sorry, Jack's been rubbing off on me. This whole situation has made me a little crazy."

"I think it's made us all a little crazy. But we have to band together, not only for the good of the town, but for the good of our lives." Said Terry.

"Anyone got any ideas on where we should rendezvous together then?" Asks Eve.

"I, for one, don't think we should all meet together in a group right away, maybe stagger the arrival in say ten-minute intervals?" Donna stated.

"Do you really think we'll be able to recruit more?" Jack was trying, and failing, not to sound downbeat.

"Time will tell." Was all Dot could say in return.

"Ones thing is for certain though. We need to be vigilant, and more aware than we have ever been before. Staying alert is key. I'd even go so far as to say that we need to act as though everyone has been infected, until we know otherwise." Donna was once more the voice of reason.

The room stood silent as everyone digested what was happening. The one thing that they all knew for certain, was that *nothing* from this point on was ever going to be the same. It was a hard truth to swallow, but it was their new reality nonetheless.

Jack resorted to doing what he always did in times of stress, organising. He had already reshuffled the contents of the counter, which amounted to odd bits of paperwork, and receipts. He was now working on the shelves, turning all the labels to face the right way, and moving all the hammers into a perfectly neat line. He wasn't sure why he did those things, but it calmed him. Ever since he was little, he could remember needing organisation. Making sure that all of his toys were in both size and colour order, and how he would become agitated if things were out of place. He's learnt, over time, that he can't organise absolutely everything though, the thought of even this frustrates him. It's something that he hasn't discussed with anyone, not even Donna. But anyone who knows Jack, knows he has his *quirks*. In both school and college, he was teased about it by the *Neanderthals* who roamed the halls. They would deliberately knock his ordered pens off the desk, or they would tip his backpack on the floor, the previously segmented contents scattering into chaos. He never let them see how much it upset him though, he would laugh it off.

"Dotty." Terry had gotten up from beside her and was walking the length of the store, attempting to get the blood flowing back to his knees.

'Yes, dear."

"Have you seen, Postie Rose today?"

"Can't say I have, but remember, I've been at the supermarket."

"Right, so you have. What time does he normally come?" He looks at his watch. "Because, it's almost 12:30 already, and I'm waiting on a delivery."

Kerwall Town

"Almost half twelve? That's my queue to leave. I will see you all later at the meeting. Stay safe." Jeremy gathers himself.

"Mine too." Said Debbie.

And with that, they both left.

"Wait, so you're saying Mike hasn't done his rounds yet?" Asked Jack, a little alarmed. Once again, he seemed to be the first alert to the potential danger.

"I don't know if he's just running late today, or is sick, but it's not like him to be late. He's normally got his rounds done by 11am. Sometimes he pops in here for a chat too."

"Don't you think that's a little odd, G'pa?"

"I don't think we should be jumping to conclusions just yet?" Donna interjects.

"I think that's exactly what we should be doing. Remember what we said not five minutes ago? We have to be acting like everyone has been infected, that's the only way we can stay safe." Total determination filled Jack's voice. There was no way he thought this was a game anymore.

"Well, the best thing we can do is see if he turns up tonight, and if he looks or acts any different, we'll know he's been infected too." Donna replies.

"You make everything sound so simple." Said Dot.

"No need to overcomplicate our enemy, right?"

While discussions continued in the hardware store, Daniel and Frances were having a conversation of their own.

The Crow's Nest was one of the largest buildings in Kerwall. It was adorned with lavish dark oak furniture, and deep reds and golds. There were six, large, high-backed booths lining one wall and the counter was in the centre, lined with bar stools. No one knew where the alcohol came from, but then, no one dared to ask. Daniel Knowles was a man who got things done by any means necessary and didn't care who he stepped on.

Daniel was wiping the counter absentmindedly, while Frances was hungrily sipping his Bloody Mary. He had said that there was no better way to start an afternoon and they filled the empty room with laughter.

"So, let me get right on into why I'm here." Frances took another sip of his drink. "I've heard that you like to get things done, and that you're a man of authority."

"Yes. I am a man of authority." Repeats Daniel.

"That's what I thought. And I know that when you were Deputy Mayor, you were *dreadfully* stifled. You were the real brains of the town; I can certainly see that."

"I was the brains, that's for certain." His eyes are locked onto Frances', hanging onto every word.

"How would you like to be the Deputy Mayor again? But this time, you'll have all the power you can handle."

"I would like that very much." Said Daniel, in a tone that wasn't quite his.

"This is most exquisite. You will be the eyes of the town when I or Victoria aren't around. You are my right-hand man, and I'm sure I can count on you to get things done, by any means. Now mark my words here, Daniel. Tonight, we are going to implement some new rules, and it will be your job to make sure that they are followed to the letter. Am I making myself clear, Daniel?"

"Perfectly."

"Good. I knew Victoria I and could count on you. Welcome to the head of the table." Daniel gleefully

Kerwall Town

takes Francis' now outstretched hand. He had power once more, but this time, it was unbridled.

"I can give you my word, that you will have model citizens by the end of the week." A sardonic smile stretches over his face. He was already salivating at the prospect of flexing his heavy-handed muscles, with zero consequences. He had finally been given cart blanche to do his dirty deeds out in the open.

"I have no doubt that you will. Now, I must be going, there is other business to attend to before the day is out." He drank the rest of his beverage greedily and then wiped the sides of his mouth with a handkerchief he fished from his pocket.

Before he left, he retrieved something from the inside of his blazer pocket and slid it over the counter.

"What's this?"

"This, is the place to dump the people who are not *wholly* agreeable to the cause. But, if you do, just make sure they have a pulse." Francis' cackle hung once more in the air around him.

"What would be the point in that?"

"Never you mind."

"No, I shouldn't mind."

"Precisely."

With that, Frances left the establishment, having planted a rather delicious seed in Daniel's head.

As soon as Frances had left, Daniel grabbed the closest baggie of coke from under the counter. He inhaled two lines in quick succession, followed by a primal roar.

"Now that's good shit." He laughed into the empty pub.

12

New Rules

Frances knocked gently on the door to Victoria's chambers. It was an oversized, dark red-brown, double door with two concentric circles in the middle. The bottom half of the door was coated in a multitude of iron carved diamonds. The head of the door was half-moon in shape and the intricate designs and patterns seemed almost delicate against the rest of the frame. In the centre, was a sleeping bat carved out of oak. It was generations old, and the blood of many a victim was stained into the deep grooves. Whichever house Victoria and Frances inhabited, that door followed.

"Enter."

Frances obliged, and opened the door with his free hand, balancing a lavish tray that supported a tall glass of dark red liquid in the other.

"Supper time." He enters, bowing slightly once he is fully in the room.

It would have been pitch black, had it not been for the many candles set about in a maze-like fashion. The candles, of every size, gave the room a dull glow. The wallpaper was a dark hue of purple with more intricate design work embroiled into it.

Kerwall Town

Perfectly central to the room was a long coffin. It was impossibly black in colour, with oil green piping adorning the exterior, coordinated crushed velvet lined the wooden casket.

Victoria was upright within it and, as Frances got closer, she moved the coffin towards her with a simple hand gesture, so it stood vertical upon the base.

"Thank you, Frances. Freshly made. I assume?" She took the glass from him with both hands.

"Fresh from last night, and chilled all morning in the stores. Just as you like it."

"Good."

She sips at it, savouring the thick texture as it slides down her throat. With each mouthful, her pupils dilate more, replicating a predator, which, ultimately, is exactly what she is. She knew it too. She took great glee in being the most dangerous thing on the planet. A perfectly crafted killing machine, with limitless potential. However, the old saying 'more wants more', could not be truer for Victoria. She has been hunting for the Sceptre for decades, and was secretly beginning to doubt its existence at all, after all, humans aren't the only species who told their children bedtime stories and folk tales. It has become her sole mission in life. She had a staunch belief that the Sceptre, if it is real, is *hers*. It was her right, stolen from her family's possession almost two hundred years ago. That was when large numbers of the Viridi line covered the globe, living in packs. Whole dynasties would rule over towns all across the world.

There was a strict code which Vampires live by, and ancient laws to follow too. Victoria didn't like the rules. She thought she was too good for them. She wanted ultimate power, and hated the thought of anyone, or anything, being stronger than her. The code decreed that no Vampire should harm another of its kind, nor shall they invade the territory of another family. Victoria broke both rules, she's now on the run from the rest of her kind. Hunted. Which makes Kerwall the perfect place to be. As far as she was aware, the rest of the living Vampires didn't know that this place existed, and they had eyes on every corner of the world. They were the true rulers of the world. Not a single law was passed without their consent. No President, Prime Minister, Dictator, anyone, had greater control. The brilliant thing about it, was that the humans were blissfully unaware that they have been manipulated for as long as the earth has had water on it. There was no such thing as free will while the Vampires were sucking on the collective neck of humanity.

"I assume everything is ready for tonight?" She drains the last bit of the glass.

"Yes. Everything is how you wanted."

"Good. And Daniel has agreed to be the new deputy?"

"He has, yes. It was easy to manipulate him. He craves the power."

"And you're sure you can control him?"

"Most definitely. He's putty in my hands. All you have to do is give him some of that devil chalk and he's even easier to control. The town are already petrified of him, and if any of them step out of line with the new rules tonight, I've said he can do as he pleases to them. I even gave him a location to dispose of the reprobates. As long as they still have a pulse. Think of it as a kind of delivery service."

Kerwall Town

"Good. It seems as though he's going to be a fine addition to us and a useful distraction to them. You did good recruiting him, Frances."

She strokes his head as one might stroke a pet.

Victoria told Francis what she had done to Mike Rose, the postman. She had decided that he may come in handy, being so well liked and respected in the town. But on the flip side, she said that she wouldn't hesitate to snap his neck herself if he became a problem. She thought, she might just snap his neck anyway. Victoria got an adrenaline rush when she hunted and killed humans. Killing fellow Vampires, *that* was pure ecstasy. She knew that she needed *some* around for her plan to come to fruition, but if any of them were to step out of line, she had no qualms with removing them entirely. She had done it countless times before, what was a few more. Vampires, like humans, were replaceable.

At around 5:30 p.m., just as Mable Knight had said her goodbyes to the factory girls, whom she was growing closer to every day, she felt as though someone was watching her. She didn't know for certain, and she couldn't put her finger on why she knew, but it was an uneasy feeling. The sort of feeling like she was in a crowded place and had just realised that her top was inside out. There was a foreboding dark cloud filling the sky and the sun was nowhere to be seen, having made an early exit for the day. The wind was beginning to lick at her clothes, throwing dust around her ankles. She hugged herself at the elbows and quickened her pace, checking behind her every few seconds. With each passing moment the sense that someone was watching her was growing. She felt as though she was being stalked like weak prey. There was no one else on the street, no one she could shout to for help. If she was attacked this very second, she was sure she would die alone.

A hand gripped her shoulder and she shrunk at feeling, screaming at the top of her lungs. *'This is it.'* She thought. She scrunched her eyes tightly closed as she turned around and balled her left hand into a fist. With no purposeful precision to her reflex she connected snugly with the assailant's nose, stretching it across their face.

The attacker screamed out in pain, she opened her eyes and was full of instant regret.

"I'm so, *so* sorry, Vicar!" She gushes, pulling a handkerchief out of her smock and pressing it to his bloody nose.

"Not to worry. I'm just glad to know you can defend yourself." He says, trying to laugh it off.

"I just got spooked. I've never hit anyone before, let alone a Vicar! Oh, gracious, am I going to hell now? Oh, please no!" She starts hyperventilating, hitching her breath. Henry becomes the comforter. He takes the handkerchief off of Mable, and holds it in his left hand, placing his right on her shoulder.

"Don't be silly, my child. It was just an accident. God cannot punish accidents, and I can already see that you are full of repent."

"Oh, I am! I really am! I'm so sorry." The words manage to escape through more hitched breaths and sobs.

He gently rubs her shoulder.

"Come, my child."

"Where?"

"To my house, silly. I'll make you a sweet cup of tea, you've had quite the shock."

Kerwall Town

"Yes, I have had quite the shock." She says passively.

He leads her gently by the arm to his house, just a short walk away. Mable realised, as they walked, that she no longer felt as though she was being watched.

Mike Rose was just waking up as Mable had punched the Vicar. He looked at the clock on his bedroom wall and was, at first, confused. It read half past five, but it looked dark outside. He jumped out of his bed stark naked. Mike has never been late in all of his life. It was something he was proud of. His school nickname, 'reliable Mikey', had followed him through life, even into Kerwall. Some residents even set their watches by him.

"I can't have overslept!" He shouts to the empty room. He pulled his shorts on, completely forgoing his boxers. He managed to find a pair of socks and shoes but couldn't for the life of him remember where he put his shirt. He hunted high and low for it, eventually finding it in the bathtub.

He quickly brushed his teeth, then went to see what sort of state he looked like in the mirror. Mike screamed. There was no neat black hair and brown eyes staring back at him. There was nothing at all. He looked down at his body but everything was still there, present and accounted for. He pinched his skin so hard that it drew blood to the surface.

"Ok, I'm not dreaming, that fucking hurt." He says, rubbing his arm. He puts his hands to his face, just to make sure. Everything was there too. So why couldn't he see his reflection. The mirror was clean, the wall behind him was being reflected back, so why wasn't he. The realisation dawned on him. Maybe, what he thought had been a dream last night, wasn't a dream at all. 'But that's impossible,' he thought. He put his finger in his mouth, and found his cuspids. They seemed longer and sharper than they had been yesterday.

"So, it wasn't a dream?"

He moved his fingers to the side of his neck, finding two small round scars forming a bumpy texture over his skin.

"What the fuck!"

He didn't know much about Vampires, he didn't even know they existed, and now he was one. Mike tried to remain calm. He got a pen and paper from the kitchen draw and listed the changes in himself since last night. When he was done, the adrenaline grounding him evaporated and he burst into tears.

Despite it all he felt fresher. No, not that, it was more, he thought. He felt *Alive!*

It was all coming back to him now, the events of last night. He remembered going to Denise's house at almost 3 a.m. How he had plucked up the courage to knock on the door, and finally ask her out on a date. It seemed as though his new found power gave him a confidence too. The memories were gaining clarity. He had hammered on her door, but to no avail. By luck, he had spotted that her bedroom window was open. Almost instinctively he morphed, his body transforming into a small bat to fly through the narrow opening. Mike had been invited into Denise's home many times before, so nothing stood in his way. Once he was inside her room, the new hybrid version of himself had reappeared and he stood tall against the wall. With his newfound vision, he saw everything in a perfect lucidity. The lamp on her bedside table, the waterbed she lay on, the beige blanket that she had cocooned herself in, and

175

Kerwall Town

her brown hair barely visible over the top of it. Her plump red lips and her soft, delicate neck had started his heart pounding. He recalled licking his lips, and his cuspids lengthened to a sharp point. It was her neck. It was desperately tantalising. He had glided to the side of her bed, and watched her. Taking in all of her silent beauty. Many people in the town no longer remembered how stunning she was. He had carefully stroked her hair back and away from her neck. There was something about her neck, it had forced his blood to race, as if a primal instinct had taken over his body. Mike had sunk his newly formed teeth into her flesh and drank. His teeth cut through as easily as a straw would pierce a juice carton. To his amazement, she didn't wake up, didn't struggle, didn't move. At the time, he had thought nothing of it, but now, his mind was going a million miles an hour.

"Oh God, what if I've killed her!? What if I didn't do it right? It's not like there's an instruction manual!" The question snapped him out of his memories, but the empty room didn't answer him back. The silence mocked him.

"I've got to see if she's alright!" He boomed into the void.

He got to Denise's in record time, and entered the same way as he had the previous night. Nothing in the room had changed. The lamp stood untouched, the chair stacked with clothes was undisturbed, and to his amazement, she still lay over the bed unmoved. Panic tried to cling to him like a parasite. He stood staring at her. Despite the power he now possessed, he was still a scared postman, from a small-town, gazing at the woman he was too scared to ask out.

"Sloppy. Very sloppy." A voice from the shadows taunted. Mike jumped, adrenaline pumped through him, transforming him into his bat form. He flapped around the room seemingly unable to control himself.

"Yes, you have much to learn." It wasn't quite mocking, but it was close.

Mike got a hold of himself. He forced a sound and it echoed back within milliseconds, his ears contracted sharply, funnelling the noise with precision. He had found the source of the voice. He flapped his wings in front of the figure.

"A quick learner I see." The man from the shadows stepped out from the seclusion and clapped his gloved hands with a distinctive laugh.

"It's *you!*" Mike stuttered in disbelief as he reverted back to his human form.

"Who else were you expecting, Father Christmas? I believe he lives in a different town."

"I don't really know." Then, remembering why he was here, Mike rushes over to Denise.

"It's too late. She's dead. Has been for hours." Said Frances, without a trace of empathy.

"No! She can't be! How?" Mike flung himself onto Denise's lifeless body. Her eyes were mercifully closed, if it weren't for the blood-soaked pillow and spilling holes in her neck, her death would appear peaceful.

"Drinking and turning are two completely different things. Looks like you tried to do both. That's what we call a rookie error. Some Vampires want it to be punishable by death."

"Vampires? So... That *is* what I am now? Oh, God! What have I done?" He buries his head further into her body.

"I've just told you, you killed her. And yes, you are now among the *greatest* species that has ever roamed the earth, and there is much for you to learn. The first thing we need to do, is make this look like an accident. As if *she* did it. It shouldn't be too hard for everyone to believe that she would do this. The only thing people will say is they thought she would have done it sooner."

Mike was stunned. Yesterday he was the reliable postman of Kerwall town. Tonight, he's a Vampire covering up his own murder victim. She was more than that to him though, he had wanted a life with her. What was he thinking coming here last night? He was her only friend, and he killed her.

"I killed her." Mike repeated. The words hung thick in the air like London smog.

"Yes, you certainly did. Now come on, we need to be quick. I've got a town meeting to attend to in less than an hour."

"Town meeting? I didn't know about this?"

"Obviously your attendance, like everyone else's, is mandatory. Now, go downstairs and find something, *anything,* to make this look more…natural."

"Me, why me?"

"Your mess. You fix it. Consider it part of your training." He scolded.

Frances didn't want to doubt Victoria, or her decision for Mike to join the greatest species alive, but he was certain that even she would struggle with her reasons from this sorry evidence.

Mike rushed downstairs and into the kitchen. He knew for certain that she took some sort of medication, so he began hunting for that first. He riffled through the cupboards carelessly, the additional mess making little difference. Stains on the work surfaces, overflowing bags of rubbish piled in the middle of the room; Mike thought that it resembled a crack den, minus the needles. The smell was unbearable to his heightened senses, but he soldiered on with the task in hand. Then, he had an idea. He stopped, closed his eyes, and visualised what he was looking for. Something in him led him directly to the small cupboard under the sink. He opened the door and found a stack of tablets inside. Mike took all of them, and the bottle of bleach which stood nearby. Then, as a last resort, he got a large kitchen knife from the draw too.

"I trust you have everything?" Frances scoffed, when Mike returned to the room.

"I hope so. Oh, Lord forgive me for what I'm about to do and for what I have done."

"Don't be so stupid, the Lord has no power of you. And he won't forgive you."

"The Lord loves everyone!" Mike insisted.

"Not Vampires." Frances flatly retorted.

Mike scattered the tablets around Denise's limp corpse, over the counter, and across the floor. He strategically placed the bleach above her, balanced on the table.

"What are you doing?"

"Making it look like she overdosed."

"And when they do the toxicology report, what do you think they will find? hrmmm." His laugh, for once, seemed fuelled by frustration. A sardonic, almost satanic smile rose on his face.

Realisation dawned on Mike.

"Oh, no!" He pleaded, "I can't do that!"

"You must and you will."

"I must." Mike repeated.

Kerwall Town

He gathered some tablets from the floor, opened her mouth with some effort, and crammed them in, stroking her throat to help them go down, and apologising profusely while he did it. His eyes were wet with tears, hands shaking.

"More." Insisted Frances.

"More." Repeated Mike.

This time he took a handful of tablets and forced them into Denise's mouth. He pulled her lip upwards with his other hand and parted her teeth just wide enough to drop them all in. Mike's tears fell more freely now. When he looked up at Frances, the response was a hand gesture, telling him to carry on. So, Mike did. He took each set of her teeth in both hands and pulled. The cold air was filled with a cruel sound as her jaw snapped from its hinges, filling Mike with horror.

"Oh shit!"

"Don't worry about it. Drop the tablets in."

"No, I won't worry." Mike repeated once more.

He once more dropped the tablets into her mouth, and this time there was no need to sooth her throat as he did it. He poured some of the bleach down her gullet after them.

"Good. Now, with the knife make it look like she cut her wrists."

Mike, who wasn't looking directly at Frances, this time didn't repeat and carry out the order.

"I can't." He broke down again. This was all too much. He was already in too deep. He didn't ask to become one of these *things,* and now he's one of them, covering up the murder of his friend. Sick threatened to pass his lips, but he pushed it back down.

"You can, and you will. What else were you planning to use the knife for?"

'To kill you and then probably me.' Mike thought.

"To kill me and you?" Frances' sly cackle urged Mike to protest.

Mike was taken aback. He could have sworn that he hadn't said that out loud. Could his private thoughts now be read by this parasite? He tried to wipe his mind blank.

"You have been given the greatest gift that this world can offer, and you want to squander it all after five minutes? You have much to learn, but we will teach you. We will show you that being a Vampire is simply the next step in the evolutionary line."

"We?" Mike still held the knife close to him, down by his side. It glinted when the moonlight struck it, showcasing its severity.

"Yes. There are few of us right now. But soon there will be more. Many more. And you *will* help us. You have been chosen."

Mike was growing tiresome of that punctuating laugh. He wasn't sure whether it was mocking or encouraging him. Didn't care to find out. Frances put a hand on his shoulder and Mike looked up, into his eyes. Frances held him in his gaze. Mike didn't struggle to break out of it, he melted into the power of the man stood before him.

"Now. Cut. Her. Wrists."

That is exactly what Mike did. He seemed to be in a trance now, methodically cutting her arms. The rigor mortis was already setting into Denise's ashen body, the blood didn't flow, it had coagulated onto her skin. Not even this sight could bring Mike to tears now. He was a man-Vampire hybrid on a mission. The cuts stretched up and down both of her arms and when he was done, he dropped the knife by his side.

Kerwall Town

"Good. Now it's time we left. Do yourself a favour and change your clothes before the meeting."

"Yes. I'll change." Repeated Mike.

With that, they both turned into their bat forms and flew out of the open window once more.

At 7:30 p.m. sharp, all of Kerwall was again gathered together. This time, on the green in the centre of town. Some residents had brought folding chairs from their homes and others brought blankets to sit on.

Frances was stood on the newly constructed platform, flanked by Daniel. Victoria was perched once more at the back of the stage, surveying and taking everything in.

The Kerwall (J.)J.A.D.E.'s, Peter, and Debbie sat apart from each other. Dot and Terry chose to sit together, knowing that if they were apart it would arouse suspicion. They all agreed to observe different parts of the meeting. Dot and Terry were in charge of watching the platform, the original JADEs were in charge of looking at the left quadrant of people, Jeremy was tasked with the front three rows, and Debbie and Peter took the right side and back row respectively.

The sight of Daniel on stage, alongside the two new overlords, caused commotion. It was stamped out immediately when Frances spoke.

"Friends." He stretched his hands out wide as if embracing them all into a warm hug.

"As you can see, we have elected a new member to our team, you all know him as your friendly landlord of The Crow's Nest. Well, now his former title has been reinstated, Deputy Mayor. Come on up here, Daniel."

The crowd were stunned into silence.

Daniel strode up to the lectern with a broad smile.

"We're going to make some beautiful changes to our town."

He received a lukewarm round of applause in response. Some were only doing it because the people next to them were.

"And, it will be for the better."

His voice was thunderous and commanding. The threatening tone under the smile was not lost on anyone.

"Thank you, Daniel. Please take a seat." Daniel duly obliged with Francis, like the good little puppet that he is. On the far corner of the stage was an a-frame. It was about four foot in height with red permanent marker scrawled over it.

"As you can all see." Francis glided over to the sign. "These are the new rules of our fair town. And you *will* all abide by them."

Curfew is 9 p.m. sharp

Those who are fit and able to work, shall do so.

Those who are unable to work will be given alternate tasks.

Under no circumstances are you to leave Kerwall town or speak to anyone from outside of Kerwall town.

"I'm sure that some of you are wondering why these rules have been put into place. Well, I'm afraid we have no choice." Frances was lapping the attention up, taking his time, making the crowd hang onto every syllable. Most residents were captivated by him, regardless of these new rules.

"For I am afraid that I have some terrible news, and these rules have come in effect because of this. Our dear resident, Ricky, owner of the petrol station, has been found dead."

Cries of shock reverberated over the town common, the occasional sob rising above the noise. Ricky was

Kerwall Town

known by all of the town citizens, and almost universally liked too.

"There will be a service for him at the church this Sunday. That will be the only permitted time for gatherings of more than four people to take place. And of course, our meetings, which will become more regular. We, as your Mayor and Mayoress, want to be transparent and fair."

"Who murdered Ricky!" Someone cried out. Victoria, who was scanning the townsfolk, found it to be one of the factory workers, and a friend of the late Ricky, Olli Trotter. She made a note to pay him a visit.

"Calm down, there is no need to jump to conclusions. The police are investigating and have ruled that it is *not* suspicious." Said Frances, calmly.

"Bullshit! Seems suspicious to me!" Olli was now on his feet, and making his way past the stunned crowd.

"Please ... Olli, is it?" Victoria confirmed this with a quick nod. "Olli, please, remain seated." Olli had no intention of staying seated and he wasn't looking at Frances at all. His head was down and he was on a mission. If it was possible for steam to come out from people's ears, then Olli would be rivalling a New York steam vent. His face had turned a peculiar crimson colour. He made his way onto the stage and strode up to Frances, pointing a long finger into his chest.

"There weren't any murders in the town before *you* arrived. And in just a few days, we have one!" He roared in his face, showering Frances in spit.

The Mayor, remained the epitome of cool, calm and collected. The whole town were aghast. Nothing of the sort had ever happened in Kerwall before and they were eager to see how it played out.

"Please, Olli, go back to your seat. I implore you."

"You *implore* me, do you?" He mocked, still looking down. He reached into his coat pocket. It was the last thing he ever did. The sound of a handgun echoed through the streets. The residents screamed and ducked for cover. Olli collapsed in a heap to the floor, a hole torn through his scalp.

Daniel strode back up to the podium, the smoking gun still in his hand.

"See that." He pointed the gun at Olli's lifeless body. "That is what will happen if you don't cooperate. Failure to comply with any rules and I will not hesitate to put a bullet between your eyes." No one had dared leave; they were all scared to look up from their hiding spots.

"To make sure you all understand I'm not bullshitting, I want you all to repeat after me a simple phrase. 'The Greater Good'. It's only three words, so you illiterate fucktards won't forget it. Now, why have we all got to abide by these rules?" He clasped a hand to his ear.

"The Greater Good." The crowd responded in unison.

Daniel noticed that not everyone had participated. "You!" He screamed, pointing at one of the crowd. By now, Frances had taken a seat on the back of the stage next to Victoria. It wasn't what they had planned, but they had to admit, it was effective. The new subject of Daniel's rage looked both shocked and terrified.

"Get your sorry excuse up on this podium." He roared.

It was Evan, Abigail Trent's 15-year-old son. Abigail clung to him and begged him not to go onto the stage. Evan was like a deer caught in headlights.

Kerwall Town

"I haven't got all day. Get. Up. Here. NOW!" Daniel was pacing like a wild animal. He was ready to uncoil.

Evan, with all the strength that he could muster, stumbled to the stage on spaghetti legs. Once there, he fell to his knees, sobbing.

"Let me ask you a question. Do you think you're better than this town?"

"No!" The word escaped through his tears.

"Then why the fuck didn't you repeat a simple instruction?" He placed the gun to the side of Evan's temple. "Let's see if you can repeat them now, when your life depends on it."

Even gripped onto Daniel's legs and begged for his life, tears falling freely from his eyes as he pleads. "I'm sorry!"

"Why are we doing this?" Daniel was calm. The crowd were stunned into silence. The gun still planted in the temple of one of the youngest of Kerwall's residents. Abigail was sobbing into the arms of Evan's older brother, Trevor, who was equally inconsolable.

"For Kerwall!" Evan begs, still clinging to Daniel's legs.

"Exactly!" He pulls the trigger. The front row of the crowd is showered in brain matter and blood. The screams are deafening.

Abigail and Trevor collapse into each other.

At the back of the stage, Frances and Victoria are smiling. The only ones to notice are the JADEs, and they will never forget it. In that moment, their fears were confirmed, this isn't a game, and they need to be taken down, along with that psychopath Daniel.

13

The Tupperware Party

On the Sunday after the murder of one of Kerwall's youngest residents, there was a triple service at the church. It was officiated by both Henry and Reginald and the whole town attended dressed in traditional black. Despite Ricky and Olli having little family, everyone mourned their loss. Abigail was inconsolable and Trevor was a walking shell. Dr Brian Sharpe's concrete composition shattered, collapsing into tears over the loss of his son. They sat on the first pew, never taking their eyes off of the coffin encasing Evan. His candle had been blown out far too soon, and in such a reckless manner. None of the broken family had been able to get more than twenty minutes of sleep at a time since it had happened. They were plagued by nightmares, their brains playing the event over and over like a sick torture. They took no notice of the other people in attendance and, at times, Trevor thought he was in a dream once more. They knew that there would be months ahead, when they would think that they were done crying their last tear for Evan, only for a whole new batch to come. Grief has no time limit. A piece of their heart had been ripped out, right in front of them,

Kerwall Town

in cold blood. Trevor wasn't sure if his mum agreed, but he had a very clear thought; he was going to seek revenge for his little brother and kill Daniel.

The following evening, in Dot and Terry's living room, more people had gathered than they had anticipated. Staring back at them were not only the familiar faces of the Kerwall JADEs, Jeremy, Peter, and Debbie, but others too. It warmed their hearts to see so many but deep down, Dot in particular, was getting worried about the severity of the situation. She had begun to wonder whether they were leading lambs to the slaughter. She pushed the niggling thought to the back of her mind. She hated dealing with negatives but that was all she seemed to be met with these days.

There were a dozen varieties of those handy plastic storage containers around them. They were on the centre table, staked up against the walls, and spilling into the kitchen. That morning, Dot had made a cheese fondue, which was now on a table next to the television. Next to that were a handful of glasses of wine. For all intents and purposes, this was a legitimate Tupperware party. It just so happened, that it was also a covert meeting to expel the Vampires sucking the life from the town.

Playing softly in the background was a Swedish band. The lyrical irony was not lost on anyone as the knowledge that they knew very little had taken hold.

Some of the guests were idly dipping their long-stemmed bread forks into the communal pot, while others were sipping at their wine. All of them wondering the true reason for being here. The Saturday before the triple funeral the (J).JADEs, Peter, Dot, and Debbie had covertly recruited members of the town to attend. When Dot asked Andy, he had raised an eyebrow and asked if there was more to it. Dot only gave him a look in response, it told him that he had better come and find out. Dot loved that the tables had turned.

In the far corner of the room, was an a-frame not dissimilar from the one now displaying the new rules of Kerwall. This one, however, was covered in a simple black cloth. Dot clinked her wine glass and a hush fell over the room in an instant. She moved to the corner where the mysterious a-frame stood.

"Good evening, everyone. I'm sure you're all eager to know why you're here, and I shan't keep you waiting any longer." In one swift motion, she removed the black cloth to reveal four simple words: *The Owls of Justice.*

"What's 'The Owls of Justice'?" Patty had found out about the meeting when Jeremy was serving her and Linda ice cream yesterday. He had watched how they abhorrently looked on at the meeting but had tried to hide it. It was the same way that the rest of them tried to hide it, and he knew that he had to ask them. He was under strict instructions to only ask them about coming to a Tupperware party, and at first it took some convincing, but when Jeremy had told them there was more to it, it piqued their interests. They were then told to keep this top secret, even from their factory worker comrades.

"I'm glad you asked." Dot continued. "However, I think this is better coming from someone who is a little more clued up on the ins and outs. I advise you listen, and listen well, what you are about to hear is unbelievable at first, but if you take this warning lightly it may just cost you your life."

Jack and Donna stood next to their Grandmother and thanked her. Donna spoke first. "My grandma isn't wrong. What we are going to tell you may seem like make believe, but you have to trust us. There is a danger in this town. You saw a glimpse of it the other night, but that is only the surface."

"Why are you only telling us?" Andy probed.

"Because, simply, we think you are the only ones we can trust. We've been watching and discussing for a couple of days, and we feel that the people sat in front of us, the people next to you right now are the only people in this town that you can trust." Donna explains.

"What about our work friends?" Added Linda.

"Keep them out of it for now. Don't even discuss what you're about to hear in front of them, for your sake as well as theirs."

"Well get on with it then." Trevor's first words of the evening cut the air. There was a strange look in his eye that no one felt comfortable with, but equally, no one could blame him either.

"Right, of course. There's no logical way to say this, and I can't stress this enough for you to believe us, but we have *proof* that Victoria and Frances are Vampires." The words spilt from Jack with a desperate urgency.

"Oh, come off it!" Andy lacked his usual sass. He made a move to get up but changed his mind.

Mutterings spread round the room like wildfire. There was a strange balance in the living room. Half the room were already convinced, and they were anxiously hoping that the other half would believe them, or at the very least not walk out and call them crazy. To their relief, none of them did. It became quickly evident, that they had elected Andy to be their spokesperson.

"What's the proof?"

Nora, Damien, and John, the towns police officials, were sat almost in the middle of the two groups alongside Bill, forming a Venn-diagram of sorts.

It was John, much to the surprise of most, who spoke next.

"I believe I, or at least the royal 'we', can help with that." He gestured to his crew. "You heard about the murder of Ricky, but you didn't hear the one about Denise."

The room fell silent as they all tried to take in this new information. The Kerwall police were alerted to Denise's death yesterday morning. One of her former neighbours had been complaining about a foul smell coming from the house. The three of them had arrived at her house expecting a faulty pipeline and were horrified to discover Denise in her bed with blood, bleach, and pills all around her. Right away they knew that it wasn't self-harm, but a set-up, it all looked too particular. Once again, it was Bill who noticed the puncture wounds to her neck. Not as clean as the first ones on Ricky, but there, nonetheless. For the briefest of moments, John wondered if it was the work of The Skin Snatcher, but again it didn't fit the M.O.

"Wha...What happened to Denise?" Peter stuttered in a small voice.

"Much the same as what happened to Ricky. She was staged to look like she took her own life, but on closer evidence, Bill here found they had two distinct things in common." Nora responded.

"They both had two puncture, or *bite* marks on their neck." Finished Damien.

"Well, shit." Said Andy contemplatively.

"I thought Vampires were meant to drain the blood of their victims and then they turn into one too?"

Kerwall Town

Questioned Linda. Patty looked at her, a little surprised. "What? I had older brothers. They showed me all kinds of shit." She said defensively.

Debbie handed around a few books and told them to pass them on, like a teacher would in a school. One of the books was a 'World Book', Debbie had brought it as a reference, just in case.

"What are we supposed to do with these?" Patty was sceptical.

"These? These are the most powerful weapons at our disposal. Knowledge is power after all." Debbie beamed with pride.

"But this is just made up mumbo jumbo, surely." Patty had more than a hint of doubt in her voice.

"Do not doubt what is so clearly in front of you. Just because something enters your world that alters what you know, does *not* make it any less true, or in fact, diminish what you already know." Dot side eyes Peter.

Some of the guests flicked through the books handed to them, but they were more interested in what was going to be said next. Andy still felt his questions were unanswered.

"How sure can you be on this? It's a very serious, not to mention a strange, thing to accuse someone of."

"Trust us. We couldn't be more sure." Answered Jack.

"Ok, so say for a moment that we humour you and believe this. Why are they here… In *Kerwall* of all places?" Queried Linda.

"This is where it gets a little scary." Eve winced.

"As if murderous Vampires wasn't scary enough." Laughed Andy.

192

"Right, but we think they're after a Sceptre that grants them even more power. It's said to be hidden here somewhere."

"And that's why you think they're here?" Inquired Linda.

"Well, we think so, yeah."

"If this Sceptre thing was here, it'll be in the mines somewhere, surely." Said Bill, thoughtfully.

"What was that?" Jack wasn't sure if he'd heard him properly.

"Oh, I didn't mean for that to be out loud, sorry." Bill sinks back into the dorsum of the room. He wasn't good with large groups of people, it made him itchy all over, as if a thousand ants were marching on his skin.

"No, no, don't apologise, it could be important." Jack leaned towards him.

Bill smiled at him and shuffles forward, keeping his head down, making infrequent eye contact.

"Well, I was just saying, that it could be in the mines. I mean, who knows how old this place really is, and mines have been known to dig up all kinds of stuff."

"If it's in the mines, then, they probably already know it's here." Linda mulled.

"What makes you say that?" Abe's was interested now.

"Haven't you heard? They've reopened the mines and got us all to do double shifts down there, no exceptions." Patty mimicked the latter half of the sentence with distain and petulance.

"Oh, shit, oh fuck! I forgot." Jack panicked. How could he let a vital piece of information slip through? By the looks of it, the rest of them had forgotten that too, he thought. Was it said at the town meeting? It

Kerwall Town

must have been, he thought, still not remembering clearly.

"Jack, dear, watch your *bloody* language!" Said Dot curtly, but with tongue firmly in cheek.

"Sorry, G'ma." He misses her joke.

"It doesn't actually mean they know about the Sceptre though." Donna was trying to get things back on track.

"True, they have said they want Kerwall to be prosperous again." Chimed Terry.

"I don't care about any of this quite frankly. I'll join your cause on one condition." Trevor had been so quiet that the others forgot he was even here. That went double for Abigail, who cut a forlorn figure in the shadowy corner of the room.

"What's your condition dear?" Asked Dot.

"I want to kill Daniel." He said without hesitation.

No one dared to argue with him. The day that his brother was murdered, he was just a year older at sixteen. Not even a week has passed, and he now looks like he's aged several years. There's steel determination behind his brown eyes.

Taking the silence for the yes it resoundingly was, Trevor stood back next to him mum and put his arm around her.

"It's one thing killing a human-" Andy began.

"-He's not human." Trevor's voice carried from the shadowed corner.

"Right, of course. Anyway, it's one thing killing *him*, but how do we go about killing ancient Vampires?" He concluded.

"While we're on the subject of killing, I hope we get a get out of jail free card." Jack looked to the police contingent.

"I think we'd be awarded with a key to the city." Said John, smiling despite the situation.

"Say if we all do decide to join this 'Owls of Justice' thing, what are we expected to do?" Asked Patty, with her head adorned with pink curlers this evening. "Also, Dot dear, mind if I smoke?" She fished them from her purse.

"I don't mind at all, as long as it's outside."

"Maybe stand at the back door, just in case." Terry added.

Patty gives him a nod in the affirmative and asks Linda to come to the back door with her, which she duly obliges. She had been hankering for a smoke too.

As Patty and Linda were heading to the back door, they heard Dot ask if anyone actually wanted any Tupperware items. It created an instant shift in atmosphere. Who wouldn't want plastic storage boxes which would soon become more lids than boxes, and not long after a whole draw just full of lids with just a smattering of boxes that now had unidentified stains on them.

"What do you think of all this then, Lind?" Patty lit up a smoke.

"Seems pretty bloody farfetched to me, but I wanna see that bastard taken down for what he did to that poor lad." Linda ignited her own. They were leaning up the side of the house, lazily looking out across the garden. The only light source coming from the cigarettes. The plumes of smoke spiralled up into the night sky, reaching towards the stars.

"But do you trust them?"

"I trust them a fuck load more than I trust the Mayor and *that* woman, urgh, she gives me the creeps!" She shudders.

Kerwall Town

"Yeah." Was all Patty replied. She would do whatever Linda did, because, when all was said and done, she loved Linda, and not in a 'just friends' way either. She's never had the courage to act on her feelings, and most importantly, she feared that Linda wouldn't love her back. She feared that it would create an awkward void between them. No, she would suppress her feelings for her friend and their friendship, they were stupid feelings anyway, she told herself.

"I think we should do it." Linda took Patty from her thoughts.

Alarm bells rang in Patty's head. Did she just hear right? Did Linda just ask her to 'do it'? How could she read her thoughts?

She remained calm. "Do what?"

"Join The Owls of Justice thing they're on about. I've still got a lot of pent up anger from my divorce, and I'm sure you've got some anger inside you too. After all, no one fucks with our town and gets away with it!"

"Right, yeah, join the owls thing. Sure. Good idea." Patty was still trying to remain cool.

"What did you think I meant?"

For a moment, Patty was stuck for words and her tongue had gone incredibly dry, it was threatening to stick to the roof of her mouth. "Sorry." She manages. "I was away with the fairies. Lost in my own head."

"Well, I can't be losing you." Linda replies and puts a hand on her shoulder, sending a wave of tingling inside her. "C'mon. Better get back inside." Linda continues, stubbing her cigarette butt on the wall, instantly making it that much darker outside.

"Who do I speak to about buying a juice container then?" Linda smiled when they come back through to the living room. The whole vibe of the room had changed, what was once thick with dread, now had an easy going and almost happy atmosphere. It could have been the wine, the Tupperware, or the concoction of different fears evaporating as they dared to think this could be ok. That they could *actually* do this. Perhaps it was as simple as letting go of what had just been discussed. Dot gives Linda the juice container and in return she hands over some money.

"Ok, everyone, may I have your attention for just a moment." Jack fights to be heard over the noise, not only of the guests but of Elvis on a whirlwind carousel. 'You can say that again', Jack thought. The trusted residents hadn't heard Jack, so he did what his G'ma had done earlier and clinked his glass. It quieted the living room to a hum, and then to a full silence.

"Thank you. It'll only take a minute, I promise. I, well, we." He gestures to his family and friends. "We were wondering where you all stood with regards to joining our cause. We're not going to lie here, man, we could use all the help we can get. We need you. All of you. I'm not going to say it's going to be easy because it won't be. But nothing easy is ever worth fighting for, right? There's a saying my G'ma and G'pa have always told myself and Donna, and it goes like this: 'It's not what happens in the event, but how you change from it'. Tonight, will be the start of a turning point in this town. And what we decide to do in this room, will change the course of history. So, do you want to be a part of it?"

The room erupted into applause. Even Trevor and Abigail were clapping.

"I take that as a yes then."

Kerwall Town

The evening ended on a high, and they arranged to meet again in two nights time. They all promised to keep this meeting a secret and to stay vigilant.

Dot told Terry, as they lay in bed, that they had made more money in one night than they had for the past two months in the hardware store. Dot didn't think that money would soon become inconsequential, so enjoyed the buzz of being a one-night entrepreneur.

When the Trent's arrived home, Trevor made his way into the kitchen and poured himself a glass of milk. Abigail stood by Evan's door. She put her hand over the door knob for the first time since he was murdered. She took a deep breath and opened it, just a crack. That was all she could handle. She broke down into tears. Moments later, Trevor comforted her. He shut his brother's door and sat down beside his mum, holding her tightly.

"It's ok." He said as she cried into his chest.

"I can't even go in my son's room." She whimpered, regaining a little more control over herself.

"Don't worry about it. When you're ready, we'll go in there together. I'll hold your hand and keep you safe. Just because you can't see him anymore, don't mean he's not here. He's probably watching us now, wondering why we're sat by his door crying." Tears of his own brimmed in his eyes. "C'mon" He says, rising to his feet and holding out a hand to his mum. "Let's have a cup of cocoa."

14

The Skin Snatcher

When Police Chief John Hunt got home that evening, he went straight to his personal files lining his office. It was a small room, with a desk at the back next to the window, flanked either side by a bookshelf and filing cabinet. He retrieved the case that had been haunting him for years. The Skin Snatcher. He went over the cases obsessively at least once or twice a month. Trying to connect dots that seemingly weren't there. It seemed to him, that wherever he went, The Skin Snatcher followed. During one particularly dark evening, he had convinced himself that it was all in his head. That he hadn't been to the dozens of crimes committed, that in reality he was serving time in an institution. There was another time where he convinced himself that *he* was The Skin Snatcher. That was when his sobriety had stumbled though, and he was burning the midnight oil in his old town.

Looking at them this evening, he tried to make tenuous connections to the killer that has plagued him over the years to the new waking nightmare in Kerwall Town. 'Could they be the same thing?' He thought. The evidence suggested that they weren't, but he still clung

Kerwall Town

onto the idea. There were some similarities like the way they are tortured their victims first. There was one glaring difference. The bite marks. Unless the maniac had added a strange new kink to the already demonic killing method, John had to accept that they were two different cases. Which meant that by proxy, acknowledging that Vampires were real and trying to take over his town.

The one person who wasn't at the town meeting, nor had reported to work for a few days, was Mable. She was currently hanging upside down in the basement of The Skin Snatcher. She knew him by another name. The night that she thought she was being followed, was the last night she had seen the stars. The last real thing that she remembers was bumping into the Vicar, and then going to his house for a coffee. The last thing she noticed in the room were his crosses hanging on the wall, they looked different somehow, handmade. She couldn't remember leaving his house, but she must have. This was the first time she has been fully conscious for days. Catching her bearings, she realised her arms were bound by chains as the blood flowed to her head. She struggled in vain to break free, thrashing. The sound of the chains echoed in the hollow basement. Mable screamed in frustration. There was nothing around her that could help. The only thing in the room with her was a work bench. It had a plethora of tools on it, drenched with what looked like blood stains. A horrible thought came to her, 'I hope that's not my blood'. A quick inspection of herself, as best as possible, and she couldn't be so sure. There were deep lacerations on her limbs, and what looked to be a huge chunk of her skin missing from her left forearm. Seeing this a new wave of panic rose in her, and the pain that followed was psychosomatic.

"Help!" She screamed with all her effort. There was no answer. She tried again and again, but it garnered the same result. The basement was cold and damp, she now realised she barley had any clothes on too. What she *was* wearing wasn't hers. That freak must have undressed her, and God knows what else too, the notion lingered like an unwanted touch. The white top she now had on was stained with blood. This time, she hoped it *was* her blood, 'in case she caught something,' was where her mind turned. She caught herself, 'funny how the brain works sometimes'. Her ears trained on another noise. It must have been accompanying her all this time, a steady drip. She had come across water torture from a friend when she was younger, but thought they were making it up, and this was too much of a coincidence. Her friend had told her that they made the drips land on a specific part on their victims' forehead for hours on end. Forcing the sensation of being weathered away like the cliffs of Dover. This was different. The *drip, drip, drip* wasn't dripping on her, but now that she'd noticed it, she couldn't un-notice it. The way it was always a *drip, drip, drip*. The same three taps over and over. She watched the little drops of water fall slowly to the basement floor, pooling into itself. *Drip, drip, drip*. Over and over. She forgot all about the pain in her arm, the drips were all she focused on now. She forgot how her head was swimming with the blood rushing to her brain. All that she could care about now was the *drip, drip, drip*.

After what seemed like forever, and it might well have been, she passed out again. She was awoken by the

Kerwall Town

sound of footsteps on the basement stairs. They were light steps. Ones that she had begun to know well.

"Ahh, it's nice to see you awake." Said the Vicar, who didn't look like one at all now, save for his clerical collar. The only other thing he was wearing was a butcher's apron. It just about came to his knees, and she couldn't help but notice the blood stain splatters. There was something about it. The texture. It was the same as the crosses adorning in his living room upstairs. Henry noticed her staring at it.

"Oh, do you like my new apron?"

"Why are you doing this? Let me go, please!" She begs.

He bends down to her face slowly and strokes it with a sweaty hand.

"Now, now, Mable. That's not fair now is it? After all, I've taken you in and looked after you. You would be dead if I didn't save you from that stalker, wouldn't you?"

Mable spits in his face.

"That stalker was you and you know it. You've been following me for weeks; I just didn't see the signs. When my friends find out I'm missing, they'll find me and.-"

"-And what? You've already been gone almost a week. No one is coming to save you. You've already been saved, by me, from a life of sin and debauchery. I've seen how you swan around town, thinking you're beautiful. Letting the scum perv on you while you pretend to be coy about it. It makes me *sick!* It makes God sick too."

He slaps her across the face with his glistening hand.

"That's for spitting on me. Filthy animal."

Henry methodically walks over to the work bench and picks up what looks like a potato peeler. Only this is used to flail skin from bone.

"Now, Mable, hold still. I need some new gloves."

She realises what he's holding, and she screams, thrashing at the chains.

"No! No! Nooooo!"

It was in vain once more.

He put the skin peeler at the top of her thigh, just below her knee, and pressed downwards. The skin came off. The ripping sound was accompanied by lashings of blood spattering the room and Henry's face. He licked at it and swallowed it gleefully. Mable's soft white skin fell off like meat from a kebab. The pain was instantly unbearable. Mable passed out, and Henry hummed merrily.

Once he was finished stripping her skin from the leg bone, he hung the flesh over the makeshift drying rack standing in the corner of the room. He stroked the peeled skin with the back of his hand and kissed it passionately. He did this with the epidermis he peeled from all of his victims.

"Yes, these will make a fine pair of gloves, I'm sure of it."

He walked back over to Mable, who was now showing very little signs of life, and stroked her cheek again. He then shoved his tongue down her throat.

"We could have been beautiful together." He said to her unconscious body.

Henry walked over to the work bench and picked up a riding crop. He knelt down by the side of her.

"I'm so sorry. Please forgive me, Father, for I have sinned." He brings the whip down across his back with such velocity that it drew blood instantly. He did it over

Kerwall Town

and over again, striking the same place each time. As he did it, he said how sorry he was. After a while, he too passed out from the pain. The only sound remaining in the room was the *drip, drip, drip*.

Henry came to an hour later. There were huge welts across his back, and he got up with a loud grunt. He poked Mable in the cheek with his finger to see if she was still alive. There was no response. He grunts again, this time in annoyance. Henry walks over to the workbench and selects a scalpel. He blesses it with holy water and says a quick prayer before kissing the sharp blade. He walks back over to Mable. He presses the blade into her cornea and pulls it out with a *plop*. Mable screams for the very last time. With her one eye, she sees him take hold of her tongue and cut it right out of her mouth. The blood and the pain were instant. She tried to scream, but no sound came out. She tried to run, but the chains wouldn't allow it. She tried to cry, but there was nothing left.

So she stopped, accepting her death.

All her plans in life, all her dreams, stopped. She would not know what her first kiss would feel like, nor would she hold her new-born child, or get married. In just a few moments, she would fall from this world without ever really experiencing it. Her heart ached for what could have been, and the things that she never got to say. She had a moment of pure reflection. She realised that she wouldn't see or speak to her parents again, nor her lovable ginger cat, Tinkey.

By the time that Henry was done, there was an assortment of body parts now lying on the makeshift rack. Henry liked to use as much of the body as possible, and what he didn't use to make clothing or furniture, he would boil into a stew. He found that earlobes and the pelvic bone made a rather nice broth, accompanied by a dusting of coriander. Oh, how he dreamed of hosting dinner parties and serving it to his guests. He fantasised of how they would marvel over his culinary excellence. From time to time, the '*blood*' he would offer to the congregation, was just that, blood. He would mix it with a few spices so people wouldn't notice. It had worked a treat for over the many years he'd been doing it so far.

He hung his butcher's apron on the hook by the door. Walked bare ass up the stairs and into the shower to get cleaned up. He rubbed his skin raw in an effort to remove all the blood. His own blood had amalgamated with that of Mable's. He detested when the blood got under his fingernails. It was the only part that he *truly* hated, that and the uncleanliness of it all. The actual killing, and torture, part he enjoyed. He was particularly fond of the stalking stage. He would follow them for weeks without them suspecting a single thing. He had learnt how to stalk his prey from his dad when they had gone hunting when he was little. Of course, his father was none the wiser that he had been teaching his son how to take out bigger targets, like humans. Henry can't quite remember when his lust to kill first spoke to him, but he knows that when he thinks about it, he can't remember a time that it wasn't there. The *need* to kill people was as essential to him as breathing. The clothes and furniture he made from them came by way of necessity, he needed a way to dispose of the bodies. His hatred of waste fuelled the eating of the leftovers.

He took an instant liking to the taste. He had always been a culinary whiz it was something he got from his mother. Again, his mother wasn't expecting that all the lessons she had passed down to him would help him prepare human bodies. He remembers one particularly nasty incident, when he was first starting out. He had tried to boil one of his victims alive, like a lobster. He bound the victim's arms and legs with rope and stuffed an apple in their mouth, creating a fanciful look more than anything. The nasty thing about it was the taste. He just couldn't balance out the blood, no matter what he tried. It's something he has sworn to never do again, it ruined his whole evening. More than that, the boiled human body that he was *so* looking forward to eating was ultimately an extreme waste. He disposed of that body in a river almost three hundred miles away.

A couple of years ago, he wanted to add thrill to his life, so he started leaving small clues for the police to find. At first, he was unaware of John Hunt. But, as the years went by, it became a challenge to see how much he could mock him, it was a long-distance torture. Some of the clues he left were whole bodies, stripped of their skin, sometimes teeth, and sometimes it was just a foot. He would watch how it was tearing John apart. He graduated to leaving notes for John. It was an ironic twist of fate that they had ended up in the same town together. But Henry has needs, and John getting closer to discovering him wouldn't stop him. It made the situation all the more exciting. He had even kept an empty space on his wall, just for John. One of Henry's absolute favourite things to make from his victim's flesh was a cross. He had dozens over his house, and once or twice he had worn them to his services, each time he was complimented on his craftsmanship. His mum had taught him to sew perfectly as well as cook. There was no real reason why he picked the victims that he did, he just enjoyed the sport of it. He didn't even care what gender they were. Although, he would go on record and say that, for some reason, the female body tastes sweeter than the male counterpart. Along with keeping trophies of his victims he also kept newspaper articles pertaining to his murders. He would laugh at the sensationalism of them all and howl at the inaccuracies. One particular article claimed that The Skin Snatcher was a woman, and that they had mental illness because they had sex with the female victims too. That town was a few ants short of a picnic, he had decided. It was one of his first human kills.

The thing he likes making the most from their skin was dressing gowns. He's made countless robes and enjoys wearing them to bed. Henry once tried to make slippers too, using hair to form the fluffy part, but they gave him a rash and he put them in the Church incinerator. He had made a mental note to never make slippers again. He put it down to the hair having lice, but even then, it wasn't worth the hassle. One thing he was sure to do, as well as collect all the by-products from his victims, was save their hair. The hair, he had found, made the perfect thread to stitch up his back, making sure to first wash the hair thoroughly to avoid another lice incident.

Henry decided that along with the traditional cross and the gloves, he was also going to make a new collar for Church out of Mable's porcelain skin. He had a craving for lasagne this evening, so that was what she was also going to become. He laughed to himself.

"People kill to be in many places at once, and here I am, doing it for them without them knowing." It was a crazed laugh, one that belonged to a wolf in the dead of night.

He looked at the clock in a start and realised that he was going to be late for his service. He quickly got ready and, at a moment's notice, decided to take one of his skin crosses.

By the time Henry arrived at the Church, he was around fifteen minutes late. His congregation were flocking outside in the cold evening air, wondering what was going on. Their disgruntlement turned to genuine joy when they saw him. Henry was loved in this town, and no one had a bad word to say about him. By all accounts, he was God's perfect disciple.

"I'm so sorry I'm late, dear lambs." He stretched his arms wide to them all.

He weaves in and out of his flock to make to the door and unlocks it. They were all happy to be inside, even though it felt a lot colder in the Church than the open. They blew and rubbed their hands to make them warm. When Henry next spoke, they could see the cold on his breath in the air.

"Please, take a seat everyone, I shall just find the switch for the heater. I recommend we all sit a little closer tonight to keep in the warm." They all did as he commanded, and he found the switch for the heater which whirred into life in a splutter. It would be at least thirty minutes before they all felt the benefit. Henry was relying on the placebo effect of telling them that the heating is now on.

Henry caught Reginald scowling at him from the corner of his eye. It wasn't uncommon for him to be scowled at, nor for them to be at each other's meetings, but Henry still felt uneasy. He clutched at his skin cross the same way that he had when he met Victoria that day. 'Oh, Victoria', he thought. Yes, she was to be his next one. What a fine trophy she would make. There was much he could make from her.

"Why were you late... again!" Berated Reginald, breaking Henry from his fantasy.

"Sorry, I lost track of time."

"Been doing that a lot lately. Kick the habit." Reginald walked off towards the front without waiting for a reply. How he would love to kill him sometimes. But his skin was too worn. He couldn't make anything good from worn skin, and the flakiness of it too, it was enough to make him heave. He had thought about killing him just for the sake of it, but he didn't think God would forgive him for that one. He believes that God allows him to do what he does as he wastes so of the people he kills. They are bad people anyway, like that promiscuous Mable. She was asking for it for sure. Just like Victoria was. He believed that a woman should know her place. He absolutely loathed the idea of a woman in charge.

As Henry strode down the aisle, robe flowing behind him, meeting his congregation quickly as he did so, a funny thought struck him. He wasn't at all prepared for this evening. When he rose to the pulpit, the eyes of his flock were staring in earnest up at him. He decided to wing it and hope for the best.

"Good evening, my lambs." He's not sure where, or why, he started calling them lambs, but they all loved it, so he continued. To some of them, he was like a Rockstar. It was evident in the coldness of the night as he stood before an almost full house. He hadn't realised when he had said that they should gather at the front that some would take it literally. They sat cross legged, in front of the pews.

Kerwall Town

"A lot has changed in our fair town over the past few weeks. Some for the better, but as you all know, some for the worse. We have lost some dear friends." He signed the cross on himself. His lambs did the same.

"I am reminded about Jeremiah's teaching of hope, and I feel it rings true now more than ever. I see many of you staring up at me this evening wondering about plans. What good are they if they keep changing? Well, 29:11 of Jeremiah may help guide some of you. *For I know the plans I have for you, declares the Lord, plans to prosper you and plans to harm you, plans to give you hope and a future.'* You see, God knew that our town was going to have some harm in it. But he also promises that there is going to be more hope for the future, and we shall be prosperous once more. So, I ask you not to be scared about the loses, but to treat each one as a step closer to our overall happiness."

The whole evening, he had them eating out the palm of his hands once again. Even without a plan. As they were leaving to go out into the cold night air, he stood where he always did, at the exit, wishing them safe travels. He once again got compliments on his cross, and someone tried to touch it. He grabbed their hand away just in time, and smiled at them, saying that it was a treasured and a very old item. He told them that it must only be touched with special gloves or by blessed hands. The lamb apologised profusely, begging for forgiveness. Henry laughed it off and said that there was no need to. But, for a brief moment, that's not what his eyes said at all. There was fear and hate within them in equal measure, his lamb was too worried herself to notice.

It wasn't the first time that the mask of Vicar Henry Blackburn had slipped.

15

The Other Vicar

Those who truly know Reginald Dundon would tell you that the man he has become is a far cry from the man he once was. But then again, he was much older now. When he was an adolescent, he had served in the war effort to help the country he was so proud to call his own. That's what he told people anyway. One day, when he is stood in front of St. Peter at the gates of heaven, he will tell the truth. He used to enjoy the killing. Until one day, when an enemy soldier felled him in the woods. He had begged for mercy and, to his surprise, he was granted it. The enemy soldier had taken pity on him. Once the war was over, they became good friends. More than friends. They got married in secret three months later and two years after that, the only person Reggie every truly loved, Hershel Kopf, died of AIDS. Reggie asked God why He took the only good thing away from him, but he got no response. He began to think that perhaps he was being tested, and it was at that point that he gave up the pursuit of love and took up the cloth of God. He left his friends in his old town and travelled in search of a new life. He came across an advert in a national newspaper about a new town

Kerwall Town

waiting for citizens. It promised them a new life and the guarantee that they could be anything within their own imagination. Reggie took it as another sign and drove the hundred or so miles to this brand-new government created town to start a fresh life. That was the day that *Vicar* Reginald Dundon was born. All that he had to tell them at the sign up was that he had served in one of the wars and they gave him the chance to choose who he wanted to be, just as the advert had said. He remembers how easy it all was and how friendly the sign-up people were. They had been dressed in clinical whites, clutching at clipboards. The women had bouffant hair and the men had slick crew cuts.

At first, he was known as the fun vicar, he was also the *only* vicar until a few years ago. It was around three years before Henry came on the scene that he had started to sour on this town. He began to see through the bullshit and bureaucracy. He wanted more than rules and regulations, he wanted to be happy. He wanted to be his true self again, he just had to find it buried deep in hate and cynicism.

When Reggie got home that evening, he was filled with a sense of unease. It was different from what he had been feeling since the new Mayor and Mayoress arrived. This time, it was emanating from Henry. He had noticed that he was taking less care with his sermons and was becoming increasingly late to them. The altercation with his "lamb" confused him. To Reggie, they were residents, not farm animals. What Henry didn't know about Reggie was that although he may be old, he was wise, and when he wasn't talking, he was looking, observing everything. There was something peculiar about the cross he wore tonight. He remembered that Henry had worn it before too. It was made out of a material he wasn't familiar with, and when Reggie asked him where it came from the first time that he wore it, Henry just laughed a strange laugh and said that it was hand crafted. That didn't seem something to laugh about, but Henry had found it hilarious. Reggie had almost dismissed that memory, until this evening when he wore it again. Henry was precious about it, he was protective.

Reggie de-robed for the evening, put on his pyjamas and slippers, and made himself a cup of *Lyons Coffee*. It was his favourite brand of coffee, and one he drank exclusively. He drank it while sitting in his high back chair watching late night television, as he did every night. He was a true creature of habit. But tonight, his mind was wondering elsewhere. Not only towards his fellow vicar's strange behaviour as of late, but the town itself. He sensed a change in atmosphere, a mood in the town, and he was no detective, but he can pinpoint the precise moment it changed. The day Victoria came to see him and Henry at the Church. He had noticed how Henry was practically falling over himself for her, but he intentionally remained stoic in his demeanour. When Henry had said that was strange, Reggie had said that it wasn't. He didn't say who he was referring to. Of course, the Mayoress wasn't acting strange, that was true, but Henry was. He has seen that look in his eyes but a few times, he has seen it reflected in his own too. Lust. When that emotional feeling isn't controlled, it can do terrible things.

He looked at the picture of his late husband, framed on the table next to his favourite chair, and cried for the first time since his funeral. The day he had buried his

Kerwall Town

husband was the day he buried his feelings, and now, for some reason, they were beginning to surface again.

A knock at the door startled him back to reality.

"Just a minute." He said in a voice that wasn't quite his own.

He got up out of his chair with some effort and made his way to the door, wiping the tears from his eyes. The door kept knocking.

"I'm coming, for goodness sake!"

Elsewhere in the town, Linda was sipping coffee at Patty's house. It had become somewhat of a tradition as of late, she would come over after work and shoot the shit with her best friend. The television was on low in the background. Patty's living room was what an estate agent would call 'cosy'. Common code for, 'good luck fitting all your crap in this room.' It worked fine enough for Patty. Since her husband had passed away, she didn't have much in the way of possessions, especially in the living room, save for a small television, a glass cabinet to store her knick-knacks, and a few framed pictures. Then there was the necessity of her two-seat black leather sofa, bookended by small coffee tables. The carpet was orange shag pile and the curtains were huge floral numbers. There was no door to the kitchen, instead, Patty opted for hanging beads, which were a nuisance more often than not. The worst part about them, she found, was that she could never shut them to create an exclamation point in an argument.

Linda was twisting one of her bare feet into the shag pile rug while sipping her coffee and listening to Patty. Several times so far this evening, she had to remind herself not to give Patty the *love* eyes. She had decided at the Tupperware party to give up her pursuit of Patty.

She *almost* plucked up the courage when they were having a smoke, and when she said they should '*do it*' she was absolutely not talking about The Owls of Justice. But she had seen the alarm in Patty's face and decided, with regret, that Patty just wasn't into her that way. So, Linda bottled up the feelings. The feelings she has harboured for her best friend for almost twenty years. The most important thing to her was her friendship with Patty, and she would not let her love get in the way of that. After all, she wondered, how many people are secretly in love with their best friend? Patty guessed it was at least a dozen. Not in Kerwall however, there was only one other gay person she knew in this town, and he was a he. She had no interest in men, they were too complicated and caveman like for her. She wanted a *woman*. She wanted Patty. 'No!' Linda told herself. Stop doing this to yourself!

"What do you say we make the coffee a little Irish?" Patty interrupted her thoughts.

"Oh, ur, sure." Linda shook off her internal reflections.

"Wanna smoke too?" She said through the kitchen beads. Linda said agreed again, and they went out to the back door and lit up.

Linda watched Patty put the cigarette into her mouth, and she could have sworn that no one did it sexier. There were no curlers in her hair this evening, her chocolate brown locks were on full show, falling just past her ears. Linda tried to look away, to not torment herself any more, but it was hard not to.

"Are you ok?" Patty could see her friend had gone a peculiar white colour.

"Ye… Yeah, I'm good. Honest."

"Something on your mind?"

Kerwall Town

"Nothing of any importance." Linda lied once more.

"You know I can tell when you're bullshitting me, right?" Patty said with a smile.

"Ahh, fuck you." Linda smiled back.

"There we go!" Patty pushed her arm playfully.

"What do you mean?"

"A bit of your spark retuned then. I've missed that spark."

"I didn't realise it had gone."

"You've been missing inside your own mind these past few days, but I'm glad you're starting to come back."

"I'm sorry."

"No, no, it's nothing to be sorry about, I just wanna see you happy, that's all."

"Ditto" Replied Linda equably, the antithesis of what she was really feeling.

"Come on, let's go make those coffees more Irish, shall we?" Patty extinguished her cigarette on the brick wall and Linda follows suit.

"We've got work in the morning though. Maybe I should go."

"Nonsense, when has that ever stopped us. The night is still young, and so are we!"

"Well, If you're sure about this."

Patty pours some liquor in their coffee mugs; it was an answer as good as any.

Around the time that Linda and Patty were making their third coffee Irish, Abigail Trent was once more outside her late sons' bedroom. She too had been drinking some adult courage juice. She stood outside the door with bated breath and put her hand on the doorknob. It turned. The door creaked open. Her stomach dropped as if it was on a rollercoaster. The tears splashed onto her cheeks as her right foot touched the brown carpet. It was as far as she could go before the panic struck her. She broke down again and slid down the door frame. Even though the door was now open a crack, she refused to look in. She couldn't look in. The sound of footsteps on the landing startled her and, for a confused moment, she called out Evan's name.

"It's just me, mum." The voice sent a shiver down her spine, and then she looked up and realised it was Trevor. He sat down beside her. She held him tight and buried her face into his chest.

"What was you doing going in there on your own? I thought we had a pact to do it together."

"I... I thought if I drank enough, it would give me some strength... Why? Why was he taken form us? He was too young! It's that *bastard's fault!*" She spat the words out, shaking with rage.

"We'll get him, we'll get him for Evan."

"And we won't stop there. I want the Mayor and Mayoress gone too."

Trevor held his mum tightly.

"We'll make this right." He promised. "And when you're ready, we'll go in there together... Unless there was something you wanted from in there now? I'll go in and get it for you... If you want." Trevor seemed to be in the anger stage of grief, but the anger wasn't directed at his younger brother, it was squarely aimed at his murderer.

"Thank you, but I couldn't ask you to do that."

"You didn't ask, I did." He replied, trying to give her a reassuring smile. But truth be told, he too was scared to go into the room.

Kerwall Town

She said no more words to him that evening. What she wanted to say to him couldn't be articulated in the same way that a mother's hug could.

By the time Reggie got to the door he was furious with the late-night visitor, and he made sure they knew that when he flung the door open.

"What?" He bellowed at them furiously.

The person on the threshold of his doorway was sobbing, but not because of Reggie. Stood in front of the vicar, at almost 11 p.m. was Shelly. He vaguely recognised her from one of his sermons, but, at first, he couldn't place a name with the face.

"What is it?" He still sounded a little pissed off but tried not to show it in his face.

Her reply came through hitched sobs.

"I... I...I'm sorry." Was all she could muster. She put her shaking hands up to her face and he noticed that they were covered in blood.

"Jesus, Mary and Joseph." He swiftly crossed over himself. "Come on inside, quickly before someone sees you."

She did as she was asked, and once inside, she stood still in the doorway, looking down at her brown shoes, crying silently, and repeating the words *'I'm sorry.'* Comforting wasn't really in Reggie's wheelhouse. He patted her left shoulder.

"Come on into the kitchen. I'll make you a hot drink and you can tell me what happened." Despite being interrupted during his evening alone time, he was beginning to thaw. She followed him meekly into the kitchen, still looking down at her shoes, and still repeating *'I'm sorry,'* under her breath.

He pulled out one of the wooden kitchen chairs from the circular table and told her to sit. She obliged again without a fuss. The water is still warm from his own drink not fifteen minutes ago, so it didn't take long to reheat. He poured himself a new cup of coffee and made her a sweet tea, for the shock. Reggie put the drinks down on coasters and slid her drink over to her as he sat down opposite.

"Thank you." She manages.

"You can thank me by telling me who's blood is on your hands for a start."

"Right… of course." It was as if she had only just realised that her hands were stained with red. She took a sip of the tea with shaking hands. "It's my blood."

"What do you mean, *'your blood'* Who did this to you?" He was growing ever concerned now. He ran his bony hand through his thinning hair. A few flecks of his scalp fell to the floor.

"I… did this." She says in a small voice. It was at this point, now that he could see her in pure light, that he noticed that she was wearing an oversized orange cardigan. It certainly didn't belong to her, so it was most probably her husbands, he decided.

"You're not being clear. For me to help you, start from the top." His usual bluntness had left him. There was so much blood on her hands, and probably more under the jumper. He took a sip of his coffee.

"Sorry." She utters. "It's my husband. He…" She broke down once more. Her blonde hair was hanging all around her face this evening, lacking her usual lustre, and it looked damp too, but he didn't think it had been raining.

"Take a breath. And power though." He said and almost added, 'It's the middle of the night so stop

Kerwall Town

bloody stuttering and hurry up.' But that was too much, even for him. Was he softening in his old age?

She once more did as he asked, and like a late-night miracle, it worked, mostly.

"My husband found out I... had been unfaithful to him a few weeks back, and since then... oh God... oh, shit, sorry." Her face goes as red as her blood covered hands from the embarrassment, Reggie waves for her to carry on. He was beginning to get a little frustrated with her if truth be told.

"Since then, he's been taking advantage of me... sexually... and beating me too." That's all she could manage before breaking down again. Once she regained control over herself, she told Reggie how her husband had impregnated her, something she had always wanted. Then, this evening, pushed her down the stairs in a drunken rage. That was where the blood had come from, from her unborn child. She had run from the house and didn't know where else to go, didn't even know if he was following her, but she was too scared to look back, and definitely too scared to go back to the house. Reggie asked her how she had time to put a cardigan on. It was at this point that she too realised that she was wearing it and shrugged her shoulders in response. She said that she may have grabbed it off the hook as she ran out the house, or she might have already been wearing it. She couldn't be sure. He told her that she can stay on his sofa for tonight and then tomorrow morning, when Dr Brian Sharpe was open, he would take her down first thing. She thanked him for his kindness, and they finished their drinks in relative silence. Reggie marvelled the amount of blood on her hands every time she lifted the cup to her mouth. It glistened in the kitchen light and it transported him back to the war. He excused himself so that he could go to the bathroom.

For the second time that evening, Reggie broke down.

16

Mining Your Own Business

The second Owls of Justice meeting didn't take place in the evening as planned, instead it took place in the afternoon, in case messages were being listened to. Luckily, the members had all got the memo and were all present and accounted for.

On the board today was not the name of their little group, but a single word. A word that not even a week ago, was thought to be exclusive to comic books and fairy tales. *'Vampires'*.

"Ok, everyone, welcome to Vampire 101, I am your teacher, Jack." He says with a false bravado smile.

"Stop being a dork and get on with it."

Jack stuck his tongue out at Donna and pulled a face.

"Before I start with my news, do any of you have any more names to add to our list of recruits?"

They all shook their heads in the negative. Stood in this room were all the people that they could trust, it was a harrowing and sobering thought.

"Groovy. Thought as much. Ok. What do we know collectively about our new neighbours, the Vampires?"

Jack had a pen in hand, ready to write their suggestions. It took them almost a full minute to think of anything.

"They're persuasive...?" Andy said without much conviction.

Jack wrote it on the board and added one of his own. After another ten or so minutes had passed, the board contained the following words:

persuasive
can turn into bats?
fly?
mind control
can only be invited in
strong
sharp fangs
can either turn you or kill you
different types
want the Sceptre

Admittedly, some of it was guess work, and most of it had come from Jack's extensive knowledge of comic Vampires. They also recapped on the methods to kill a Vampire, and a little hope was starting to surface. But hope can lead to complacency, and complacent people cause deaths. Some would find that out the hard way.

Once Dot had handed out more refreshments, the room was beginning to feel more optimistic again. Donna had been thinking.

"Is there anyone you suspect is now a Vampire? I know it's not a nice question to ask, but it's our new reality."

The room fell silent for a moment. Terry was the first to speak.

"Has anyone seen Mike? Because I haven't seen him for a few days, and you know how reliable he is."

It was a question that he had asked before, but it didn't seem to have occurred to anyone else, despite all receiving their post from Mike for as long as anyone of them could remember. Finally, Patty is the first to admit that she hadn't. John argued that he could just be ill, his voice was thick with doubt.

On another part of the board, making two columns three, Jack wrote *'possible Vampires',* adding Mike's name to the list first.

"We've also decided to all take a job down the mines." Abe said flatly.

"What!? Why?" Dot asked with a worry warped voice.

"Debbie and Bill said the Sceptre might be down there, right?" Eve began.

"And we all think that they don't know it's here." Contributed Donna.

"So, we're going to beat them to it." Continued Abe

"And then destroy it." Jack finished.

Abe flashed him a destructive look which went unregistered.

The meeting was the furthest thing from Abigail's mind as soon as it was over. She was sat at her kitchen table. The last of the afternoon's sunlight was a strip across the old wooden table. Trevor was sat beside her, both with a cup of coffee in their hands. The thought that he was perhaps a little too young for coffee didn't cross her mind. After all, not long ago, he had promised to kill another human being.

"I think I'm ready." She was staring out into the living room.

"For what?"

"To go into Evan's room."

"Are you sure? It's barely been a month."

"I know... But if things go the way I think they will... with this *Vampire* business... I don't think we'll have a month."

"You can't talk like that."

"We have to be prepared. We weren't prepared and look what happened. Before I die-"

"-Stop! Don't say that!" He fought back tears.

She waved her hand dismissively and continued. "-*IF* I die, I want to be able to say to Evan, when I see him again, that I, *we*, were brave enough to go into his room." What was really eating her inside was that they hadn't put any of his personal belongings into his coffin, save for his favourite snack and trainers. She was determined to right a wrong, no matter how hard it was.

"Ok, we'll do it. For Evan."

"For Evan."

They were stood outside his door for what felt like eons. She took hold of the doorknob and gave Trevor a look which conveyed every emotion. He put his hand over hers, and they opened the door together. Their stomachs bracing for the drop.

The scent of stale air, amalgamated with teenage boy, hit them instantly. Instead of being repulsed, it was like greeting an old friend. With the door fully open, they could see everything. They held each other, letting the tears fall freely. The first step in anything, is always the hardest. That is doubly true for a grieving mother and brother, entering a parted family members room for the first time. Everything remained untouched, exactly where Evan had left it. His bubble-gum cards and *Pez* dispenser on his desk, clothes clumsily freeze

Kerwall Town

frame falling out of his wardrobe, and his bed unmade. All of it, unchanged. The window was ajar, and the slight breeze was dancing with the curtain. On his bedside table was his pet rock, Rocky. Abigail walked over to it and hesitated to pick it up, she settled for kissing it instead. She then put her hand on his bed, still indented with his body shape, and moved her fingers up to the pillow. She sniffed. The scent of her late son came in waves, and fresh tears fell. Trevor stood by her side, sobbing silently. To him, standing there brought home the importance ridding Kerwall of its Vampires. Daniel too.

Abigail wrapped her arm around him, checking that he was ok.

"Do you want to take anything? Put it in your own room as a keepsake?"

"Maybe one day. Right now, though, I want to leave it just how it is."

She numbly agreed. They sat on the edge of the bed for another few minutes, almost hovering so as not to disturb Evan's outline. Then being there became all too much once more.

They left the room almost exactly as they had found it and shut the door.

The next day, in their own homes, the Kerwall J.A.D.E.'s woke as the clock struck 4a.m. They had previously been blissfully unaware that there were two 4 o' clock's in the same day.

After the ringing alarm tore them from their sleep, Jack and Donna made their way into the kitchen. Jack made the coffee, while Donna made the toast. They shuffled around the kitchen in a zombie like fashion, barley picking up their feet as they walked. As Jack got the mugs from the cupboard and put the coffee grounds into them, he noticed one of them had food caked to the bottom of it, as if someone put it there for safe keeping. Donna had a similar experience when she opened the fridge, the house keys were in the butter dish. They looked at each other a little confused. A small voice from the kitchen door made them jump.

"I guess you found my secret."

"What do you mean, G'pa?" Jack was trying to regulate his heartbeat. He was most certainly awake now. Terry looked ashamed to answer.

"I've been keeping this from you both, and I'm sorry. I thought I could handle this on my own, but it seems as though it's been running away from me these past few weeks." He made his way to the kitchen chair, put his ageing hand on the back of it to steady himself, and sat down. He was fighting internally with the tears, not wanting his emotion to be seen. Jack and Donna each put an arm around him.

"Don't worry, we'll get you the help you need. We won't leave until we find you the best help we can, and I'm sure Peter and Grandma will be supportive too." Donna spoke softly to console him.

Terry looked quizzically up at them, and then realisation dawned on him.

"Oh, no, no. It's not me who needs the help, it's poor Dotty. I try to get up early and clean up the things she does at night, so she doesn't see it in the morning. She would be ever so embarrassed if she found out what she was doing. I wanted to tell you both, I really did, but we've had a few more... urgent things to keep us occupied for the moment."

They tightened their grip on his shoulders, giving him a light squeeze, then asked if he wanted to join them for coffee and toast. He smiled warmly, appreciating his grandchildren's kindness. Jack and Donna set about making him breakfast.

"How long have you known about this?" Donna was once again reaching for the butter from the fridge.

"Oh, I'm not sure. Maybe a few months, on and off. Sometimes it's food she hides, and other times it's things like remote controls or the newspaper."

"So is it…" Jack tried to think of the word, but sleep still plagued his brain.

"…Dementia? It's ok, you can say it … I think so. I haven't spoken to the Doc yet. Maybe when this is all over, we can take a trip there and get her some help."

The three of them agreed, determined to support their beloved Dot. None of them verbalised the doubt they all harboured for *this* being over. It had reared its ugly head once more, like an unwanted spot on prom night.

The Kerwall J.A.D.E.'s gathered together and joined the queue to the mine at 5 a.m. They knew some of the others in the line, but none by name. Eve wiped sleep from her eyes and stretched her mouth into a yawn.

"Not used to being up this early?" Abe looked bright eyed and bushy tailed.

She grunted in his direction. Which she would ordinarily deem un-lady-like, but this early in the morning, she really didn't care. Eve needed her full quoter of sleep, complete with her peach tinted face mask. She was far from a diva, as some called her, she simply enjoyed sleep and took pride in her appearance. She would lose that trait if she followed in her mum's footsteps she decided. She was a little uncertain if it was possible to change personality in an instant though.

Doubt was becoming their constant companion, sticking to them like an unnatural shadow. The distrust was festering in their minds, often without them even knowing it was there. Impossible to shake off. It was burrowing deep inside each member of The Owls of Justice, sucking away the goodness and turning their once colourful world view into a black hue.

Abe was the only member of the group who looked awake. He seemed entirely refreshed.

He was determined to find the Sceptre. He had no plan to destroy it though.

All of his life he had wanted power, and if there was a chance that he could have it now then he was going to grasp it with both hands. He'll have his mum right by his side, and together they will do what's right. They will right the wrongs in their life and smite those who stand in their way, he had decided. Abe thought that he should have the Sceptre's power to use it for good. He also argued profusely that *Darth Vader* was a good guy and a great father. His friends believed that his life barometer was fairly skewed, but Abe would hold onto the idea of his mum ruling by his side. All that they could ever want was just a few meters away from him, there was no doubt in his mind.

The line into the mine moved agonisingly slowly, and even wrapped up for the weather, Jack Frost was still trying to nip at any and all exposed pieces of flesh. Moonlight provided them with a little light, supported by a smattering of stars. Eve continued to complain about being up so early, forcing Donna to quietly reminded her as to why they were all here. They were,

Kerwall Town

in a manner of speaking, under cover after all, with the fate of much more than Kerwall on the line.

By the time that they got into the mine itself, it was almost 5:30 a.m. They were flabbergasted at the enormity of it. The mine stretched into darkness far beyond their eyes. They were given helmets at the makeshift reception area, along with a few essential tools. They were each given a small hand axe and torn gloves, worn by countless other before them. The residue of other people's sweat at the fingertips soaked their skin as they pulled them on.

After Jack tripped over a mine cart sleeper track on their way to meet their supervisor for the day, they were all a little more careful where they placed their feet. The JADEs found themselves in a tight huddle of people much older than them. They spoke to each other as if they'd known each other over many years, and many in-jokes had already been established. That didn't bother them the group too much, especially Abe. His mind was a single track, he didn't know how to get there yet but was sure that inspiration would strike. He was hoping that it would be today, but then came the uncertainty.

Their boss for the foreseeable future was a large jawed man with a booming voice. His brown hair was tucked imperfectly underneath his coal stained safety helmet. He begrudgingly introduced himself as Stanley Everett, a former foreman at the toy factory. He talked passionately about his joining the cause for Kerwall. He had done it especially for his wife, Pam, who was expecting their first child any day. He was addressing the newbies mostly, and those who had heard it many times before were having their own loud conversations. The atmosphere was rambunctious and lively, filled with testosterone. Donna could count all the women saw down there on two hands, including herself and Eve.

As they moved deeper into the mines, they noticed canary birds trapped in cages, barely able to stretch open their wings. Eve was curious what they were doing here. One of the men explained, in no uncertain terms, that if the bird died then it was time to worry. The jolt of realism woke her up.

Stanley was leading the pack, commanding workers as they walked. Once they received them, they immediately did as they were told, often whistling as they went. After the pack was whittled down to the JADEs and two other workers, they climbed into two mine carts. Stanley rode with Jack, Abe, Donna and Eve, while the two unknown workers hopped into the cart behind them.

"Easy job for you all today." He boomed in his trademark voice. Jack was certain that the mine was going to cave in he was talking so loudly. He had never understood why people felt the need to talk with such volume, did they not know that it pisses people off, he thought to himself.

"You two, keep an eye on these four, that's all you gotta do today." Stanley shouted over to them. The carts squeaked along the track. When they got to their destination, Stanley firmly pulled the break, jolting them forwards. They clapped their hands to their ears for salvation from the grinding of the metal on metal.

"You four, you have an even easier job." He hitched up his jeans, which were also stained with coal and whatever other gubbins was lurking on his denim. "All you have to do is take your pick axe, and hammer it into the wall, you can even use your little *princess'* axe if you so wish, you know, the one dangling from your

Kerwall Town

belt. If you find anything interesting, or shiny, tell one of those two and they'll sort it out."

"How far does this go down?" Abe was barely listening.

"I don't fucking know. Probably all the way to China. What does it matter, kid?"

"Just taking an interest in my job." Abe was trying to sound jovial.

"See if you change your tune about the place by the end of the week… If you make it that long." With that, he walked off and ushered over the babysitters, for that was all that they really were today. The JADEs were sharing jokes and laughing, paying no mind to them at all. After a few moments, Stanley looked over, and saw that they weren't working.

"You know, the axe works a lot more effectively if you plough it into the wall. Or do you need these two here to do that for you?" The two by his side, burst into laughter, before they turned around once more. Jack quickly cottoned onto the fact that they were all the *stooge*. He had heard his dad talking about it a couple of years back, when he was reminiscing about one of his first jobs. The basic idea, if he remembered correctly, was to hound the new guy until you make him quit, in the hopes that others would fall into line. He had heard that some film directors did this too, but they would deliberately hire someone to fire them in front of everyone on set. Jack was under the impression that it was common practice in most workplaces. It added an extra layer to their desire to stay on and do the job.

Within the first hour they had produced more sweat between them than they thought was humanly possible. While they worked, the two babysitters were sat on crates playing cards. The group had never felt such intense stagnant heat, the two lads had stripped off the top layer of their clothing, not that that stopped the sweat running down their burning bodies. The girls wrapped their jumpers around their waists. It was still too much so they put them in a pile on the floor, not caring how filthy they would become. The boys soon followed suit and added their own to the growing heap.

"Think we can make a break for it?" Abe expectantly asked, wiping beads of sweat from his brow.

"I doubt it, especially on our first day here." Eve gasped.

Abe had thought considered this fact too, but it was still annoying to him. He was desperate to get his hands on the Sceptre this instant, every moment without it, was a moment wasted. It was starting to become an obsession; he couldn't help the overwhelming desire to hold it. He wondered whether the others were obsessed with finding it too, and if they were, he wanted to know what were they going to do with it. Questions like this had been keeping him up at night for days now.

"Have any of us thought about the possibility that this thing may not even be here at all?" Donna was ever the voice of reason. "I mean, we've gotta be realistic."

"Realistic? What's the point of us even being here if we've got doubts? Don't chicken out on us just because it's getting a little too hard." Abe was becoming fiery, not that he noticed. He seemed perfectly rational to himself, so when Donna snapped back, he took it personally.

"I'm not saying it's 'too hard' at all, jeez, relax!" Retorted Donna. They were now eye to eye, and the tension was thick.

Kerwall Town

The two babysitters didn't bother to look up from their card game. The taller of the two side-eyed the situation.

"I'll wager that the girl hits the lad."

"Oh, yeah." His rotund friend replied. His dark eyes were almost buried underneath his enormously bushy brow.

"How does a note sound?" The taller card player flashed the note in front of his friend's eyes.

"I'll take that bet, why not. Nothing better to do."

"Deal"

"Guys, c'mon, c'mon, focus. Donna, why don't you see if you can get some air or something?" Jack wasn't used to being his sisters' voice of reason. He made a mental note to remind her of this later, and to bring it up in awkward situations, like a good brother should, he thought. Donna wanted to question why she should be the one to get some air, but went to speak to the babysitters anyway.

"Hey, is there anywhere I can go to… you know, *go?*" They didn't register her question at first, eventually bushy brow spoke.

"There's a can over there, squat over it if you think your aim is good enough." The two of them laughed.

"Ha, ha. Unlike you two knuckleheads, *I'm* a woman. And women don't squat. So, I'll ask again, and I'll ask it slowly so you can understand. Where. Is. There. A. Place. To. Gooooo!?"

At this point, Jack heard her sarcastic tone and decided to intervene. He put his hands on her shoulders.

"If you will, please excuse her. She's urm, having, you know…" He whispers to them loud enough so the whole gang could hear too, "…Lady troubles." He tipped them a wink.

"Ohhh, errr, gotcha." Bushy brows blushed.

"Take a left. The first one you see, and then it's the next two rights after that. Walk on a little further and they'll be some of those port-o-loo things. It's signposted, you can't miss it." The tall man directed.

"I need to go too!" Abe joined the conversation.

"And me!" Chimed in Eve.

"Oh, for fucks' sake! All of you? what about you kid?" Jack shrugged his shoulders in response to the large man.

"I could go I guess."

"Fine, all of you go, but this is the only break you're getting for the next three hours. So, use it wisely. And don't take too long." Bushy brows continued.

"We won't." Abe said as they left.

"Two notes say they won't come back?" The taller one ups the ante.

"Deal." They shook hands once more.

Once the JADEs were out of sight, Donna gave Jack a dig in the arm hard enough to turn purple the next morning. He clutched his arm immediately and shot her a look.

"Oww! What was that for?"

"For telling them about my lady problems."

"Well, it worked, didn't it?"

"Never mind that, let's start looking." Abe was becoming frustrated with their constant quarrelling.

Donna shot him a look to kill, fortunately he hadn't noticed.

"If I was an all-powerful Sceptre, where would I be?" Eve mocked.

Kerwall Town

When they came to the first left, they look a right, knowing full well that they were doing. The workers they passed didn't look up, they were completely absorbed in their task. Some appeared to be a kind of trance. They moved, synchronised, to a rhythm. They clanged the pick axe into the wall, inspected the clump which they pulled out, and threw it into the 'keep' mine cart or the 'throw' one. A quick peer over one of the 'keep' ones showed a dusting of sparkles in assorted sizes.

"Jeeze, would you look at that!" Jack marvelled at them. He did a quick sweep of the line, and noticed that no one was looking, so he picked one up. It was the size of a small coin, so he put it in his pocket.

"Jack, you can't do that!" Eve was outraged.

"No one's gonna know." He shrugged. "And besides, we can take it as payment." He was right, no one would ever know, the people surrounding them were far too engrossed in work. They all took a piece of treasure and put them in their pockets. They carried on down the line, walking passed countless numbers of people, all doing the same monotonous thing.

Hit the wall with the axe, inspect it, put it into the right cart.

Over and over. They reminded the group of bees in a hive. The reminded them of more than that. It looked as though they all moved as one single being. It was eerie to watch.

"Did any of you know that we had this many residents?" Donna asked in a hushed tone.

"Nope." Jack whispered back.

What they found even eerier, the further down the line that they walked, was how quiet they all were. Not a single sound from any of them, just the clanging of their tools into the wall and the thud of their findings being put into the carts. It was constant. It was strange.

Then, as they had almost become accustomed to it, a worker looked up, and into the Jack's eyes. Staring back at him were pure black, soulless eyes. Jack screamed. The *thing* staring back at him didn't flinch. It didn't even seem to register his existence. It was only a brief glance, but it was more than Jack ever wanted to see. When that *thing* looked at him, it was as though it took something away. The thing went about its business again. It remained unchanged.

"Di... Di... Did you see that!?" Sweat glistened on Jack's palms. He looked at them, with pleading eyes, but they had seen it too. The mine suddenly felt claustrophobic.

"You don't think they're all..." Eve trailed off. She couldn't bear to say the word.

"...Vampires?" Donna finished.

"And where did they all come from?" Abe was genuinely curious.

Jack's knees struggled to support his shaking frame. Donna placed a hand on her brothers back.

"I have a feeling that our Mayor and Mayoress have been here a lot longer than they've been telling us."

"But what do they want from the town then, if they don't know this Sceptre is here... or might not be here?" Eve asked.

"It *is* here. I can, I don't know, it's like I can *feel* it somehow." It was the first time that Abe was able to articulate his feelings on the matter.

"What do you mean *'feel'* it?" Donna probed, with an ounce of sarcasm in her tone, she wanted to be clear that she was still a little pissed at him. Walking along the line slowly, they all checked their surroundings more

Kerwall Town

and more frequently. There was an overwhelming sense of being watched, but no eyes were trained on them. The *things* were working on either side of the group, all to one soundless rhythm.

"I… I, just can. It's hard to explain, but just trust me."

"Where does your feeling think we should go?" Jack voice began to return.

"Down."

"Of course, … Not up, down. Man, this is not cool, *not cool* at all!" Jack decided to stop trying to hide his fear. When the time came, he would be brave, but until then, he allowed himself to be afraid.

"Down it is then." Donna was determined.

The further underground that the Kerwall JADEs walked, the tighter the grip of claustrophobia. The walkways became narrower, only permitting one set of workers on the left, and passers-by to the right. The workers merged more and more into just one being.

They had lost all sense of time now. Two hours could have passed, or four, or maybe just the one, there was no way for the group to tell. Donna noticed that there were no canary birds this far down. She thought that perhaps it was because Vampires didn't need them.

A sense of foreboding hung over them, and doubt rattled around in their heads. Around thirty minutes ago, or an hour, two left turns back, they had taken off their gloves, succumbing to the heat. The sweat still poured off them, stinging their eyes. Donna had the foresight to pack a bag, with drinks and food for them all. They drank from the bottles greedily, the warm liquid serving as a placebo.

S.D. Reed

"How much further, Abe?" Eve was dragging her feet more than the others. She hadn't had a good enough night's sleep and was paying for it tenfold now.

Abe, leading the line, stopped in his tracks. The others tumbled into each other, there was a quick round of the blame game, but Abe quickly shushed them. The mine was completely silent, save for the repetitive clanging of axes into the walls. The was something else though. Something you could only hear if you knew what you were listening to.

It was the sound of a heartbeat.

It was getting louder.

"Do you hear that?"

"Hear what?" Jack wasn't really listening.

"The town. It's alive."

17

The Stalking Game

On the surface, Kerwall was almost dark. Terry and Dot were growing worried as to the whereabouts of their grandchildren. Dot paced up and down the kitchen, her slippers slapping against her heel. Peter, Debbie, and Jeremy were sat in the kitchen with them. The others weren't able to wait.

"Why aren't they back yet?" She muttered once more. It was more of a question to herself, than to the room. Another look at the clock confirmed that they should have been home hours ago.

"I knew we shouldn't have let them go! It was a foolish thing to let them do." Dot said again, this time to the room.

"Don't worry, they know what they're doing. And they're smart kids too. Have a little faith." Jeremy hoped to sound reassuring.

"They know what they're looking for, so it's just a matter finding it, which they will. I'm sure of it." Debbie suppressed her unexpectedly shaky voice.

Terry wrapped his arms around his wife and kissed her cheek. It was all that he needed to do. As with many things, it was often what was done and not what was said that mattered most to them. She savoured every one of his kisses.

The guests stayed for a further hour, leaving at around 8:15 p.m. Dot bid them farewell at the door, promising that she would call them as soon as they heard anything. She sighed as she shut the door, and moved back into the kitchen where she had left Terry waiting. He wasn't there. The house was quiet. Her chest became tight as her eyes widened.

"Tez!" She shouted.

Silence answered her back in deafening tones. She ran as best as she could from one room to the next, calling his name. The only sound was the *clack, clack, clack* of her slippers against her heels, taunting her.

There was a knock at the door. The panic gripping her heart tightened.

Terry hasn't been himself as of late and it was scaring the hell out of Dotty. Ever since this whole Vampire mess had begun, she had noticed that his grip on reality had almost entirely diminished. A few days ago, Peter had confided in her that he thought that Terry might need to seek a doctor's help for his growing forgetfulness. Just yesterday, Peter had told her that Terry had completely forgotten his name. When Peter had tried to talk to him about it, Terry had thrown a small paint can at him, narrowly missing his head. Dot had told him that she would try to deal with it as best she could. She was sorry that she didn't tell him sooner. She wasn't at all surprised to learn that Terry had told Peter that it was in fact *her* who had onset dementia.

Her heart ached for the lost memories of her husband.

Kerwall Town

The change in his attitude was evident, he had become a little volatile at times, but only to her. He hadn't hit her yet but he had been close on a few occasions. Late at night, when they ordinarily lay in bed together, she would hear him get up and go to the kitchen. He was presumably moving furniture around, or storing food in unusual places. It was a wonder that he didn't wake the whole house up with the noise. She would lie in bed listening to it and cry silent tears. On more than one occasion, she cursed God's name for inventing the cruel disease. It was robbing him of his humanity and dignity. Dot thought that it was especially cruel that it seemed to effect loved ones on a much larger scale.

"I'll get it!" Terry's voice was jovial.

'Where was he and why didn't he answer?' She thought. Dotty tried to beat him to the front door, but by now she was at the back of the shop. By the time that she reached the hallway, he was stood at the open front door greeting the late-night visitor.

"Don't let them in!" She screamed from down the hall. She broke out into a trot but it felt like she was running in treacle, it was the fastest that she could go. An icy grip clutched at her. Terry didn't hear her; it was as if she wasn't there. 'Where in the world was Peter', she wondered. It had been that very thought, the thought of help and hope, that ultimately slowed her down, allowing her husband to beat her to the door.

"To what do we owe the pleasure of the Mayoress at our door at this time of night?"

"We need to have a little chat. May I come in?" Her enchanting voice lulled him.

"No!" Dot shrieked.

It was too late. Terry had already invited Victoria in.

Very little escapes Victoria's notice. On this night, however, she failed to realise that she was being followed. Across the road, leaning against the alleyway wall, was Henry Blackburn.

He had trailed her on and off ever since he had finished with Mable's remains. This evening, to stop his fingers from getting cold, he was wearing his new gloves. They were the latest addition to his collection. It was the first time that he had worn them and they fit snuggly.

Henry was yet to establish what brought Victoria to the Smith residence so late in the evening. He concluded that it must be Mayoress business. She had been talking to a lot of people this evening and the evening prior. Every night since last week she has been making house calls until as late 9 p.m. He couldn't understand what was so imperative, but he also didn't care. He had become a hunter, and she was his latest prey. Like a true trophy hunter, he would get his kill, no matter what. He fantasised about the feel of her skin, imagined inhaling her scent, but most importantly he wondered what she would *taste* like. Even the thought of it made him salivate.

He knew that he couldn't stalk her much longer, his need was becoming all too consuming. In Henry's bag was his favourite mask. One of his very first kills. He pulled it on, and silently entered the Smith residence.

Unbeknownst to them, Dot and Terry's residence was the place to be tonight. Nora and Damien were also watching the house. When they became aware how late home the JADEs were, doubt had paid them a visit. It had nestled into their subconscious and planted a tree. Nora couldn't shake the feeling that they were all in immense trouble. For the first time in what seemed forever, she forgot her torture fantasies for Doctor Sharpe. They were just about to rush in when they saw Victoria head inside, but stopped when they saw Henry enter the house too. They had stationed themselves adjacent the hardware store in an unmarked car and had been watching the residence for most of the evening.

"What the hell is that all about?"

"I don't know, but we better find out!" Nora spoke with all the urgency in the world.

They got out of the car as quickly as they could, and rushed to the house.

Victoria flicked her wrist nonchalantly at Terry, pressing him to the wall. She strode up to Dotty, who seemed unable to move. Victoria overpowered the elderly woman effortlessly. Before Dotty could release the breath that she had been holding, Victoria was behind her with her neck firmly in her hands. The more that Dotty tried to struggle, the tighter Victoria's vice grip became. Terry, now free from the wall, attempted to desperately wrestle his wife free, but Victoria pushed him to the ground with one hand, His head hit the skirting board with a sickening *thud*, knocking him unconscious. Blood trickled out from the back of his cranium.

Henry stood perfectly still, watching from the front door, his mouth is open aghast, unable to speak. *'She's a killer too, like me. We're perfect for each other'*, he thought. Before his thought could reach a conclusion, she looked up, and stared at him. Their eyes locked, it was far from a lovers look. Victoria watched him with utter contempt. She snapped Dot's neck. The sound of tendons tearing and bones crunching were the last sounds her body made. She fell to a lifeless clump on the floor. Her eyes still open, unseeing, stared at the closed eyes of her husband.

Victoria flew at Henry, and in one smooth motion she flung him to the ceiling and then slammed him down to the floor, all with a flick of her wrist. He lay, barely moving, barely breathing on the floor. He tried to stretch his skin gloved hand to her legs. She stood on his fingers with the heel of her boots and they snapped on impact. Henry whimpered in pain. With his one free hand, he reached for the cross that was tucked inside his shirt. She pulled it free from him and wrapped it around his neck without touching his own flesh. He tried to claw at it, but she wound it tighter and tighter. Under his mask his face was turning purple and he was gasping for air. She lifted him off of the floor and forced him up against the wall, his boots trying in vain to touch the ground.

He slumped to the floor, still wearing his haunting mask.

Damien and Nora were crouched behind a parked car. Nora was the first to break free of her fear, she got up slowly from her cover position. She emptied her clip into Victoria, aiming directly at the heart each time. Victoria snickered, swatting some of the bullets away before pouncing on Nora. In an instant, she was dead. Damien tried to run. There was little point to his efforts, and Victoria had met him within seconds.

Her laugh echoed off the buildings surrounding her. Before the night was out, she hunted almost all of the members of The Owls of Justice. All except for her mole and, because the intel was so good, as good as they had promised, she would spare their life, as per the deal.

18

The (De)Sceptre

By the time the Kerwall JADEs had reached the epicentre of the mine, Victoria had broken the neck of an innocent and defenceless elderly woman. She knew where Dotty's grandchildren were too, but as requested, the mole was going to take them out.

Abe wanted the Sceptre as soon as they had learnt about it. The knowledge that his friends would want to destroy it drove him to the brink of insanity.

Three nights previously, Abe lay restless in his bed, he couldn't stand it anymore. The thought of his *goody-goody* friends destroying his one chance at happiness was all too much. Hate bubbled away in his stomach, like magma ready to force its way past the surface. He decided there and then that he was going to eliminate them before they killed his dream.

Abe was no longer himself.

He got out of bed and shoved on the clothes that he had worn earlier in the day. He picked up his socks and gave them a quick sniff, the smell that invaded his nostrils was strong and vinegary. He rummaged in his sock draw to pick out a fresh pair. The last thing he

Kerwall Town

wanted to do was to offend his potential new masters. Abe sneaked passed his mum's door, who was snoring lightly, and crept down the stairs, careful to avoid the ones that creaked, without turning on the lights. Once he was in the back garden, he got his bike out of the shed and made his way to make a deal that would change the rest of his life.

There was no doubt in his mind.

At 11 p.m. he stood outside the house of Victoria and Frances. He used the kickstand on his bike to rest it on the path and confidently strode up to the huge dark oak front door. The knocker was wrought iron shaped into a man's face; its sinister grin invited Abe to use it. The oil green appeared to glow in the moonlight. Abe grabbed it and banged it firmly against the wood three times in quick succession. He stepped back politely. It was as if he was a carol singer waiting angelically, not someone there to make a deal with the town's devils. He didn't have to wait long until Frances opened the door, greeting him with a smile similar to the door knocker. Frances noticed that it didn't frighten Abe one bit.

"To what do we owe the pleasure of a visit from you at this hour, Abe?" His silky tone, had little effect. His laugh no longer grated Abe's ears.

"Information." Abe replies, monosyllabically.

"Then you better come in and make yourself at home." The grin exposed abnormally large teeth, confirming to Abe *what* he really was.

Frances gestured Abe inside and once in, he shut the door behind them. The entranceway was beyond opulent. Abe didn't know what the floor was made from, but he could see his own reflection looking back at him in it. Both of their footsteps echoed throughout the house. In the middle of the sweeping entranceway a grand staircase stood, made from pure white marble. It split off to separate wings of the house, and in the centre of the first floor a wall length window is covered by red satin drapes. The banisters are made from carefully handcrafted wood. Abe noticed, among the carvings, was a bat in mid-flight. Hanging from the vaulted ceilings is a diamond and crystal chandelier, Abe swore that it was bigger than his fridge. Directly under the ceiling jewellery, on what Abe now thinks is a marble floor, is a huge decal depicting a compass with a filigree pattern. The green stood out prominently on the white marble.

"Like what you see?" Frances looked at him with that same shit-eating-grin, making Abe jump a little.

"Huh ... oh, yeah." Was all Abe could manage to say, the proverbial bat had his tongue it seemed.

"What information do you have for me then, young Abe?" Putting his black gloved hand on Abe's shoulder, it made him squirm a little internally.

"I've got information for *both* of you." The words spill from Abe with confidence.

"You have some fire in you, boy. I like it but let's not get ahead of ourselves here. You tell me the information and I'll deem whether it is worthy of bothering Ms Viridi with, hrrmmm?" His tone was condescending, not that Abe noticed as he made a point to not look directly in Frances' eyes.

"I know what you are. What you *both* are! Is that enough?" Fire rose in his voice and he shrugged his shoulder free.

The sound of Frances' cachinnation reverberated in the entranceway.

Kerwall Town

"And pray tell me, *what* are we but the same as you?" He hooks his eyebrow into a sharp arrow and tilts his head expectantly.

"Vampires!"

"Whatever do you mean dear boy? Vampires only exist in movies and comic books."

"Ha, yeah, sure. I'm not going to grass on you both, nothing like that. I want *in!*" Abe looked directly into Frances' eyes; black circles stared back at him.

"What on earth is all this racket... Oh... Abe... Correct?" Victoria elegantly walked down the staircase. Her long black dress pooled around her feet and was adorned by a classic cape flowing behind her.

"Abe here thinks we are Vampires."

"How preposterous."

"Does Sceptre of the Dark Gods ring a bell to you?" Abe says, daringly.

Victoria and Frances' poker faces were non-existent.

"What do you know about that!?" Demanded Victoria greedily.

"Ahh, so it *is* true. All of it. I knew it!" Abe jittered excitedly like a child on Christmas morning.

"I think we should address this in the drawing room. After you Ms Viridi."

The three of them moved into the drawing room without a sound. Abe was once again blown away by the grandiosity of the room. Another gaudy yet tasteful diamond chandelier hung in the centre of the ornate ceiling. The walls are white with gold gilding, the red and gold floral carpet looked as though it had never been walked on. The white and gold sofas and high-backed chairs that flanked the deep bay window appeared untouched. Running across the opposing wall were bookshelves from floor to ceiling.

S.D. Reed

"Please… Take a seat," Frances invited. It was said innocently enough, but Abe felt a little threatened by the tone. He obliged all the same … not that he had much choice in the matter.

"Look before I say anymore, I want some assurances."

"You… Are making demands… to *us* even though you claim us to be *Vampires*. How very brave of you." Victoria snarled.

She sat down bedside him and crosses her legs, seductively twirling her long pale finger over Abe's knee, it sent a shiver down his spine.

"I am … yes …"

"Well, before I hear them how do I know I can trust you… a *human*?" She spat the word with distain.

Abe pulls the collar of his shirt down, exposing his pasty neck. Victoria and Frances can't help but stare at the thick jugular vein pulsating from his neck. It would be easy for them to take him out now, to be done with this little freakshow, but they were also deeply interested in whether he was being truthful. Watching the steady beating as his blood was pumped around his body gave them a clear insight into whether he was being deceitful. Abe wasn't … at least not to them.

"I want to sacrifice myself. I want to become one of you. I want to join your legion and be part of your rebuilding. I want my mother safe too. In return, I will hand you the Sceptre that I know you've been searching for most of your life. The Sceptre that was *stolen* from you."

Abe leans back on the sofa and Victoria continues to move her finger on his leg. Frances moves towards her to whisper in her ear with a cupped hand, then steps back in place.

Kerwall Town

"Very well. But you must kill your friends while you're in the mine." Victoria made murder seem sexy, as if you'd be a square to not partake.

"Deal." Abe sticks out his hand.

Victoria eyes his glistening hand with dirt under his cracked fingernails.

"We will not shake hands, it is so... primitive." She continues in the sultry tone. She leans over him, kisses his chest, and tickles him lightly behind his ear with her long index finger, forcing him to lift his chin. She grabs him by the scruff of his neck, making his veins protrude even more flagrantly. Victoria whips her head back and extends her jaw, her sharp fangs sink deep into his nape and she drinks greedily from him. After a few moments, she stands up licking the blood from her lips. Without look back or breaking stride she commands Frances.

"When he comes to, give him a blood box from the stores and find out what else he knows."

Before Frances could respond she left the room.

Since then, Abe had been living as a Type B Vampire. It had been him who had made sure that the meetings were after dark. No one thought to question why. It was the reason why he had become so in-tune with the town, why he was the only one who could feel the pulsating black heart of Kerwall.

They were now so deep into the mine, that they were the only ones in the tunnel. The lights on their helmets, and the odd overhead bulb, were the only thing keeping them from absolute darkness. They eventually come to a fork in the mine, the heat had become so intense that beads of sweat stood out on their skin like pearls.

"Well... Which way is it?" Jack still questioned Abe's judgement.

"Left."

They took the left track, and Abe led on once more. The track led them to a dead end. It had sent them into a circular room, with only their helmets for light. They shone over different sizes of rocks and large clumps of dirt.

"Guess we took a wrong turn somewhere." Eve was far too hot and tired to add any disdain to her voice.

"No, it's got to be here!" Abe looked frantically round. He clutched the ground hysterically digging at it with his hands.

"Come on, man, maybe it's just not here -"

"NO! It *is* here." Abe said this with such venom that Jack fell back a little from the shock.

The spotlight on his helmet dashes to and fro. Just before he gives up hope, the light trains on a small wooden box in his newly created hole.

"There!" The voice wasn't his own. The others shone their lights onto the box. There was no telling how old it was. It was about one and a half foot in length. Abe pounced on it with a survival instinct. He was too quick for any human, but of course that wasn't what he was anymore. The Vampire blood was still fusing with his own, he wasn't at his strongest yet. But the Sceptre would grant him ultimate power, and once he had his hands on it not even Victoria could stop him.

Jack, Donna, and Eve noticed how fast Abe moved. Jack was the quickest to realise what was happening once again.

"Abe! Wait!" He shouted.

Kerwall Town

Abe looks up at his friend, someone who he has known almost all of his life, with eyes as black as coal. He smiled at Jack, it was void of any love, fuelled only by hate. His newly formed fangs were on full show now. Jack's heart sank, and Abe heard the hypnotic rhythm increase.

'Oh, how nice that sound was'. How he would just love to drink his blood and kill him. *'Who would have the last laugh now?'* Abe thought cynically.

It was true that Abe had been jealous of his friend for many years, but now the tables had turned and he would go on to become the most powerful being in the world. So, he determined, when he was done draining the blood from his friends, he would crush their mortal skulls under his boot.

The Abe that Jack was looking at wasn't the one that they grew up with. Not the one they had campfires with. Not the one they went to the cinema with. This Abe was different. He was more dangerous than they could imagine.

He thrust open the box and there it was, the Sceptre. He could feel the power pulsating from it. He snatched at it with both hands. It felt like it was always meant to be in his possession, like he had found a missing limb. He makes a bee-line for Jack.

"Kneel before me." Jack tries to resist, the veins standing out on his neck and his face turned a deep beetroot. Eventually his knees take on a mind of their own, and he kneels at his friend's feet. His lips are close enough to taste the dirt on Abe's shoes. A thought arises in Abe's mind, he tells Jack to kiss his dusty boots. Once again, against his will, Jack does as he is commanded. Grief rolls down Jack's face, and a snot bubble pops from his nose. In his urgency, his veins stand out on his neck even more prominently as he tries to stop himself. Abe licks his lips at the sight.

"Don't try to fight it, Jack! It's no use! Come and join the superior race. All of you." His arms were outstretched, like a preacher. Not five minutes had gone by and he was already drunk with power. That was one thing the book couldn't tell them.

The Sceptre of the Dark Gods prayed on the weak willed and infested their mind with a million power hungry thoughts, while simultaneously draining them of whatever power they had. In the wrong hands, all it really is, is a parasite. The power it drains from the fragile minded increases its own strength. No one on this earth could be more powerful than the Sceptre because it wouldn't allow it, it was omnipotent.

To Abe's detriment, and at the Sceptre's discretion, he had lost sight of Donna and Eve. They lurked behind him, each with a huge rock in their hands. Donna smashed the left side of his head, and Eve the right. The rocks were so pointed and heavy that they caved in the sides of his skull. Abe fell to the floor, his brain spilling from the right side of his head. Needless to say, he was dead even before he hit the floor. He fell clutching the Sceptre. His strength had been drained, rendering him to have the same power as a bed-ridden ninety-five-year-old. Abe never stood a chance.

The Sceptre was silent in his grip.

"Shit! Fuck! You killed Abe!" Jack cries, dusting himself off from the floor. The world doesn't feel right to him now, but he tries his best to shake the internal cobwebs free.

"And good job too. That wasn't Abe anymore, and he was going to kill us all, and you know that!" Donna would have never let him hurt her brother.

Kerwall Town

Jack notices the brain matter and blood coming out of his now dead friend, and runs to the side of the room to be sick. It comes up in watery chunks. Eve is still holding the bloodied rock in her hand. She's looking down at the lifelong friend that she just murdered. She knew that the image before her now would be one that plagued her dreams.

Jack wipes the corners of his mouth free from sick. He continues dry heaving from time to time as he's hunched on his hands and knees. He looks like a cat trying to get rid of a rather troublesome fur ball. He doesn't even notice that the drenching sweat has stuck his shirt to his back.

"So, what do we do with this?" Donna didn't want to pick up the Sceptre, so she kicks it instead. As her boot makes a connection, she felt a surge of power, it repulsed her.

"We destroy it, just like we came here to do!" Jack said, flatly, rising to his feet. His bearings were returning to him now and he leans on the wall to regain his balance.

"Are we sure he's, you know...*dead?*" Eve's was yet to look away from the recent corpse. Her mind is elsewhere, anywhere but here.

"He looks pretty dead to me." Jack concluded, marking the sign of the cross on himself.

"I know, but aren't you supposed to, spear their heart with something?" Eve's mind was still on another planet, a sane one where her former friend wasn't just murdered partly by her hands, but what she's seeing is a complete juxtaposition.

"She's got a point. How many times have we seen the false dawn in horror films?" Donna agrees.

The others both nod solemnly, and look for something sharp in the alcove of the mine they find themselves in. The axe's that hung from their waists were seemingly forgotten. After a moment, Donna's light shines over an old, rusted pick axe. She picks it up with both hands with a grunt. She was both mentally and emotionally exhausted, they all were.

"Anyone want to do the honours?" Donna didn't believe her own words, but uttered them anyway.

Jack and Eve put a hand each on the pick axe over Donna's without saying a word, they moved it directly above Abe's heart with shaking hands and plunged the tip right through his chest. They punctured his heart.

There was now no dispute, they had officially killed their childhood friend. As they pulled the blade out, the remaining JADEs fall into a heap, sobbing in silence. After what felt like almost too long before someone spoke, Jack lifts his head.

"Abe, before the Vampires got to him, was a good man and a great friend. Let us not forget that."

"Never." Came the choral reply.

"Now what in the hell *are* we going to do with that?" Jack echoes Donna's earlier question.

"It looks pretty brittle. Maybe we can just snap it?" Wonders Donna.

"Snapping an ancient artefact just doesn't sit right with me. I know it's evil, but it's like ripping a book, it's taboo." Eve shudders.

"It's worth a shot." Says Jack. He picks up the Sceptre hesitantly, wrapping it in his damp shirt, and tries to smash it against the wall. It remains fully in tact on the floor. Jack picks it up and tries again, nothing happens. Donna tries too, yielding the same result. Eve tries to smash it with a rock, but to no avail.

Kerwall Town

"Shit! What are we gonna do!?" The trepidation in Jack's voice was paramount and his insides felt like he was swimming against an insatiable wave.

"Why don't we take it with us and hide it in the next town or something?" Eve posed, with absolutely no conviction in her voice.

"I'm not picking it up! My foot is still tingling from when I kicked it earlier." Donna didn't even want to look at the Sceptre, she would rather look at the corpse of Abe for the rest of her life than take another glimpse at that *thing*. She could swear that it was alive somehow, that it fed off the energies of the people who held it.

"Well, we can't just leave it here... Can we?" Jack wanted to be as far away from it as possible.

"No one knows about it other than us and the rest of The Owls of Justice... I say why not?"

Donna said the words that none of them had truly considered.

"I'm all for leaving it here... But what about Abe?" It was a question they didn't want to deal with.

"I guess we leave him here too, until we can get someone to help us lift him out. His mum deserves a burial at the very least." Jack's tone is sombre and his heart ached for Chrystal. The others nod in agreement.

The three friends moved Abe to a more dignified position, none of them touching the Sceptre. They put the box it was found in over top of it. As they silently began leaving the alcove, almost instantly, the mine was no longer so silent. Deafening moans are being emitted. Jack, Donna, and Eve run along the tracks, trying to remember their way back up to the surface.

It wasn't long before they found the source of the sounds.

19

The Wailing

The sound coming from the Vampires is deafening and disorientating in equal measure.

As they wail, they fall to the floor their bodies decomposing into dust. If the remaining JADEs had dared to look, they would have seen that the Vampires were not only disintegrating, but melting. Skin slipped from their bones with ease, as if unseeing hands were tearing them apart, like chicken torn from the bone. Not all of them tuned into pure dust either, there were remnants of skin, bits of eyes, fingernails, and teeth could all be found amongst their remains.

"What the fuck, man!" Exclaimed Jack.

"Is it to do with the what we did to the Sceptre?" Eve's eyes were wide.

"Who the hell knows, all I care about is getting as far away as that bloody thing as possible!" Donna's hair stood on end, she appeared aged by fifteen years. Much like anyone who has just gone through a traumatic event. Her world view was changed, her soul too, the same was true for her friends.

Kerwall Town

They were sprinting down the narrow corridors of the mine. Before long, they were back in the section with wailing workers on either side of them. They were being showered by the Vampiric remains, like they were in some kind of awful celebration or sadistic carnival. The smell was putrid, like a combination of rotten flesh and sour milk. The stale air and the sweat seemed to amplify the nauseating scent.

Luck must be on their side, they managed to find the exit of the mines. Stepping over the piles of human dust and bodily juices now encasing their shoulders, they ran towards the hope of freedom. They were greeted at the exit by Stanley. He was a shell of the man they had earlier met.

"Whaa … What's happening to them!?" He rambled to no one in particular. His head was in hands, he was rocking back and forth. There are other miners around him, all with the same expression on their faces, some were walking in circles muttering to themselves incoherently. One miner has the remnants of someone's eye socket stuck amongst his hair. He didn't seem to notice it though, a small mercy in an otherwise clusterfuck of a day.

They hurried back to Donna and Jack's grandparents' house as quickly as their aching legs could carry them, dropping their toolsets and headgear somewhere along the way. Jack had an awful feeling in the pit of his stomach and he prayed that they weren't too late.

Doubt flooded his mind.

Elsewhere in the town, Victoria felt a part of herself die. It stabbed at her from an unknown place. She knew that the Sceptre had been damaged and that Abe was dead. The Vampires that she turned were all connected to her in that way. A part of their souls entwined and they would feel each other's pain. Victoria has become so used to this aching that it was like a calming lullaby to her now. With it, this time, all her hopes of everlasting power diminished. Yet again, she was so close to taking full control but had been thwarted. Kerwall was no longer safe for her, and that pissed her off more than anything else this evening.

She screamed a guttural roar. No one saw her in Kerwall again.

Victoria needed a place to rest, to regain herself. It would be a long time before she would be seen by another person again. She vowed to seek revenge on The Owls of Justice and to return to Kerwall one day, to reclaim what was hers. At the moment, however, she is weak and crestfallen. She will rebuild, she's done it before, it's how she's survived this long, but she needed time.

Frances felt a snap in his heart, it was stronger than Victoria's pain, after all, he's weaker than her. Frances roamed the streets searching for her, but it was to no avail. He scoured their make-shift home but she wasn't there either, her casket lay empty. For the first time in his renewed life, since Victoria gave him the gift of Vampirism, he sunk to his knees in his now empty mansion and wept. He was alone in this strange town without his only confidant. He knew that he couldn't stay here long, it wasn't safe. The secret was out, and sooner or later, the pitchforks would appear. He'd seen it before and had no intention of seeing it again anytime soon. Frances decided to leave Kerwall behind and find

Kerwall Town

a new place to live. Alone again.

The sight that that meets Jack, Donna, and Eve at the house, stops them in their tracks and freezes their hearts. Before long, they began to howl like the Vampires in the mine. Without the salvation of disappearing out of this world and away from the crushing pain.

Terry gradually comes to, opening his heavy eyes. They lock instantly with those of his wife, the eyes that he has stared into for almost all of his life. He reaches out a hand to her and traces her face with his gnarled fingers. Her once warm skin is now ice cold. He calls her name softly, she doesn't answer. She couldn't answer. He tries again. The silence greets him back like an unwelcome guest. He is unaware that he is being watched by his grandchildren and Eve. His whole world is shattered into tiny pieces. He kisses his wife's forehead, and sobs uncontrollably.

Jack and Donna broke free of their horror. Eve's eyes were now firmly resting on her dead mum. Her dislocated eye socket was touching the middle of her bicep, blood tricked from her ear and had congealed into a pool on the floor. Eve walks over to her, struggling against an unknown force. She carefully picks up her mum's snapped neck and holds it in her arms close to her chest. The bawling broke free despite her best efforts to contain it. It would be yet another image that would permanently be engrained onto her retina. She gently rocks the fragile cadaver back and forth in the middle of the road, stroking her lifeless hair and muttering.

"It's going to be ok." It was far from the truth but it was all she could say as she looked at her mum. She had no idea how she was going to pick herself up from this, but she knew she would, eventually. She was certain, now more than ever, that she was going to follow in her late mum's footsteps.

Terry's still comforting his wife when he is enveloped in an embrace from either side by his grandchildren. No words are exchanged. What they wanted to say, more than anything, was, *'I'm sorry.'* In this moment, however, the words were better left unsaid. So, instead they sat silently holding each other long into the night.

Daniel is oblivious to all the goings on in Kerwall, sleeping soundly in his bed. He's woken by a sharp slap to the side of his face, making his ears ring. He opens his mouth to speak, but still nursing a heavy night of drinking and coke sniffing, his room spins in and out of his view. The headache is beyond anything he has ever felt before. He attempts to sit up, not yet registering the impending danger looming over him.

The barrel of a gun is jammed into his mouth. It almost touches his tonsils and he gags on it. Water brims in his eyes as they struggle to focus, until he gets another slap on the other side of his face. He screams out in pain his eyes stunned, open wide, and he sees Trevor standing over him.

Before Daniel could speak, Trevor pulls the trigger.

His brain splatters on his headboard. Trevor shoots him again with a guttural roar, emptying a slug into Daniel's black heart. He was showered with blood for his effort.

"For Kerwall." Trevor spat and walks out of the room. For the first time since his brother was taken

Kerwall Town

from the world by that sorry excuse of a man, Trevor felt a weight lift from his shoulders. When he slept that evening, it was a long and deep rest. He saw his little brother in his dreams, with a huge smile across his face. They hugged each other tightly without saying a word. Trevor noticed that Evan had the beginnings of wings forming on his back and he beamed with pride.

Terry continued to search for Dotty, he would shuffle from room to room, calling out her name. His brain, riddled with the terrible disease, couldn't accept the passing of his wife, so it completely erased the memory of her death. It broke his grandchildren's hearts every time they heard him say it. Peter took on the role of looking after him full time, whilst running of the shop too.

When the search party retrieved Abe's body from the mines there was no mention of a box or of the Sceptre. Eve, Donna, and Jack were all part of the retrieval effort and they too couldn't find the box. It was as if it had never been there, but Jack knew better. Someone had taken it before they got there and there were two guesses as to who that could be. Just like Victoria had vowed to seek vengeance on The Owls of Justice, the remaining members vowed to defend their town. If it was ever threatened again, they would be ready.

One of the few positives to rise from fair Kerwall's fatal events, was that Linda plucked up the courage to ask Patty out on a date. She screamed with excitement and accepted in a heartbeat. During the date, Patty confided in her that if she been asked, she was going to do it herself. Seven months into their relationship, Patty got down on one knee in her kitchen and asked Linda to be her wife. The self-governed town passed the unprecedented law to allow same sex couples to marry. Patty and Linda were the first. Kerwall was taking its first steps to becoming inclusive, the residents all knew that a united town was a strong one.

It would be a few weeks until Kerwall town would return to some sort of normal. A full investigation was carried out, but the talk of Vampires was redacted from any official records. Andy Cooper was appointed as the new Mayor of Kerwall and he graciously accepted the honour bestowed upon him. He promoted Abigail to the new manager of Cooper's store and appointed Peter his second in command. He accepted, promising that it wouldn't interfere with his other duties.

After a few weeks in office, Andy posed a question to the town:

'Should Kerwall come out of the shadows and join the rest of the country?'

The vote came back as a resounding no. For all the faults that the town had, they all felt that they were better off without the input of the rest of the country. After all, Kerwall always found a way to look after itself, because, like its residents it was alive.

Kerwall Town

S.D. Reed

Kerwall Town does not exist ...

Kerwall Town

A note and some acknowledgements

I am often asked where I get my ideas from, and normally I give a shrug and say, 'I dunno, some kind of *cosmic force*', but for this one, I can tell you specifically where I was. It was at a family gathering, Boxing Day 2019. There was a football game on T.V. and I had a strange thought, 'what if those were the only people in the whole town. How would they survive and what put them there?' I wrote down a few notes on my phone with excitement. The end product is a little different, but the bones of the idea are still there.

I began writing this book around three weeks before the global pandemic shook the world, and I was surprised by how much my fantasy was starting to mirror real life… minus the Vampires, of course. While a lot of research was done to make this fictional town from the '70s come to life, I must stress that this is a work of fiction, and any connections made to real people is purely coincidental.

It has always been a dream of mine to write a book about Vampires, and I just hope I did the genre justice. It has been great fun writing it and living in Kerwall town for the past few months. I've been fascinated with monsters and ghouls ever since I was young and when the opportunity came to write my own version I jumped at the chance.

Once again, I would like to say a huge thank you to a few special people. They are without doubt the best kind of people and my life is better for knowing them. BETA Readers – Thank you all for taking the time out of your busy lives to go over my novel and make it the best it can be for the world to read. Your opinions have been invaluable.

TJ- of course. You continue to inspire me and support me. This book wouldn't have been written without your constant cheerleading and input. I am so lucky to be able to call you my soulmate. Words will never express how much you mean to me.

Kathleen - Along with TJ, you have an opinion I can always rely on, you too are an ever present and your kindness is unwavering. I am privileged to call you my earth mum.

Rachel and Iain – You are a formidable team and I cannot thank you both enough for all the help you bestowed on me with this novel.

Linda - You know how much your support means to me, and a simple thank you doesn't seem to suffice. You have a very special place in my heart.

Liz - You are my American rock and support. Thank you for always being there through the good and the bad.

I'd also like to thank Tony, Diane, Susan, Nicola, Sarah, Lisa, Christine, Jay, Viv, and countless others. You know who you are and how much you mean to me. You all rock.

Finally, and most importantly, I'd like to thank you, *dear friend* for supporting me on this journey. You have trusted me with your hard-earned money to tell you a story. I just hope it was worth the admission fee.

I pride myself on being the *'Purveyor of literary ice-cream'*, which basically means that I'll be writing all sorts of genres for you. Little did I know that five months after writing my first author's note, I would be writing my

S.D. Reed

second one. So, here's to the next one!

Stay safe and well my friends! I'm sorry if I scared you
but that is what we're here for, right?
Make sure those curtains are drawn at night!

Your friend,
S. D. Reed.

23rd April 2020

You are invited to join S.D. Reed behind the scenes

Online:
www.sd-reed.com

Facebook:
S.D.Reed.Official

Instagram:
sdreedauthor

Twitter:
SDReedAuthor

YouTube:
S D Reed Author

If you have been affected by any content within this novel here are some places you can contact for support:

UK

Samaritans

Telephone: 116 123 (24 hours a day, free to call, UK & Ireland)

Email: jo@samaritans.org

Mind Infoline (confidential mental health info services)

Telephone: 0300 123 3393 (9am-6pm Mon to Fri) or text 86463

Email: info@mind.org.uk

Victim Support (crime or traumatic event support)

Telephone: 08 08 16 89 111 (24/7, every day of the year, free to call)

USA

Suicide Prevention Lifeline

Telephone: 1-800-273-8255

RAINN

Telephone: 800.656.4673

Printed in Great Britain
by Amazon

48365559R00163